THE
Shakespeare
REQUIREMENT

THE
Shakespeare
REQUIREMENT

Julie Schumacher

DOUBLEDAY

New York

www.doubleday.com

DOUBLEDAY and the portrayal of an anchor with a dolphin are
registered trademarks of Penguin Random House LLC.

Book design by Michael Collica
Jacket design by Emily Mahon
Jacket photograph by eye35 / Alamy

Library of Congress Cataloging-in-Publication Data
Names: Schumacher, Julie, 1958– author.
Title: The Shakespeare requirement : a novel / by Julie Schumacher.
Description: First edition. | New York : Doubleday, [2018]
Identifiers: LCCN 2017051695 | ISBN 9780385542340 (hardcover) |
ISBN 9780385542357 (ebook)
Subjects: LCSH: College teachers—Fiction. | GSAFD: Humorous fiction.
Classification: LCC PS3569.C5548 S53 2018 | DDC 813/.54—dc23
LC record available at https://lccn.loc.gov/2017051695

MANUFACTURED IN THE UNITED STATES OF AMERICA

2 4 6 8 10 9 7 5 3 1

First Edition

For Lawrence Jacobs: *Free Jay Fitger*

THE
Shakespeare
REQUIREMENT

ONE

Economics Department to Celebrate
Grand Reopening of Willard Hall

—*by Madelyn Rao*

The Campus Scribe (September 3, 2010): Payne University's economists will soon be toasting the completion of a yearlong renovation of Willard Hall, celebrating with a ribbon-cutting ceremony and reception hosted by Econ Department chair Roland R. Gladwell.

"It was a long and difficult year," said Professor Gladwell, reached in his spacious new office. "The second floor of the building was gutted, and we had to beg a year's lodging from our friends in Geology. But you can see that the result is well worth it." The Economics Department's portion of Willard Hall now includes state-of-the-art technology-enhanced classrooms, a fully equipped computer lab, elegant seminar and meeting rooms, faculty offices, and a café.

Stunning mosaic tile floors and skylights were underwritten by the Morse Foundation; digital LCD wall displays were donated by philanthropist-alum Bill Fixx.

Asked to comment on the nearly completed project, University President Nyla Hoffman praised Payne's corporate and private donors and said she looks forward "to a renewed era of growth for the Department of Economics, a jewel in the crown here at Payne."

Willard Hall is also home to the Department of English, which occupies the lower floor.

On the first—unrenovated—floor of Willard Hall, Jason T. Fitger, recently elected chair of the Department of English, stuffed his copy of the *Campus Scribe* into the shredder. He had recently returned from a visit to Econ's portion of the building, where he had been mistaken by one of the clerical staff for a vagrant or tourist—another gawker come to admire the hot-and-cold water fountains and Orwellian flatscreens, the espresso bar, and the sunshine filtering gracefully through the skylights and casting itself in subtle patterns on the tile floor. Descending the stairs again to English, he left behind a silent, air-conditioned Erewhon and reentered the grim and steamy underworld that served as heart and soul, at Payne, of the liberal arts.

Muttering, Fitger flipped the switch on the shredder. Nothing. His office—the entire administrative "suite," or English Department headquarters—was barbarically hot, and he had just spent forty minutes duct-taping a rusted, squeaking fan in his window and tracking down a series of extension cords (the outlets in his office were only sporadically working) which, end to end, snaked their way to a distant receptacle in the hall. He'd had to prop his window open with a dictionary and several rolls of toilet paper: due to two broken sash cords, it functioned more or less as a guillotine.

Careful not to yank the fan from his window, Fitger crawled under his desk to fiddle with the plug on the shredder. The semester—including his own freshman class on "The Literature of Apocalypse"—would begin in four days. Sweat cascading down the neck of his shirt, he reminded himself that there were benefits to being head of the department: his new office did not abut the men's room; his teaching duties consisted of two classes per year instead of five; and he had been granted permission to select from a glossy catalog an ergonomic chair that, should the photo turn out to be accurate, would not be crisscrossed with electrical tape that adhered to his pants. Still, these perks were a handful of penny candy sprinkled over a minefield: English, one of the most ungovernable academic units at Payne, had a reputation for discord and dysfunction going back forty years. Fitger's predecessor, Ted Boti, recruited during a moment of administrative despair from the Sociology Department, had abandoned his post after only nine months, racing out of the office as if his head were on fire. He had bequeathed to Fitger a scrim of dead insects on the desk, a defunct computer, and a file cabinet containing a Sudoku puzzle book, eleven pencil stubs, and a tube of psoriasis cream.

Fitger's ex-wife, Janet, comfortably employed by the plutocrats in the Payne University law school, had warned him against beginning the academic year in a futilitarian mood: that is, in her words, could he try not to be such a fatalistic ass? English was, she pointed out, in an enviable nowhere-but-up situation. True, Fitger probably lacked the respect and goodwill of the Payne campus (as a novelist, not a scholar, he was generally regarded as a member of a subordinate species), but he was the chair, for god's sake; the ship might be ugly and battered, but he stood at its helm, his colleagues—unwilling to serve as chair themselves—having held their breath, plugged their noses, and voted him in.

Now, deep in uncharted territory under the desk, Fitger came face-to-face with several fossilized apple cores and the remains of what appeared to be a cheddar cheese sandwich. He flicked them away. English might not thrive under his watch, but he would take up the pen and the sword to defend it. Among the department's immediate needs were two tenure-track faculty hires, funding for the (defunct) literary journal, an increase in student fellowships, and the reinstatement of the (recently eliminated) creative writing degree. The complication: most if not all of these housekeeping improvements required approval from administration—in the personage of, among others, Philip Hinckler, the dean. Janet, for the past six months, had been sleeping with Hinckler. Was their relationship serious? Fitger had put this question to his ex-wife one evening in August, after the two of them (Fitger and Janet), perhaps not thinking entirely clearly, had ended up in his bed. Janet hadn't reacted well to his question. Jamming the shredder's twisted, irregular plug into the extension cord, he tried not to think about his ex-wife boinking the dean.

"I hope you're not trying to use that shredder." The office adjoining Fitger's—the two small spaces divided by a sheet of unpainted wallboard into which, inexplicably, someone had fixed a Plexiglas window—was occupied by his administrative assistant, Frances Ignatieff, aka Fran.

"What?" The shredder rattled noisily to life. Inch by inch, Fitger fed it the *Scribe*. He was on his knees, smacking the neck of the machine to speed things along. The shredder paused, coughed, set its own dials to *reverse*, and vomited ribbons of half-digested paper all over the rug.

"Un-fucking-believable," Fitger said.

"I can't hear you," said Fran.

A Frisbee *thwocked* against the window. Clutching the edge of his desk, Fitger stood up, shreds of newspaper drifting across his shoes in the sluggish breeze from the fan. What was it about Frisbee, he wondered, that undergraduates never tired of or outgrew? Year after year, chipper and shirtless on the quad, they hurled a plastic disk back and forth while the planet hurtled toward its fiery end.

Stuffing the mangled remainder of the paper—with its smiling photo of Economics chair Roland Gladwell—into the trash, Fitger torqued his shoulders left and right, his vertebrae sounding off like a marimba. He peered through the Plexiglas window into Fran's office. Support staff at Payne, he had found, tended toward eccentricity as well as recalcitrance; Frances Ignatieff scored high on both counts. She was a short, gnomelike person whose preference for baggy sleeveless dresses gave her the appearance of a sack of flour with legs. Her shower sandals—Fitger didn't want to dictate office fashion, but there was something draggletail, he thought, about rubber footwear—revealed ten oddly shaped and prehensile toes. Having been on her own in the office for most of the summer, Fran seemed to consider the newly elected Fitger, though he was her boss, as an annoying impediment to her work—whatever that was.

He tapped at the window between their two offices. Fran sighed. New department heads were as helpless as infants. Fran had been at Payne for eighteen years and had broken in four of them, having been shuffled as if across a battered checkerboard from one hapless department to another, drilling these supposed intellectual giants in their ABCs. She had strenuously resisted the relocation to English—everyone at Payne had heard the stories—but as a reward for grooming Fiamatu, the woolgathering leader of Studio Art, she had been appointed assistant to the university's number-one loudmouth and notorious crank.

He knocked again. It was eleven-fifteen; Fran had a to-do list a mile long. She had been hoping to take an early lunch in order to go home and check on Gloria, a cockatiel (Fran was a member of an animal-rehab cooperative), and here was that idiot's face in her window. He had spent most of the morning pacing back and forth in his office, fiddling with extension cords and turning the light switch on and off, without even glancing at the documents she had put in his in-box. He probably had ADD; a lot of chairs did. They started the year with a missionary's zealous drive, but soon turned bitter and disillusioned. The bunion on Fran's left foot had lit up like a fuse.

With the air of a person climbing out of a manhole, she pushed herself up from her chair and trudged around the divider to Fitger's portion of the office. And there he was, resembling a toddler left alone, standing bewildered in a

6

mess of his own creation and looking to Fran to put it to rights.

"I told you not to use the shredder," she said. "It doesn't work."

"I don't remember you telling me anything about the shredder. And why is it here in my office if it doesn't work?"

Why, why, why, Fran thought. *Why* was not the right question. At Payne, the only question that could reasonably be answered was *what*. *What* was that in the corner of the chair's office? A broken shredder. *Why* was it broken? The second question had no response. It was simply broken; many things were; it had not been fixed. At forty-four, Fran felt too old to be revealing to yet another budding leader the secret handshakes and koans that served as policy at Payne. She had never intended to work at a university, which everyone knew was full of misfits with badly swelled heads. Her dream— impractical but not yet abandoned—was to become an animal behavior consultant, which most people didn't think was a real job, but of course it was. Fran already possessed much of the requisite experience, having fostered cats, dogs, rabbits, birds, reptiles, and voles, but she lacked the degree. "There's nowhere else to put it," she said.

"What about the trash can?" Fitger asked.

"It's not going to fit. And the trash collectors don't accept machinery."

"How about the hallway?"

"Blocking the hall is a fire hazard."

Fitger stirred the gray confetti on the floor. "Do we own a vacuum?"

Did. They. Own. A. Vacuum. Fran tugged at the door of

the supply closet—marked very clearly with a sign that said SUPPLIES—and dragged from within it the gray Electrolux tank that appeared to have been manufactured during World War II. She parked it next to the plastic bucket full of cleaning products that she had already set near the door to Fitger's office, (re)explaining—because in her experience department chairs were slow to absorb information—that custodians were responsible only for the building's bathrooms and public spaces. If Fitger wanted his office cleaned, he would have to tackle the shredder debris and any other detritus himself.

Eleven-twenty. Gloria would be waiting in her cage in the kitchen, her pretty tricornered feet nimbly gripping the perch. Fran tried not to get too attached to the animals she fostered, but Gloria (considered hard-to-adopt; she was a biter) had already lived in a cage in Fran's kitchen for almost a month. And she was such a smart bird, with a truly fun-loving personality. Sometimes she liked to stand on one foot, like a drunk about to fail a sobriety test. Her previous owner had given her up because "owning a bird was too much work." People were assholes, Fran thought. She had spent the past few days teaching Gloria to whistle the tune to "Three Blind Mice."

"Is there anything else you need?" she asked.

Fitger stared at the vacuum, its cylindrical hose like an elephant's trunk. "Yes." He wanted to know if she'd heard from Tech-Help yet, about a replacement for his computer.

Fran took a deep breath. She had explained the computer issue already. "We can't order a new one until they send someone to diagnose the old one. If they decide the old one is definitely broken, they'll send an e-mail to Central. Then you can fill out an online request for a new computer."

"You're saying I should submit an online request via a computer that's no longer working."

Fran looked at the behemoth on Fitger's desk; it must have been twenty years old and probably weighed three hundred pounds. "I wonder if somebody pulled a switch on you," she said. "That's not the computer that was here last summer. You should have brought the computer from your faculty office when you moved in here."

"I tried to," Fitger said. "But about ten minutes after I became chair someone changed the lock on my office and loaned the place out to that visiting Norwegian."

"I thought he was Swedish," Fran said.

Fitger shrugged. Arnljot Johansen, a skeletal man with a shock of white hair and elongated limbs so fragile he seemed almost transparent, was a visiting interdisciplinary scholar; no one seemed to know anything about his field. The contents of Fitger's desk and file drawers had been moved into storage.

"Anyway," Fran said. "Until your computer is up and working, I'll be keeping your calendar. What's your password on P-Cal?"

"I don't use P-Cal."

Fran stared. Everyone at Payne used the university's calendar and scheduling system. How would he keep track of his appointments? In a paper logbook?

Fitger pointed to the paper logbook on his desk.

"That's not going to work," Fran said. "All the other chairs and the entire administration run on P-Cal. You might as well move your office into a cave."

"I'm going to keep a paper calendar," Fitger said. He watched Fran's face assume a Procrustean look. "I *will* be making use of a computer, however, so I would appreciate it if you would put in a second request to Tech-Help."

And so it begins, Fran thought. In the early days of each of her administrative postings at Payne, there came a moment when she was forced to draw a line in the sand. Fiamatu had once brought his five-year-old twins to the office (they had probably been expelled from kindergarten) and hinted that Fran might like to entertain them. And What-Was-Her-Face, in Anthropology, had floated the idea that Fran might work on occasional (unpaid) weekends from home. Now here was Fitger, effectively canceling her lunch hour, a period of time during which Gloria—probably at that very moment cocking her head and listening for the sound of Fran's key in the lock—might as well starve to death in her cage. It was no way to treat a foster bird.

"I gave you the Tech-Help number," she said, careful to look him in the eye. "It's on a yellow sticky note, right there on your desk."

Fitger tipped back his head and regarded her through a pair of filthy black plastic readers. The floor and the desk in his office were covered with paper, the in-box stacked about nine inches high. His shirt had an ink stain on the pocket, like a navy blue nipple, and was otherwise near-translucent with sweat. "Ordinarily," he said, "I would be delighted to initiate a search for that sticky note and then dial the Tech-

Help number myself. But—perhaps this will come as a surprise to you, but I'm not sure that it should—my phone isn't working."

Fran shouldered past him and lifted the receiver; she heard a mechanical voice requesting that she enter a code. "You just have to clear the old voicemail and set up a password."

Fitger explained that he had attempted to do just that; but lacking high-level security clearance and a degree in cryptology, he had failed to penetrate beyond the insistent request for a code. "Which is why I am asking you, as my assistant, a person employed by this university to aid and support me in the operation of this office, for your invaluable help."

A Frisbee slammed—again—against his window, dislodging the rusted screen, which tumbled out of its casement. The screen was accompanied on its earthward voyage by the rolls of toilet paper that had helped to prop the window open; thankfully, the dictionary remained firmly in place, as did the fan. There was a shout from below.

Fran started toward the open window but reversed course when a column of insects drifted balletically in on the breeze. "Whoops," she said. "Looks like you've got wasps."

Precisely above Fitger's office, on the second floor of Willard Hall, where the temperature was a calming seventy-one degrees, Professor Roland Gladwell made an editorial note in the left-hand margin of the *Campus Scribe* and buzzed his assistant, the rigorously lovely Marilyn Hoopes, who immediately knocked twice—*tap tap!*—and then opened the door.

"Econ," Roland said, pointing with his Montblanc to the

Scribe's opening paragraph. "The *Scribe* has referred to us as 'Econ.' We are the Department of Economics."

"I'll call it in," Marilyn said. "Do you want a printed correction?"

"No." Roland held up the meaty, pawlike palm of his hand. He was feeling generous. The architectural renovation of Willard Hall's second floor was ... not perfect, but close. It had taken three years to overcome the university's quibbling legalities and regulations, but finally even that stick-in-the-mud President Hoffman couldn't deny the largesse of the corporate sponsors who—so what?—had some opinions about hiring and curricular issues and would soon see their names prominently displayed on a plaque in the hall. A certain tenacity, Roland had found, was essential to getting things accomplished at Payne.

He opened the skylight over his desk. Like it or not, education had changed. Gone was the era of young men in neckties reading Catullus; students today, justifiably anxious about rising tuition, needed to be prepared for a dynamic workplace, and universities had to adapt. Ergo, business and professional schools were on the rise, as were the hard sciences, whereas some of the "softer" departments—the language units, art, music (piano and dance lessons, Roland thought, were best left as hobbies for the weekend)—would inevitably shrink. It was a simple and necessary formula: supply and demand and competition. The university had no choice but to become more fiscally responsible and more efficient, which meant eliminating redundant or unprofitable programs. As for the thin-skinned faculty and students whose tender feelings might be hurt by a lack of inclusiveness: let them beat their drums and sing their victims' songs. Roland had no patience for those who would defend incompetence or champion all-but-moribund areas of study. As per the dean's recent memo, "The Road to Ecexellence," the future of Payne was *quality*: only the worthiest departments would be granted resources and, at least in their current incarnations, be allowed to survive.

A gentle *ping!* from Roland's electronic calendar, P-Cal: it was time to check the placement of the donor plaque. Roland had, of course, overseen its design. He had supervised every aspect of the Willard Hall renovation, from the square footage in each of the faculty offices to the selection of window shades and the color of carpet and tile. Roland understood what most academics did not: money attracts money; like attracts like. Additional, future donors—skillfully identified by Marilyn Hoopes—would, at the celebration in October, soon be anxious to see their names among the illustrious contributors on the plaque.

Roland adjusted a cuff link—unlike faculty in some of the grimier departments, he was conscientious about his appearance—and strode out through the anteroom, where Marilyn and the other staff members were working. Marilyn followed him into the hall. The plaque was eight feet wide and four feet high, a few inches shy of ostentatious. Roland had wanted it large enough so that the names attached to the various levels of giving could be easily read. A trio of workmen in overalls and hard-toed shoes held the plaque in place. Marilyn had triple-checked the spellings. Yes, Roland thought, it struck just the right tone, the typeface dignified and substantial. He turned toward her. "At the reception, we need to make sure that each of the contributors—"

To Marilyn's left, a troll-like woman stood with her hands on her hips, contemplating the plaque. She was stolid; her gray dress resembled a cement drainage pipe. "Can we help you with something?" Roland asked.

She raised an eyebrow. Most people were intimidated by Roland, if not by his intelligence or the rolling timbre of his voice then by his size, particularly the savanna of his chest and the breadth of his shoulders. But the drainpipe woman seemed . . . unimpressed. "Just looking." She walked slowly away, a pair of rubber flip-flops clapping against her heels.

Marilyn Hoopes lowered her voice. "That's Frances Ignatieff," she said. "She's the administrative assistant for English. I believe they're coming upstairs to use our rest rooms."

"English," Roland said. He hated English. He hated its sloppy, undisciplined students; he hated its lawlessly oblique course offerings; he hated its faculty, probably half of whom were insane; and he especially hated Fitger, its chair. Fitger had spent the previous year publicly pissing and moaning about the Willard Hall renovations, making a stink about the dust and the corporate funds, and now he was sending his employees up here to pee. A parasitic discipline by definition, English was a feeble, fast-declining department. If it had ever had a heyday, that day was done. Fitger and his ragtag colleagues had no business in Willard; Roland wanted to crush and humiliate them—failing that, he wanted them out.

"Would you like me to speak to them?" Marilyn asked.

Roland watched Fran amble down the corridor—a snail

could have defeated her in a footrace—her sandals still slapping against her feet. She pushed through the door to the women's room, whistling: Was that "Three Blind Mice"?

"No," he said. "Not yet." He needed to caution himself. Patience. The only way to climb the rungs of the Payneful ladder (within ten years, Roland would either become provost or leave this cut-rate institution behind) was to sheathe his iron fist in a velvet glove and seize the opportune moments when they arrived.

"Ready to go, sir?" one of the workmen asked.

Roland nodded. He turned to Marilyn Hoopes. "Put Fitger and his staff on the invitation list for the celebration," he said.

Marilyn—she was superb; he would have to see about another raise—assured him she would.

Power walking across campus during her twenty-two-minute lunch hour, Janet Matthias (she still occasionally signed her name—bad habits being the hardest to break—as Matthias-Fitger) paused at the side door of Willard Hall. Typically, starting out from the law school, where she served as senior administrator, she preferred the paths on the north end of campus, shaded by oaks; but the north end was jammed with freshmen and their hand-wringing parents, everyone sweating and pushing Payne-issued bins full of electronics (most students needing at a moment's notice to exchange erotic or animal videos with every other resident of the globe) from the upper parking lot toward the dorms.

She took her pulse: a bit fast but not bad. The daily

walk was supposed to reduce her stress and bring her pulse and her blood pressure down. But, pausing on the steps of Willard—she had just cut through the building in order to deposit into Jay Fitger's campus mailbox a current issue of the *Campus Scribe*—she felt her pulse quicken. Impossible to resist bringing to her ex's attention those few short paragraphs (Janet had circled them in red) about Econ—a delicious thorn to be inserted into his side? But now—stretching her calves on the cement steps—she thought about returning to the mailroom to take the student paper back again. Fitger had a tendency to overinterpret and, given their error in judgment back in August (force of habit: one minute they were arguing about nothing; the next, their clothes lay tangled on the floor), he might read something into her gesture that she didn't intend. Already, he had implied that Janet was partly to blame for his status as chair—which was absurd: she had simply confronted him with a series of truths, i.e., the previous academic year, culminating in the death of a favorite student, had hit him hard; his writing had stalled (the market perhaps saturated at last with egotistical male writers); and there were worse sorts of tonics for the academic soul than a three-year stint in administration. Gazing down into a planter filled with the butts of cigarettes, she felt startled, anew, that he had listened, that he had run for office and won.

A shirtless Frisbee-playing student sprinted in front of her across the sidewalk, sporting the shoulder-length hairstyle of a wannabe Jesus. She noted the nipple ring and the macramé bracelets. (Now in her fifties, Janet found herself—with no desire to fight the tendency—becoming a crank.) Fitger-as-department-chair did present problems: namely, he had no tact and no discretion, and his immediate superior was Janet's significant other, Phil Hinckler, dean of Humanities and Arts. Phil was in almost every way unlike her ex. Amiable, guileless, and even-tempered, Phil was ill-suited to academic intrigue, and was repeatedly dumbstruck by attacks from other administrators and (especially) from the faculty. He had been called (he told Janet) a traitorous popinjay; a Scaramouch; a bovine sycophant (these were PhD holders, after all); and a clueless astigmatic stooge. Still, like an oversized Labrador retriever, he walked into a room in the hope that he would be liked. Only a few days before, he had slung a beefy arm across her freckled sternum and mourned the loss of his humbler, less well-paid position in the Department of Music. Then he rolled out of bed, a soggy condom forlorn on the sheet at her side.

Janet shaded her eyes and looked up at the first-floor corner office of Willard Hall, where a rusted screen appeared to be barely affixed to its frame. When people on campus found out she'd been married to Fitger—and not as a youthful, passing mistake but for almost twelve years—she could see the astonishment blooming to life on their faces: *Jason Fitger? In English? Really? Why?*

Well, it was hard to explain, but once upon a time when they were in grad school, they both had wanted the same things—to write, to publish (Janet had long ago consigned her work to a dark shelf in the closet)—and that had seemed like enough: to be two striving artists hammering away at the door of the world. Jay had succeeded, at least for a while: he had published his novel and climbed the tenure ladder at Payne, while Janet labored on and collected rejections, her failure a wellspring of embarrassment to them both. Jay offered occasional bon mots of encouragement, which made her detest him. And then one day, when she was in her late thirties, opening a rejection letter in the bathroom where Jay wouldn't witness her humiliation, she had looked up at the tarnished mirror over the sink and seen her mother's face taking shape within her own. Her mother had been dead for three years, but there in the mirror were the doleful, yellowing half-circles under her mother's eyes, and the two horizontal lines that had segmented her mother's neck like a thorax. Janet had torn up the rejection letter (*given the volume of submissions, we regret to inform you . . .*) and decided to free herself from the tyranny and the failure of writing. She quit her freelance editing job and accepted an administrative post at the law school, for which Jay pitied her. *Let him,* she thought; her salary now exceeded his. Giving up on the writing and, a few years later, her marriage (the final straw being the publication of Jay's novel *Transfer of Affection,* which contained a very thinly disguised account of his affair with another woman on campus) had been a relief. But judging from their entanglement in August (about which Janet had no compunctions—these things happened sometimes, and she had made no assurances to Phil), she wasn't sure whether Jay felt the same.

The yellow Frisbee boomeranged onto the grass and came to rest at her feet. Janet picked it up and found herself face-to-face with the wannabe Jesus. One look at his unwashed hair and unfocused eyes and she understood why his aim was inaccurate.

"Sorry, lady," he slurred.

"That's all right," she said. "Here's your toy." Every now and then she needed that little electric jolt that came from dispensing small verbal cruelties.

She looked up once more at the corner office before deciding to leave the *Scribe* in her ex-husband's box. There was no escaping one's past within the circumscribed world that was Payne.

Sitting on the newly made bed in her dorm room, Angela Vackrey looked out her window at the perfect green rectangle of grass on the quad. Her mother had just left, having stained most of Angela's clothes with her tears, even sobbing aloud (Angela hoped none of the other girls in her dorm overheard) while stacking a new pink diary (a graduation gift from Angela's grandma), a dictionary, and a Bible on the pockmarked shelf by the bed. Her mother had wanted her to live at home and go to the community college seven miles from their house in Vellmar; but Angela, who had been homeschooled since the fourth grade, had needed a change. She wasn't sure yet what kind of change, but the world was surely bigger than the pile of paperbound workbooks (*Broad Horizon: A Christian's Historical Perspective*) next to the chicken-and-egg-shaped salt and pepper shakers on the maple table where she had completed her schoolwork at home. Angela felt guilty whenever the thought slid into her mind, but she wanted to be different from her mother. She wanted to be smarter, more interesting. Which was cruel and unfair: her mother, a single parent (Angela remembered her father as a large, inebriated shadow; he drank himself to death when she was four), had sacrificed so much to raise her. They had only twice left the state for a vacation, her mother working overtime for months to pay for a trip to Florida, where the three of them—Angela and her mother and grandma—had huddled together under an umbrella in the rain. So when people in Vellmar had stopped Angela on the sidewalk or in the hobby store where she worked, and asked, *Are you really planning to go away to college and leave us?*, she could scarcely bring herself to reply. Together, she and her mother and her grandma had prayed for guidance on the issue, which eventually arrived in the form of a full-tuition scholarship to Payne.

Angela contemplated the denim skirt she was wearing—her knees prickled with hairs—and wondered whether she ought to be wearing shorts. Her roommate (because of the silver ring through her nose and the heavy dark makeup, Angela had decided it best not to show her mother Paxia's photo) was currently hitchhiking across the country and would not be attending orientation. Angela had also kept from her mother the e-mail in which Paxia had used the word *fuck* three times and identified herself as *bi/questioning/ queer*. For the next few days, Angela would have their modest cinder-block room to herself.

Though she had already memorized its contents, Angela opened her blue-and-white *Welcome to Payne* folder and read through it again, laying everything neatly across the bed. There was her orientation schedule; her campus map; a list of her fall course assignments (calculus, chemistry, English, physics, French—*What do you need French for?* her mother had asked); a copy of the student paper, the *Campus Scribe;* and the name of her faculty adviser: Professor Jason T. Fitger, Department of English, Willard Hall. Coincidentally, this was the same professor who was teaching the Literature of Apocalypse class (her mother thought it was about the Book of Revelation) in which she was enrolled. As instructed, Angela had requested an appointment with her adviser on P-Cal, the university scheduling system, but had not heard back. Which was a relief, because what on earth would she have talked about at a meeting with a professor? She wouldn't be able to think up any smart questions, and would have been throwing away a valuable opportunity to ask for advice.

She straightened her Bible and her dictionary and tucked her diary (nothing was written in it yet) into the bottom of her underwear drawer. She put her dorm key on its lanyard around her neck, included her weeping mother, her grandma, her hitchhiking roommate, and Professor Fitger in a brief, cheerful prayer, and went out for a walk. At the edge of the parking lot, she helped a tall, dark-haired girl whose rolling bin of belongings—suitcases, computer, lava lamp, near-life-sized stuffed moose, microwave, ironing board, and beanbag chair—had a misaligned wheel. The girl said "Thanks" but didn't stop to introduce herself or ask Angela's name. But that was okay: making friends would take time, and Angela would have to learn to be more outgoing and not behave like a "daydreaming mouse," as her grandmother said. Away from home, from her room with the faded blue flowered wallpaper and the smell of the Limreys' strawberry farm drifting through the curtains in front of her window, she felt untethered, as if she'd been freed from the laws of gravity. It was dizzying. Because no one knew her here at Payne, she could be anyone, whoever or whatever she wanted. She had the sense of being on the threshold of something—as if her life hadn't yet started, but she was standing in front of it, heart thumping, her trembling hands pressed against the door.

A woman wearing a dress and running shoes walked quickly past. At a university of this size, you couldn't acknowledge or say hello to everyone you met on the sidewalk. That would be too many people. Angela took a deep breath. There was the university library, with tendrils of ivy creeping like witches' fingers up the brick facade, and there were the classroom buildings—Angela probably wasn't allowed to go into them yet—including Willard Hall, where Professor Fitger had his office. The *Welcome to Payne* folder said that freshmen should feel free to consult their advisers with any questions about their academic goals or their future. But did that include questions about being different from her mother and other people in Vellmar? Questions about becoming a person whose life could be different from the way she'd grown up, a person, for example, who—

On the first floor of Willard Hall, a window screen bucked and tumbled out of its casement, skating onto the sidewalk in front of an old man carrying an armload of books. The screen was followed by several rolls of toilet paper, which unfurled themselves like banners on the way down. The old man startled, nearly falling, and several of his books landed, with their pages splayed open, in the grass.

Angela waited for someone to help him, but one student ran off, chasing a Frisbee, and another was stuffing the toilet paper rolls into an oversized purse. She stepped forward. The man was thin and very old, his face so deeply creased she imagined smoothing out the flesh with her mother's iron. He was dressed in a black suit and black shoes and tie, as if he'd been at a funeral. She bent to pick up his books while he shaded his eyes and squinted at the building's now screen-less window. A portable fan—maybe that was the problem—teetered and revolved on the peeling sill. When she brushed the dirt and grass from his books, the old man seemed to soften. He peered at the nametag on her lanyard. "Ms. Vack-rey. Thank you. Are you new to Payne? A freshman perhaps?"

Angela nodded and blushed.

He introduced himself: "Professor Cassovan, Shakespear-ean, Department of English. I hope the remainder of your time here at Payne will be hazard-free. No more objects plummeting out of the windows." He smiled.

Angela willed herself to say something—here was her first meeting with a professor!—but ended up only scraping her shoe, like a pony's hoof, across the cement.

Professor Cassovan waited a moment, then nodded as if she had answered or even said something wise. "Well, I wish you a stimulating first semester. And thank you again for the assistance. You know what they say: 'Virtue is bold, and good-ness never—' "

Fearful, Angela thought. Shakespeare! He was quoting Shakespeare, and though she wasn't sure where the line came from she knew its author. The old man seemed to understand that she'd found it familiar, and perhaps was waiting for her to speak. But beyond the suggestion of an *F,* she couldn't bring herself to make a sound.

Back in Vellmar, when Angela's mother and grandma talked about her (which they often did after dinner, Angela listening through the heating vents in her room), they worried aloud about her shyness, which they attributed to the fact that she walked around all day with her nose in a book. Angela's mother had always encouraged her to read for pleasure—but her future, like everyone else's, it seemed, lay in the sciences and math. Angela was smart; if she kept up her grades and held on to her scholarship, she could have a career as a dental hygienist. The dentist in Vellmar, Dr. Crain, often said that for a bright young woman like her, it would be a terrific career.

The old man with the stack of books was studying Angela's face as if he were privy to this conversation and had immediately discerned the narrowness of her life, which sometimes felt to Angela like a long anonymous hallway with a gravestone planted like a goalpost at the end. He had quoted Shakespeare and she had known what it was. Though total strangers, they had understood one another via a secret, purposeful language, one that ran separate and subterranean from the clumsy dialogue Angela struggled to engage in every day. The professor nodded—it was almost a bow—and she watched him slowly climb the steps of Willard Hall, dragging the broken window screen behind. Angela wanted to throw herself down on the grass and weep. "Be good," her mother had said, before she left. "You know you can come home if you aren't happy." But how would Angela know if she wasn't happy? How did anyone know? She looked at her watch; its face was blurred.

In the middle of the lawn up ahead she saw a group of student leaders in matching blue T-shirts printed with the fresh-men orientation slogan: GET READY FOR PAYNE. Angela took a deep breath. She was going to do her best to be ready. She would be outgoing; she would meet other students and talk to strangers; she would take advantage of everything that college threw her way. And because one of the first things it had thrown her was a professor of Shakespeare, she was going to drop either physics or chemistry in favor of something that Professor Cassovan was teaching. She would send her adviser, Professor Fitger, a message on P-Cal to let him know.

Dennis Cassovan carried the crumpled window screen with which, accidentally or no, someone in Willard Hall had just tried to kill him, and propped it outside the chair's office next to a trash can overloaded with broken ceiling tiles, the remains of rusted Venetian blinds, and other miscellaneous debris. Cassovan had been on sabbatical during the previous year, fortuitously absent during the renovation of the second floor of Willard Hall. He didn't care one way or the other about the economists upstairs—they and their spreadsheet ilk were beyond irrelevant—but he detested disruption and noise. Given the poorly socialized nature of his own depart-ment, whose faculty behaved with all the decorum of a pack of wolves, Cassovan's general workplace practice was to keep his own counsel, speak cordially and briefly when addressed, and get his work done.

Opening the door to his office, Cassovan set down his books and, with a sigh of contentment, surveyed the famil-iar, if modest, surroundings. Here was the plain oak desk propped up with a brick where it was missing its right front foot; here were the industrial metal bookshelves with a full set of *Shakespeare Quarterly* and the OED; here the electric typewriter (yes, still in use); the green-shaded banker's desk lamp that had been his father's; the five-dollar clock; and the ancient, nearly patternless oriental rug beneath his wooden chair. Other than the layer of dust, presumably caused by construction, everything was, reassuringly, the same. This was the setting in which the majority of Professor Cassovan's life—the parts of it that he cared to think about and remember—had transpired. His wife, Margery, had succumbed to a heart attack in her fifties some decades before, and their only son had died of cancer in his teens. That was the outer, dispiriting shell, the objective existence that others recognized and acknowledged, thereby reducing his life to a single-line caption: *professor, widower, no heirs*. But Professor Cassovan's true existence had flowered within the confines of this dingy eight-by-ten-foot room, the faded quality of his workspace an ideal backdrop to the intellectual labor of forty-two years.

A Shakespeare scholar, Cassovan had published only two monographs, but in both instances it was as if he had wrested from the earth the hunks of clay with which he was laboriously sculpting his own psyche: his two books were more completely Dennis Cassovan than were his hobbies (of which he had none) or his face or body, now so vitiated with age. Cassovan's research was not flashy or groundbreaking but it was precise, as thorough and intricate as an ivory carving, and it was the result of decades of meticulous philological work. His readership—typically other scholars of Shakespeare's Roman plays—was small, and some reviewers had initially dismissed his more recent tome (a study of augury in *Julius Caesar* and *Coriolanus*) as "almost excruciating in its level of detail," but during the past few years, younger up-and-coming scholars had begun to cite him. He had spent his recent sabbatical at Shakespearean archives in the United States and abroad, assembling material for his third (and perhaps final) book—appropriately, given his age, an examination of memory and remembrance he had titled *Anamnesis in Three Roman Plays.* Now, reinstalled at his desk, he hoped to spend the fall semester getting the preface and the opening chapter into shape.

A knock at the door announced the arrival of his research assistant, Lincoln Young. Lincoln had a PhD in English but, now balding and fast approaching forty, had been unable to find steady work; he taught one or two sections of composition each semester at Payne and then, like an itinerant tinker or scissors grinder, traveled from private high school to community college to tutoring center in order to assemble a living wage. Because no one in English had research funds, Cassovan paid him privately, unofficially, fifteen dollars per hour under the table. Ostensibly, he was doing his assistant a favor, but he was aware, given the ravenous look that Lincoln Young occasionally gave him, that the favor he preferred would be for his supervisor to die and free up a job.

Lincoln sat down, the chair beneath him wheezing gently. Although the semester hadn't yet started, he looked a bit weary, almost waterlogged, his hair a collection of dark threads pasted across a sweaty scalp. How was Professor Cassovan's time away? Productive? Good. And this was his first day back? Had he been upstairs yet, to see Econ's refurbished part of the building?

No, he had not. He was not a professor of economics and had no business or interest in that vacuous field. Could they get to work? They were both obviously very busy preparing classes, and—

Yes, of course. Definitely. Right to work. Lincoln smiled in a sidesaddle fashion. He was one of the few people Cassovan knew who was less attractive when he smiled: he wore the pitiful, wrenching grin of a suffering clown. Before they settled on the first list of tasks for the semester, he wanted Professor Cassovan to know that he might not be teaching at Payne after the coming year.

Oh? Cassovan tried not to look surprised. Had he found a regular position somewhere?

Another torqued smile. Unfortunately, no. But word on the street—or in the windowless basement offices where the adjunct faculty and TAs were housed—was that the university's financial problems were particularly dire that year; and that the non-tenure-track instructors, come spring, would not be rehired. Lincoln would hate to leave Professor Cassovan in the lurch, especially now, when they were collaborating on a paper for the upcoming conference; but perhaps, as an esteemed senior member of the department, he might intercede on Lincoln's behalf, arranging for a two- or three-year lectureship, via Fitger, the incoming chair.

Cassovan blew his nose severely into a handkerchief. While he sympathized with the temporary instructors, who could probably earn more as forty-hour-a-week fast-food managers than they did as adjunct faculty at Payne, these rumors about fiscal and administrative crisis swept through the campus every year; moreover, it was unprofessional of Lincoln Young to suggest that Cassovan cut a back-channel deal with the incoming chair. Clearly, Fitger was a poor choice to lead the department—Cassovan wouldn't have trusted him to run a pet shop—but if and when true crisis came, he wasn't likely to respond to it by firing the adjuncts, who toiled away on endless stacks of freshman essays for miserable wages in a warren of cubicles on the subfloor.

Might his fellow instructors' anxiety, Cassovan asked, be premature? It was a stressful time in higher education, and changes, at Payne and elsewhere, were undoubtedly afoot, but personally he hadn't heard of—

Lincoln interrupted. Sometimes the instructors, he explained, who were more vulnerable than the tenure-track faculty, made it their business to learn about these shifts in policy first.

Cassovan was rankled—he didn't like being interrupted. "What shifts in policy?" he asked.

Lincoln stroked his thinning hair—a nervous tic—with his fingers. He confessed to being a bit of a computer nerd; he kept late hours and in moments of insomnia browsed through university documents online. Did Professor Cassovan know that English would soon submit its new Statement of Vision?

Cassovan pointedly glanced at his watch. The Statement of Vision was a needless make-work task imposed on all departments by the upper-level administration.

"I only mention it," Lincoln said, "because you were away last year and might not have seen it." He paused. "You have to read between the lines, but—"

"But what?"

"Well . . . they're going to eliminate Shakespeare."

"I beg your pardon?"

"I suppose it's partly a financial decision." Lincoln continued caressing the hair on his head. "And partly about teaching what the undergrads enjoy. You know—the things they find relevant."

An abhorrent buzzword, "relevance," Cassovan thought, was best confined to books about tax preparation and the literature of self-help. "Where did you learn about this?"

About the new Statement? Lincoln couldn't remember, exactly. He read so many university-related e-mails and bulletins, and he didn't want to waste Professor Cassovan's money or time—unless the professor wanted him to spend a few additional minutes . . . ?

Cassovan nodded. Then, while Lincoln Young opened his laptop and searched, he sat and waited, studying the brittle black-and-white poster of William Shakespeare, greatest writer in the English language, that for several decades had hung on his glass-front door.

At the opposite end of the hallway, outside the department chair's suite, Professor Jason T. Fitger, pant legs rolled haphazardly up his calves, was duct-taping a third extension cord to the floor.

"Just FYI." Fran peered down at him where he crawled

through the dust like a penitent, legs sticky with sweat. "I'm getting ready to spray, in the office."

Fitger ripped the duct tape with his teeth. Fran had managed to find him a semifunctional laptop, and he was determined to be able to plug it in while making simultaneous use of both desk lamp and fan. She was shaking a sizeable container—it looked like a magnum, he thought—of insecticide. "You can't use that indoors." He peeled another strip of tape from the roll.

Two junior economists, briefcases and lattes in hand, emerged from the stairwell. Confronted with a heavily perspiring man kneeling in front of the WELC ME TO ENGLI H sign, they quickly rectified their mistake and moved along.

"You have a nest of wasps right by your window," Fran said. "And you don't have a screen."

"I thought you were an animal sympathizer."

"I have no sympathy," Fran said, "for arthropods."

Fitger stood up and followed her through the anteroom into his office, and together they noted the comings-and-goings of a number of flying insects, half a dozen of which were making loops around the traylike fluorescent lights. Fitger ducked when one of the creatures flew near. "I think if we open the door and prop the—"

Fran pressed the nozzle, which seemed to misfire, and a wet arrow of insecticide—Fitger remembered an uncle describing the effects of Agent Orange—caught the rim of his ear.

"Whoops." She sent a second blast toward the ceiling, the fallout trickling onto his head, a toxic mist.

Fitger shielded his eyes and, wondering about neurological

damage, staggered into Fran's part of the office. She followed behind him, shutting the door. "Did I get you?" she asked.

He was wiping his eyes with the tail of his shirt. "You almost blinded me," he said. "And all you did was make them angry." They watched the wasps swarming and diving on the other side of the Plexiglas window.

"We'll give them ten minutes," Fran said. She took a seat at her desk, logged into her computer, and started to work.

Leaning on the file cabinet behind her, Fitger (dabbing thick, poisonous tears from his face) noticed that their two nearly identical offices resembled side-by-side containers for a pair of Siamese fighting fish. "Could we order a blind for that window?" he asked.

She continued typing. "Money for a blind would have to come from our supply budget."

"And?"

"We don't have a supply budget. Or, I should say, we have one but there's nothing in it."

Fitger gazed through the window into his insect-ridden compartment. The wasps seemed to be increasing in strength and number.

"In case you're wondering," Fran said, "I'm trying to get you set up on P-Cal. What do you want your password to be?"

"I don't want to use P-Cal," Fitger said. "I refuse to adapt every six months to a pointless new system."

Fran didn't hear or pretended not to hear this response. She explained that, once his P-Cal account was established, either of them would be able to input (Fitger ground his teeth at this unpalatable verb) appointments on his calendar, while other P-Cal users on campus would be able to access

32

(more hideous usage!) his agenda and know when he was free.

"I have a better idea," he said. Why didn't they forget about P-Cal, which he had no intention of using, and instead make a list of things he needed for the office, a list beginning, for example, with a working telephone and computer; two functional electrical outlets; a chair that didn't double as a Venus flytrap; a desk lamp that didn't heat itself up to six hundred degrees; more than one piece of stationery; and a nameplate that spelled his name correctly, on something more lasting than the back of a cereal box top.

Fran said she would appreciate it if he would keep the sarcastic tone to a minimum, and he didn't need to nag her about the computer. She had already given up her lunch hour in order to engage in a lengthy conversation with one of the techs from Tech-Help; their office was busy at this time of year but they would show up sooner or later; that was all she could do. "Huh." She sat up straighter in her chair, her feet several inches from the floor. "Look at this: your P-Cal account is up and running, but because you haven't logged in, the system has made it look like you're always available. It must be a glitch. You've got a lot of appointments with people already."

"What kind of appointments?"

Fran squinted at the screen. "Let's see. The red ones are usually mandatory or urgent: info session for new chairs and directors; convocation; faculty cabinet; humanities council; faculty appeals board; university caucus . . ."

Fitger had the sensation that he was listening to his obituary read aloud, including a detailed account of the things that would kill him. "Wait a second." He leaned over her shoulder. "That info session, in red. Is that today?"

"Hang on. Yup. Today. Mandatory session for new chairs and directors at eleven-thirty." It was two-fifteen.

Something crashed to the floor in Fitger's office.

Peering through the Plexiglas divider, he saw his rotary fan, which, having fallen forward out of the window, was thrashing like a rabid animal among the remnants of the *Campus Scribe* on the rug. "Shit." He opened the door to Fran's office and sprinted around the divider. After yanking the fan and its extension cord from the socket, he wrenched the dictionary from its place on the sill and slammed the window against additional wasps, thereby sealing in the heat and the sickening-sweet smell of insecticide.

Fran watched from the doorway.

"I want someone to explain to me," he said, "why a university would renovate and air-condition half of a building."

"Talk to the facilities people," Fran said. "Or to your friends upstairs in Econ. You have a wasp on your arm."

Fitger looked at the wasp, which stung him. Even at that moment, his electronic calendar, P-Cal, which indicated that he was free every day, all semester, was filling up.

TWO

For forty-two years, Dennis Cassovan had carefully side-stepped all things controversial at Payne. He had arrived on campus in 1968, an introverted, anxious assistant professor who had evaded the draft due to a spindly right leg—polio, contracted at the age of four. The senior faculty had warned him, soon after his hire, against becoming embroiled in "student-centered unrest"; overwhelmed with teaching and nearly sleepless following the birth of his son—a squalling, furious, elfin creature, all mouth and fists—Cassovan had kept his head down, spent every spare second on his research, and been awarded tenure and a contract for his first book by the end of the war.

Over the years, austere neutrality had become a character trait and a default. Aloof but unfailingly civil, Cassovan had accepted as inevitable the cultural shifts in the discipline in the 1970s, '80s, and '90s. He had tried to be open-minded when dealing with the department's theorists (though he wished they could write); the creative writers (though he wished they had standards); and those who would fill their syllabi with sociological studies, television shows, discussions of sexual mores, food, politics, animals, fashion, and popular culture.

Cassovan assumed that students benefitted from a breadth of electives and from scholarly perspectives beyond his own—as long as these whimsical alternatives didn't threaten the core.

Because what, he asked himself, carefully scrolling through the course catalog for the first time in a decade, were English literary studies without the core? A curriculum lacking the foundational works—from *Beowulf* to Virginia Woolf—was a hummock of flesh without a skeleton; it was shapeless, absurd.

Lincoln Young had been right about the department's new Statement of Vision: the document, purported to be an outline or overview of the department's purpose, was distressing proof that Cassovan's laissez-faire attitude toward his academic unit had come at a cost. After Lincoln handed over his time card and slumped out of the office, Cassovan had spent the hours he normally would have dedicated to refining his syllabus to a squinting consultation with his computer screen. The proposed new SOV made no mention of Shakespeare but referred in broadly meaningless terms to *inquiry, professionalization, engagement,* and *a multiplicity of perspectives in a globalized world.* It might as well have been the SOV for the Department of Health Sciences or Phys Ed. Should the Statement be subjected to a vote and approved, the result would be a scattershot curriculum almost entirely devoid of tradition or history, and the undergraduate student majoring in English would no longer be required to take a course—not even one—in the works of Shakespeare.

Cassovan closed his eyes for a moment, feeling ill. The very marrow of the discipline would be expunged. He had to hold himself partly responsible: during the year he had been on sabbatical, he had scarcely glanced at the daily deluge of e-correspondence or the minutes of meetings. But now, e-mail by e-mail, he followed a months-long electronic rabbit trail which revealed that, in addition to electing Fitger, a hodgepodge of exhausted colleagues had collectively assembled this impossible document, as if dragging a one-legged blind man through multiple layers of the committee system. Perhaps the intent had been to obey some bizarre directive from above, but the outcome was, for the students, an irresponsible freedom. No need for the English major to familiarize him- or herself with Chaucer or Milton, let alone Spenser or Donne, all of whose works had been discarded in an earlier purge; now Shakespeare himself was to be lobbed, like a tidbit of refuse, into the bin.

And what might Payne's young literary scholars study instead? Bracing himself, Cassovan returned to the course catalog. Upcoming classes included Aliens and Outlaws, Marxism 2.5, The American Soap and the Telenovela, and The Literature of Deviation. How was a student to make any sense of it? Shakespeare was the cornerstone, the fountainhead. To allow an undergraduate English major to earn a diploma without studying *Hamlet* and *Lear,* and either *Julius Caesar* or *Antony and Cleopatra,* was, on the part of the faculty, an abdication: *Read whatever you like! We aren't here to offer intellectual guidance! Our field is a come-what-may experience. Anything goes!*

And as for the bugaboo of "relevance": to allow a student to believe that the value of a work of literature depended on its superficial resemblance to his or her life! Cassovan pulled the yellowish blind in his window to block the afternoon sun.

He had hoped, by this time of day, to be heading home to a single-serving prepackaged dinner, which he preferred, after long habit, to eat at room temperature while listening to the BBC News on the radio. But something would have to be done about the department's egregious error, the ultimate responsibility for which lay, of course, with its newly elected chair. Cassovan had no compunction about opposing Fitger, who had refused to respond to a second message sent via P-Cal, and who moreover had attempted, several days earlier, to behead his senior colleague with a window screen.

Cassovan turned off his computer. On the other side of his office door—the poster of Shakespeare providing a scrim of privacy from pedestrian traffic in the hall—students were chattering, strolling, laughing, fretting, flirting, and endowing the air, all over campus, with a galvanic charge. If Fitger's intention was to sweep beneath the carpet of oblivion the heart of the discipline in which Cassovan had long labored . . . No: Cassovan had taught at Payne for more than four decades, and he was not at a loss for strategies and resources. *The arms are fair,* he thought, *when the intent of bearing them is just.*

Roland Gladwell, BA summa cum laude Cornell, PhD Princeton, had made it his business to familiarize himself with the architectural blueprints (requested during the renovation) of Willard Hall. In idle moments, even after the renovation was finished, he unrolled the plans and made notes about poorly or underutilized portions of the building. The second floor—his own department's domain—was now well

38

designed and elegantly appointed. But both the first floor and the basement (absurd that English should have two floors, even if a sizeable portion of the basement *was* taken up with heating systems, storage, and janitorial supplies) resembled a series of animal pens, with classrooms jutting willy-nilly into faculty offices, doorways opening onto bricked-up closets, and, in an obscure corner of the basement, a mysterious windowless space designated (Roland had checked the blueprints twice) as a "breastfeeding lounge."

Fallow areas were being identified via careful research: Marilyn Hoopes had reported back on English's literary magazine office, which—given that the magazine was defunct—was clearly unused. Roland made a note in the right-hand margin of the plans. He hadn't expected to end up at a mid-sized, middlebrow university like Payne, its brick posterior overlooking a sluggish, Midwestern river. But he had been on the wrong end of his advisers' favoritism at Princeton, and so had settled on Payne as a stepping-stone, a strategic interlude during which he could sharpen his administrative skills before making his way back to the Ivies or the Big Ten. This plan had become more difficult when Payne, like a listing ship, began its steady descent in the national rankings. Under the misdirected leadership of the previous president, tuition had risen almost 40 percent, much of the increase paying for a bloated centenary celebration ("One Hundred Years of Payne"), a cluster of new athletic facilities, and the grossly inflated salary of a football coach whose team had lost sixteen consecutive games. More than half the seats in the overpriced stadium were permanently empty, but Coach Klapp remained a popular figure on campus, easily recognized for his bouncing jog, the whistle that rode the paunch above his blue sweatshirt, and his well-paid underdog's grin.

To be forever marooned here, Roland thought . . . *No: impossible.* One's only recourse, when the waters of mediocrity began to rise, was to construct a personalized life raft—which at Payne was not about scholarship or teaching, but about power, authority, status, and the ability to raise funds. The university's president, Nyla Hoffman, had recently made these priorities clear. Hired as a corrective to her spendthrift predecessor, Hoffman had a PhD in psychology but had never taught, having spent several decades in the private sector. Recruited from an inscrutable job with a high-security firm that no one at Payne quite understood, Hoffman had the personal charm of a KGB agent, and was basing her "much-needed reforms" on a thorough distrust of both professors and students. Ill-prepared for the maelstrom of university politics, she had hired an army of administrators—vice provosts, assistant vice provosts, associate deans, duchesses, dukes, footmen, jesters, earls—whose job was to reward and "incentivize" potentially profitable departments and allow the others to wither like juiceless fruit on the university vine. Roland had no objections to this philosophy, which required department chairs to think like CEOs. He had already demonstrated his own ability to "cultivate community partners," making sure to share the news of his conquests with the relevant bureaucrats over his head—i.e., the tag team of administrators who had their hands on the spigots through which the perks and finances at the university flowed.

Ergo, his cordial invitation to Dean Philip Hinckler, to

whom he had extended the offer of a coveted "first look" at the Economics Department's exquisitely renovated space. The dean had claimed at first to be busy, but Roland pressed him, suggesting a variety of dates and couching the invitation as a personal favor. "An opportunity for me to thank you," he said, "to express my appreciation for everything you've done." In truth, the dean had been nothing but a pain in the ass during the renovation, posing worrywart concerns and generally behaving, whenever Roland had attempted to speed things along, like a clog in a drain. But here he was now, chatting with Marilyn Hoopes in the outer office. Roland stashed the blueprints away and opened the door.

In his early sixties, a man with a doughy physique and a breathless, repetitive way of speaking, Dean Philip Hinckler was prone to semi-sentences that expired, half-finished, in rhetorical cul-de-sacs. At university events he could be counted on for meandering, circuitous speeches about the benefits of a "broadly diverse education"—in Roland's view a steaming, politically correct pile of shit, because why would students want to spend almost $40K per year to read a few history books and take a weaving and a racquet-ball class and call themselves well-rounded, if there was no career or financial payoff at the end? They would all be better off acknowledging this basic truth, Roland thought, but Hinckler, who had risen from the undifferentiated swamp of the Music Department into the deanery, preferred to stick to the fuzzy, traditional script he'd inherited—in effect, to pretend. The two men shook hands. They strolled into the hall so the dean could appreciate the donor plaque (Marilyn Hoopes skillfully pointing to several particularly distinguished names), and Roland conducted a brief tour of the technology-enhanced classrooms and the chair's new executive suite.

"Beautiful job, Roland," the dean said. "It's well, it's just . . ." He handed Roland a tissue-wrapped parcel. "Here. A little housewarming gift. I see you don't have one of these, so—" He glanced around at Roland's wood-paneled fiefdom. "In any case, congratulations."

Roland thanked him and set the parcel aside, but the dean insisted that he unwrap it. Roland tugged at the ribbon and then—good god!—revealed a paperweight figurine of the Payne University Prairie Dog, official school mascot known to the students as "Pup-Dog" or "Pup." Roland had a personal grudge against Pup, who could be counted on to sway its furry lascivious hips and make digging motions with its foreshortened paws during football and basketball games and other functions. Once, during a convocation, the grinning rodent (presumably a disgruntled student, securely disguised) had stood beside Roland for an official photo and stroked the chair's buttocks, a gesture impossible to interpret as accidental. Why the university would have chosen for its mascot a nondescript pest that spent the bulk of its existence hunting for insects underground was beyond Roland's considerable understanding. The dean's unsightly gift, a six-inch toothsome bronze replica, was nattily dressed in a tiny blue cap and gown.

Roland was about to consign the mascot to an obscure spot on a shelf, but the dean picked it up, examined it, and set it, somewhat roughly, Roland thought, at the edge of the desk. Were Phil Hinckler's wrinkled suit and puddin'head smile a strategic facade? This was a possibility Roland would consider later. Right now, it was noon—the campus pre-recorded bells, mechanical and yet still out of tune, were tolling twelve—and Marilyn Hoopes was delivering lunch: arugula and shrimp salad, beef carpaccio, cheese, and a selection of truffles wrapped in gold foil.

"Roland, this is a . . . I wasn't expecting . . . It all looks absolutely . . . ," the dean said.

Marilyn set up a wooden tray—several meaningful inches lower than the surface of Roland's desk—and asked if the dean would care for a glass of red wine.

Well, certainly, yes, thank you, he would. Phil Hinckler smiled and spread a napkin over his lap. From Roland's window he could see the grassy center of campus and the pedestaled monument to the university's founder, Cyril Payne, whose family had made its fortune on medicinal powders and anti-itching solutions over a century before. Undergraduates were said to observe peculiar midnight rituals at the base of this statue, sibylline ceremonies involving Hula-Hoops, kazoos, and a Pied Piper–like parade whose participants, even or especially in the depths of winter, wore only hiking boots and gloves. On the front of the statue beneath Cyril's bewildered expression was his dispiriting death march of a motto: PERSEVERE.

Ah, well. The shrimp looked terrific; and he might as well enjoy it before Roland got around to whatever request he had in mind. It was bound to be something substantial: in Phil's experience, the caliber of the blandishments (the Oregon pinot noir was impressive) was directly related to the size of the perk to be discussed.

God, he was tired of being dean. He had accepted the position six years before, stepping up into the ranks of the administration feeling pleased with himself and vaguely flattered. But the administration at Payne had swelled to such an extent that even in the provost's and the president's offices it was hard to keep track of the various sub-jurisdictions— deans and assistant and associate deans were as common as nobles in pre-Soviet Russia. Worse: two months after he moved into his new office, his faculty position in the Department of Music (Hinckler was a professor/instructor of the French horn) had been eliminated. It was as if, seconds after being lured away from his home village, he had watched it torched and then burned to the ground. With no tenure line remaining behind him, he couldn't go back to teaching music; and, given his lackluster fund-raising skills, there would be no climbing the ladder, either. Unable to retire— divorced, he had two teenage sons who despised him and who would soon require an expensive education—he was stuck. The deanship had become a waiting room to nowhere, a little purgatory unto itself. The major part of his job was saying no to faculty members in search of resources for their departments. But then there were faculty like Roland Gladwell—crowned head of a department with a superabundance of money courtesy of private and corporate donors, as well as an obscenely low faculty teaching load and a suite of offices more luxuriously appointed than the provost's— presumably greasing the wheels in order to ask for something more.

Meanwhile, the cheese was superb: creamy but not runny,

with just a hint of peppery tang on the rind. What was the name of that cave-aged brie he loved? Janet had bought it for him once . . . Was it Red Rock? Grass Rock?

Roland coughed, clearing his throat, and they engaged in a little ping-pong match of preliminary conversation, ending with the usual grim prognostications regarding the Payne U football team. And then, yes, here it came, the list of items on the Econ brag sheet, Roland praising the cutting-edge work being done by his brilliant faculty, whose research was of extreme importance to one and all. This was standard fare—the chair extolling his or her unit—and Phil Hinckler nodded, his mind periodically drifting off in search of the name of that wonderful cheese. He would have to remember to ask Janet what it was called. She remembered everything, and had a mind like a steel trap. If she had entered academia not as a member of the staff but as a professor, she would have been running the university by now.

Perhaps aware of the dean's wandering interest, Roland asked if, regarding the current research in econometrics, he should pause to explain or to clarify.

"No, I'm with you," Phil said. He hadn't taken a social science class since eleventh grade, but it was his job to keep abreast of the major trends in a wide range of disciplines. Having recently attended a presentation in the Art Department that involved the painting of historical portraits on the testes of sheep, he felt capable of withstanding the quirks in any field.

Roland refilled their drinks. Hesitant to launch directly into the need for a larger share of the building (he'd had

Marilyn Hoopes check the dimensions of the dean's office, and learned that it was smaller and more modest than his own), he opted for a subtler approach. "Phil," he said, "you can see I've been fortunate. I've done well here at Payne. I've built and run a preeminent department, and I've made important, beneficial community ties."

Still waiting for Roland's ask, the dean tipped back his wine. He put his fork, which held a vinaigrette-stained leaf of arugula, on Roland's desk.

"I'm not going to minimize my own accomplishments or efforts"—Roland wanted to pick up the fork and wipe its tines on the dean's tan pants—"but I'm able to recognize that Payne has given me a lot, and I'm in the position, now, to want to give back."

This was an intriguing bit of rhetorical feathering. The dean waited; he reached for a truffle; he was not in a rush.

"For example," Roland said. "I suspect you're having trouble recruiting faculty for some of your committees."

The truffle—dark chocolate with some sort of buttercream—was exquisite. The dean bobbed his head. A core ingredient of his job was finding faculty to serve on committees; and each semester, the number of campus committees grew, even the Committee on Committees spawning subgroups with elaborate charters and mandates, like a rapidly multiplying cancerous cell. Of course he was having trouble recruiting. Some of the faculty blocked his e-mails and didn't answer when they saw the telltale number of his extension light up on their phones. Janet had looked askance at the list of assignments he had to fill and suggested that he staff at least a third of them with nonexistent professors bearing fictional names. "No one will notice," she said. She had offered him a hundred dollars to experiment with this tactic, but he had declined.

"I do need two people for the appeals board," he said, "as well as two for athletic oversight. If you have a colleague in mind who—"

"Actually," Roland said, "I was thinking of the new quality assessment program."

Phil Hinckler—known in certain circles as the human windsock—was temporarily speechless.

"I could be willing to serve," Roland said. "Not as a member, but if you're looking for someone to chair it."

"You're already chairing a department." The dean reached for another truffle. "How do you know about QUAP?"

Roland moved his hands above the surface of his desk as if smoothing a bolt of invisible cloth. Of course he knew about QUAP. People knew. Rumors about the quality assessment program had been traded in whispers across the campus for over a year, with most faculty, heads firmly implanted in the sand, preferring to consider it an urban legend or a threat.

"Technically, the program doesn't exist yet," Phil said. "And the president wants us to move slowly, for all the obvious reasons."

The obvious reasons, Roland concluded, were cowardice and prevarication. "I assume you've already asked Wyman to run it?"

Phil sighed and tossed the second truffle into his mouth.

"And I assume she refused?"

Yes, she'd refused. Wyman, the former chair of Geography, had asked for a 10 percent raise and a teaching reduction to convene the committee, and when these demands weren't met she declined to serve on the basis of "general scruples." Almost no one on campus would want to touch QUAP; a sort of wolf in sheep's clothing, its mission would be to rank every academic unit according to a "quality metric." But its methodology would clearly be punitive. Designed with Big Brother–like oversight capabilities, including the (rumored) capacity to revoke tenure, QUAP was the Death Star of university committees.

Roland thought the hush-hush hysteria about the program absurd. QUAP was simply a way of publicly and more emphatically enacting a process with which everyone on campus was already familiar: stronger, more functional departments would be rewarded; the weaker would not. He found himself repeating the acronym to himself, enjoying the feel of the word in his mouth. *QUAP:* the sound of a door clicking satisfactorily shut.

"I'll need to . . . ," Phil said. "That is, I'll have to speak to some of the other deans and the provost."

"Absolutely. Of course." Roland shoved the Pup-Dog statuette aside. The opinions of the other deans were irrelevant, and getting approval from the provost was a ruse: almost no one had ever seen Rutledge, who was said to be allergic to sunlight and for the past four years had been "working from home."

He invited Phil Hinckler to take some truffles for the road, then looked at his watch: it had been forty-five minutes since the dean walked in. By prior arrangement, Marilyn Hoopes knocked at the door to remind him of a nonexistent appointment. "I'm so sorry to interrupt," she said, "but they're waiting for you, Professor Gladwell."

"Ah! Apologies." Roland stood, extending a manicured, muscular hand.

Phil Hinckler hauled himself out of his chair, his knees creaking like hinges. He had thought QUAP would remain for another few years on the university's almost limitless back burner, but with Roland volunteering to lead it . . . Inertia could slow things down for a semester or two, but after that . . . He shook Roland's hand. The university was gradually being taken over by brawny, networking businessmen and -women who knew nothing of students, and who would turn the teaching of undergraduates into ill-paid, incidental labor. *Four more years,* Phil thought: that was as long as he could possibly last—his sons would have to borrow the money for college.

He took an indirect route out of the building, hoping to avoid faculty—especially in English, where Janet's ex-husband, Fitger, was the chair. Phil stirred the truffles in his pocket, planning to share them with Janet that night after dinner; but he ended up eating them, one by one, in his office, alone.

THREE

In Fran's opinion—not that anyone ever asked for her opinion—it was not a good idea for the incoming chair of a department to be absent during the very first week of the semester, to cancel his first class and his office hours and at least two meetings, and to tell his assistant to say he was sick (he didn't sound sick) and could be reached via e-mail at home. Fran would have been happy to run the department herself—and could have done so with one hand tied behind her back—but as a member of the staff she was restricted to the status of eternal helpmeet, her fate inextricably allied with that of the chair. Sitting down at her desk with a cup of coffee (a scrim of aspartame floating along the top), she asked herself, not for the first time, whether, in being assigned to English, she had been a target of discrimination. She was four foot ten: someone had once told her that if she had been half an inch shorter, she would have qualified, legally, as a dwarf.

An hour into the morning she heard the squeak of the outer door and looked up in time to see Fitger's briefcase turn the corner into his office. She needed to ask him about taking an extra hour at lunch: Gloria was under the weather—her tail feathers were soiled and oddly clumpy— and Fran had a 12:40 appointment at the vet. She positioned herself in Fitger's doorway. "Ahem," she said.

He looked up.

"Jesus Christ in a cradle." Fran took a step back.

"Wasps," Fitger said. He scratched himself. "It turns out I'm allergic." He was wearing a wrinkled short-sleeved shirt and a bright red tie. "How bad does it look?"

His face was dotted with welts the size of golf balls sliced in half. His right eye was swollen shut, and a bluish-red lump, like the beginning of a solitary horn, strained the skin between his overgrown brows.

"You're staring," he said.

"I can't help it. Do you need some Benadryl?"

"I already took some. These goddamned lumps just refuse to go down." His swollen left hand resembled an animal's paw. "I have to teach at eleven, but I'll probably work from home after that."

"You can't work from home. You've been out half a week. And you're in charge of the welcome and orientation for new TAs and instructors—which I already rescheduled. It starts at one."

Fitger pointed the plum-colored knurl on his head in her direction. Might Fran be able and/or willing to—

"No." She was still staring. "I have an appointment off-campus." She decided not to tell him about the vet. "Besides, leading the department is not my job. But I can give you the bullet points for the orientation. Ashkir typed them up."

"Who is Ashkir?"

"Our undergrad office worker. From the work-study office. I hired him."

But: Wasn't the hiring of staff the chair's responsibility?

"That depends," Fran said.

"On what?"

"On whether you want to get anything done. You weren't around; I had to hire him. You can meet him tomorrow. We can only afford him for ten hours a week." She handed Fitger a piece of green paper that invited him to *the first mind-bending kegger of the year.*

"No. The other side," she said. "We're saving paper."

Fitger flipped the page over and read:

ORIENTATION FOR NEW TAs AND GRADUATE INSTRUCTORS

1) You're glad they're here.
2) It is too late to make changes to their teaching assignments.
3) You are sorry about the basement office space— they should be careful of remaining scaffolding and please leave mouse- and ant-traps where they are.
4) Remind them not to sleep with the undergraduates, even when undergrads are older/hotter/more desirable than the norm.
5) No drugs or drinking with the undergrads, especially hard drugs while inside the building.
6) For all other policy matters and questions, see Fran.

"You can flesh it out and personalize it," she said, "but those are the basics. By the way, you owe me $33.50."

Fitger folded the paper into his pocket. Addressing the non-tenure-track instructors was a ticklish and morally complicated task—akin to a ship's captain going belowdecks to rouse the galley slaves at their posts. "Why do I owe you $33.50?"

"I ordered bagels and cream cheese for the orientation. You can't have an official gathering in the middle of the day without food. Not for this group." She had met a few of the new instructors, who appeared to be in need of famine relief; they had the hollow, hopeless physique of refugees.

Fitger reached for his wallet, then stopped. Orientation was a department function. Couldn't she take the bagels out of the budget?

"I think I mentioned this before," Fran said. "We don't have a budget. I hired Ashkir with our repair and maintenance funds."

He shook his head. "So when do we get our department budget?"

"After you get the faculty to vote and approve of the Statement of Vision. Every other department submitted theirs last year."

Statement of Vision: Fitger shuddered at the vacuity of the phrase. The SOV was a nebulous document intended to summarize the department's purpose—as if the teaching of literature and composition were something obscure. "We can take care of that at the faculty meeting," he said. "We have a draft, so it should be simple enough. Shouldn't it?"

"I'm not going to answer that," Fran said, "except to say that Dennis Cassovan has been looking for you. He stopped by several times in the past few days."

Fitger scratched at himself, fingers raking his chest. Amazing that Cassovan was still teaching. How old was he—ninety?

"But hey, it isn't all bad news," Fran said. "Look. You got a new computer."

Stacked in the corner of Fitger's office, which was hot and airless because the window was closed, were three large cardboard boxes, their "this side up" arrows all pointing down.

"They couldn't assemble it?" he asked.

Well, no: because when they delivered it, Fitger was gone and they needed his signature. But they would come back as soon as he requested another appointment—which, by the way, he should do very soon, because Tech-Help was busy at this time of year. "And that reminds me," Fran said. "I scheduled the welcome and orientation in room 102B."

Fitger gently kicked one of the cardboard boxes. Room 102B was a standard English Department classroom: chipped linoleum floor, teetering mismatched collection of uncomfortable desks, elementary school blackboard with half-inch remnants of chalk. "Why didn't you schedule it in the conference room?"

"The conference room's not available."

"Why not?"

Fran sighed. It was only 9:45 a.m. and already she was thinking about being at home in her gravity-free chair with a bag of ice on her legs. "You really want to go into this now?"

"Go into what?" Fitger was scratching himself again; in her

mind's eye, Fran took up one of the extension cords and fastened his twitching hands behind his back.

"There's a whole new system for room allocation," she said. "The conference room designation was changed. It's no longer designated for 'primary use' by our department."

"But it's our conference room," Fitger said. "We've been using that room for thirty years."

"That's not how it works anymore. Under the new system, departments have to bid—and yes, I'm talking about money—for the use of any 'common space.' And someone bid for the conference room. So we can't use it, because the room is reserved."

Fitger couldn't help pointing in the direction of the room. "But it's just down the hall," he said. "I'm talking about the conference room on our floor. You're telling me we have to pay to use it?"

Yes, that's what she was telling him, and she was well aware of the room's location. "But if we haven't reserved it, we can't get into it. It's locked. You need one of the new magnetic cards."

A horsefly zoomed through the airspace between them; Fitger, still gun-shy given the incident with the wasps, recoiled. His swollen eye seemed to be leaking some kind of fluid. "What about our faculty meetings?" he asked. "Have you reserved the room beginning next week?"

"Did I mention that we don't have a budget?" Fran asked. "I can't bid on the conference room until we have a budget. And along with most of the other reasonable rooms, it's probably taken by now—at least during the day. You might want to start scheduling faculty meetings for midnight on Wednesdays." She watched him absorb this information. "Anyway, for now, you're meeting in 102B, and you owe me thirty-five bucks."

"I thought it was thirty-three and a half."

Fran said she assumed that he didn't have change.

An hour later, after right-siding and opening the computer boxes and staring, mystified, at the cables and plastic-wrapped machinery within, Fitger picked up his briefcase and trekked across campus to teach his first class. He normally taught in one of the generic 1970s-era buildings east of Willard, just past the gleaming new architectural wonder constructed for the benefit of the business school; but for the current semester (perhaps because of the new room-extortion system and his department's indigence) he had been assigned to a nearly decommissioned cinder block slab on a dead-end road, between the facilities plant and the women's gym. Pavender Hall—Fitger had heard it mentioned but had never entered it before—was flanked by industrial trash barrels and resembled a colorless brick that had been pressed into the earth by a giant foot. The front entrance was locked and much of the building appeared to be unused, but Fitger eventually made his way to Pavender 001, a faintly illuminated bunkerlike enclosure on the lower floor. Perhaps last used in a low-budget horror film, this windowless chamber had an emergency showerhead in one corner and had presumably, at the time of the first atomic explosions, been a science lab. Fitger's twenty-four Literature of Apocalypse students—all of them freshmen—sat in long rows, some flanking a trough-like metal sink, others hunkered around an eyewash station or a stone-topped table equipped with levers that, when turned, released remnant whiffs of a foul-smelling gas. Pendulum chain-link lamps dangled overhead, suggestive of nooses. Putting his briefcase by the lectern and taking stock of these surroundings, Fitger heard one of the freshmen say to another, "This is *so cool.*"

All right, then: forward. After apologizing for missing their opening session, Fitger glanced at the roster, which he had meant to study in advance in order to pronounce his students' names correctly (too late for that), and confronted the two dozen young strangers armed with pristine notebooks and pencils, who for most of their short lives had been hectored about the importance of education. Having purchased a $39,000 ticket, they found themselves seated in a radioactive bunker, their instructor a one-eyed Cthulhu restlessly scratching himself and pacing back and forth on an isthmus of faded carpet at the front of the room.

Buying time while shuffling through a stack of paper, he asked them to introduce themselves and tell him something about their reasons for taking the class. Several students proclaimed an interest in "death and stuff"—there was nothing like kicking off one's college career with a cheerful survey of the end of the world—while most of the others admitted that the course had fit into their schedules. Fitger chafed at his weeping eye with his swollen hand and promised, in return for the students' full and regular engagement, fourteen weeks of scintillating lecture/discussion punctuated by six short essays the details of which would soon be revealed.

Beginning at the back of the room near the eyewash station (he was tempted to use it), he distributed the syllabus, which the students, apparently too polite to mention his disfigurement, accepted as if taking communion. After explaining due dates and assignments—and quickly calculating the number of student pages (700–800) he would have to correct—he went over his standard classroom policies: eating (no), drinking (no), late arrivals/early departures (no), sleeping or cuddling (no, and no), cheating (just try it), and the use of technology (other than mechanical pencils, not permitted; students should leave all gleaming gewgaws at home and take notes by hand, as god intended) during class.

There was a moment of stunned silence, followed by a voice softly murmuring, "Is he just talking about our cell phones?"

No, he was not. He was talking about iPhones, iPads, laptops, desktops, earbuds, tape recorders, DVD players, Game Boys, mini-fridges, pocket pets, laser pointers, calculators, e-readers, slide rules, astrolabes, and—unless they could supply a note from a medical professional—iron lung or dialysis machines. Were there any questions so far about the syllabus?

One of three students named Sam (this sort of redundancy occurred almost every semester; Fitger wondered if some joker in admissions deliberately funneled students with the same name into his classes) politely asked if, in written assignments, "you'll be grading us on how we write or on our ideas."

"Excuse me?" Fitger briefly wondered whether it might be possible to ask one of the Sams to shave his head, and another to attempt, if at all possible, a beard.

"We want to know if you'll be grading us on our ideas or on grammar," another student helpfully said.

"Aha." At the front of the room, Fitger nodded, leaned back, and settled both hands in the white debris-filled tray of the chalkboard. He so enjoyed these first, early encounters with the incoming freshmen, who were as tender and unsuspecting as asparagus tips. Pushing off from the chalkboard and immediately impressing cloudy white handprints on the seat of his pants, he explained to Sam & Company that transparency of meaning and lucid expression traveled hand in hand, like Hansel and Gretel through the terrible woods; and furthermore, that carelessness in language—syntactical clumsiness, boneheaded usage, confusion of *affect* and *effect,* *lie* and *lay*—betrayed a dubiety of purpose, threatening to detract not only from the grades they would receive on their essays but from the aggregate of human knowledge, a transgression that was, on a personal level, extremely painful to their instructor, Professor Jason T. Fitger, who suffered the death of a thousand cuts when forced to confront these myriad insults to the written word.

He clapped his hands, releasing a puff of grayish white dust. "All clear then? Is everyone with me?"

There was no response. Fine. He distributed two dozen copies of a suitably grim little work of dystopian fiction and, beginning with the first row, asked the students to take turns reading it aloud. The first student—one of the Sams— gargled his way through the opening paragraph as if reciting a dirge underwater. Fitger stood him up and started him over, twice, correcting pronunciation and posture and expression, and leading him word by word through the passage with a conductor's flair. "Next!" The second student stood at her desk and read more fluidly, but in such a faint voice that Fitger, only a dozen feet away, could barely hear. Striding forward, he was getting ready to interrupt her and to ask if he should order twenty-four hearing aids and a megaphone but, once within glowering distance, he noticed how severely her hands were trembling. Unlike most of the young women in the room, who dressed as if stopping by class on their way to a nightclub, she wore a homely denim skirt and white buttoned blouse, and her entire body was shaking as if she were standing over an earthquake that measured at least 6.5 on the Richter scale. The page from which she was reading nearly shimmied out of her grip and onto the floor.

"All right," he said, when her whispered monologue was finished. "Let's keep going. Paragraph three!" The next student tried and failed to pronounce the word "tragic." Fitger glanced at the clock. At the back of the room, under the pull chain by the shower, a student was dribbling hot sauce onto a taco while checking his phone.

This first edification session complete, Fitger released his hostages and returned, bearing twenty-four handwritten writing samples, to Willard Hall. He paused by the door of his old office, now inhabited by the visiting Norwegian, and heard a flurry of typing. Farther down the hall, he came to a stop at the double doors to the conference room. He peered through the glass in one of the doors: the room was empty, unlit. He tried the knob, then noticed the newly installed plastic panel with a blinking red eye. Though the university had no money to hire faculty or supply them with working telephones or computers, it could apparently afford a security system allowing professors to be locked out of conference rooms. The corridor was relatively quiet, only a handful of students, presumably exhausted by an hour of intellectual labor, arrayed like garden slugs on the floor.

He took a credit card out of his wallet—all things apparently for sale at Payne—and swiped it over the blinking red surface. Nothing. Perhaps he could use the card to nudge the metal toggle between the two doors . . . He knelt on the floor (his knees would punish him severely later) and attempted to jimmy the—

"Shit." The credit card leapt out of his hand and fell through the gap between the double doors, landing faceup, his full name and Visa card number available to passersby for immediate use. A few moments of physical violence against the door, though somewhat cathartic, proved ineffective. He went back to the main office for advice but Fran was out— perhaps attending an instruction session regarding CPR for chipmunks or squirrels. He considered the idea of a wad of chewing gum affixed to the end of a coat-hanger spear, but ultimately decided he had no other recourse but to beg the use of an electronic key-card from a department in possession of clout and a budget—i.e., Econ.

Fitger climbed the steps to the second floor and paused outside the OFFICE OF ROLAND GLADWELL, PH.D., PROFESSOR AND CHAIR, allowing the sweat to congeal on the back of his neck. Econ epitomized everything that was wrong with

higher education. It was the crassest form of financial training, a networking program for would-be tycoons. On the wall
to his left, as evidence, a massive bronze plaque displayed
the names of donors to the department, apparently sorted
according to available millions, beginning with the DIAMOND
JUBILEE CIRCLE and funneling resplendently along through
platinum, gold, silver, emerald, ruby, sapphire, and pearl.
(If English had a plaque, he reflected, the donor categories
would begin with Styrofoam and end with tin.) These corporate benefactors weren't only contributing funds; they were
calling the shots, making decisions about research and curriculum. It was a deeply cynical and pecuniary model, the
selling of intellect and faculty labor. Fitger sighed, then
opened the door to the inner sacrarium, coming face-to-face
with four efficient young women, all of whom appeared to
have the same fitness trainer, dietician, and personal stylist.

"I need to get into the conference room on the first floor,"
he said. "May I borrow a key?"

One of the women (he noted the nameplate on her desk—
Marilyn Hoopes) appraised him with a flicker of her eyes as if
to remind him of the chalk and sweat on his clothes and the
incipient, purplish horn on his forehead. "Your name is . . ."

"Fitger." This was gratuitous harassment; she knew who he
was. "I work downstairs."

"Have you reserved the room?"

"No. But the room is empty, and I need to get in it. I left . . .
a personal item there."

"And you don't have a key?"

"Do you think I would be here if I had one?"

Marilyn Hoopes responded with a taut little smile and

consulted her computer. "It looks like the room is reserved right now."

"That may be," Fitger said, while stepping closer— ominously, he hoped—to the side of her desk. "But whoever is using it is either delinquent or invisible, and I need to retrieve my missing item." He held out his hand.

"I'm afraid I can't help you," she said. "The room is reserved."

Fitger pictured a conga line of undergrads queueing up by the conference room door, charging a year's worth of alcohol to his Visa account. "Would you let me know who might have reserved it?"

She glanced complacently at her screen and said no, she could not.

Fitger lunged for her computer, but before he could get a good look at the screen she exited the document. "That's our goddamned room," he said. "No one's in it; it's been dark all day. Who would reserve a conference room on the English floor and then not even . . . bother . . ." He stopped.

The office had gone quiet. None of the women were typing.

"May I speak to Roland?" he asked.

No; he was out.

When might he be back?

Ms. Hoopes didn't know. She referred Fitger to P-Cal, where he could check on Professor Gladwell's office hours and request an appointment.

Fitger scratched himself and gazed, almost mesmerized, at her computer, which had begun scrolling through a slide show of university photos: Payne in the winter, spread with a tablecloth of snow; Payne in the spring, with crocuses fore-grounding Bynmarlen Hall; Payne in the summer . . . How much of his life had unfolded against this reiterative back-drop? "I don't use P-Cal," he explained. "And I would like to speak to Roland for five minutes, without the intercession of a machine. Therefore I am hoping you will let me know when I can find him here. In the meantime"—he held out his hand—"I would appreciate your giving me the key to the conference room, so that I can retrieve an item left therein."

Ms. Hoopes cleared her throat. "I can't give you the key, and I don't make Professor Gladwell's appointments." That was what P-Cal was for, she said. It was a university-wide sys-tem, which every member of the Payne campus was required to learn.

Fitger was reminded of one of the shorter works from his apocalypse class, with its depiction of mindless automatons marching across a continent in lockstep as if the planet were a prison yard. "Here we are," he said, taking another step toward Marilyn Hoopes so that he was peering down at the top of her unresponsive head. "Two human beings, inches apart, and yet what you're telling me is that I need to go back downstairs to my own office, to my computer—except that I don't have a working computer—and spend thirty minutes searching for a website that will allow me to send a message that you could simply write down with a pencil on a piece of paper, right there on your desk. Do you find that strange? No? You might as well send me to Western Union for a tele-gram. Or suggest that I pound with a broom on the ceiling: a message to Roland in Morse code. Perhaps I'll send him a smoke signal from the hall outside the conference room, by

64

pouring a can of gasoline over my head and setting myself on fire."

Ms. Hoopes refused, steadfastly, to give him the key.

But ten minutes later, two uniformed officers of the campus police did manage to open the conference room door and retrieve Fitger's Visa card. They waited while he tucked the card into his wallet, and then escorted him past the new TAs and instructors who had gathered outside room 102B for orientation ("We'll be rescheduling," Fitger told them), ultimately delivering him to the university's Office of Mental Health and Wellness, where over the next hour and a half he assured one and all that he was not in danger of self-immolation.

Late that afternoon at home, after pouring himself a sizeable drink, Fitger picked up the phone to call his ex-wife, Janet Matthias. He probably owed her an apology: the campus police, using outdated information, had contacted her as next of kin, asking her opinion of his mental well-being, including his likeliness of wanting to burn down Willard Hall. She had apparently vouched for him, though one of the campus officers had later told Fitger that she seemed "remarkably unsurprised" about the questions they'd posed.

He let it ring five times; Janet didn't pick up. Was she avoiding him? Only a week or two earlier she had put a copy of the *Campus Scribe*—folded to the article about Econ—in his campus box. There was no note attached, but he knew that Janet was its source: even before the divorce, she took time to celebrate his humiliations.

He topped off his drink. Outdoors in the alley, his elderly neighbor was engaged in a weekly, inexplicable ritual: washing his garbage bins with a scrub brush, bucket, and a hose. Probably a post-retirement hobby, Fitger thought. Wearing fishing waders and suspenders, the neighbor appeared to be talking to himself; he circled the second, already immaculate container, then wiped the bottom of the upended bin with a cloth.

The fading daylight stretched itself across the sky like a band of spun sugar. When the neighbor shielded his eyes and looked up, Fitger waved from the window. "Nice night," he called.

By way of response, the older man scowled in the direction of Fitger's two garbage bins, which were mismatched and usually smelled of the spoiled remnants of takeout food.

Fitger picked up the phone and hit *redial* for the pleasure of listening to Janet's message. *("You know what to do at the beep.")* He suspected—after nearly a dozen years of marriage, he knew his ex-spouse's tactics and foibles—that she was probably home and deciding whether to answer. Even if she didn't pick up, he thought, this was a form of communication. She would understand that he wanted to reach her. She would know that he was enjoying the sound of her voice, that he was thinking about her, and that he had called.

FOUR

In the southernmost corner of the Willard Hall basement (the building was shaped like a giant letter *E*), Zander Hesseldine, literary theorist and scholar of postcolonial film, scrutinized the agenda for the English Department's first faculty meeting of the year. As usual, the department appeared to be committed to a semester's worth of milquetoast conversation devoid of substance or import. At a time when education and the pursuit of knowledge had become the objects of a sneering disdain, when most Americans seemed eager to ship intellectuals—especially anyone with a PhD in the humanities—out to break rocks in the countryside, the English Department's course of action was to tinker with documents that mattered to no one. When they should have been manning the barricades, they were scheduling a vote on that meaningless treatise, the Statement of Vision.

Disgusted, Hesseldine unbuttoned the top of his shirt—his office was as hot as a kiln—revealing a thick pallet of chest hair. He refreshed his browser. He had sent Fitger half a dozen P-Cal messages in the previous two weeks in an effort to include on the agenda a number of more urgent items that did not appear: Hesseldine's stagnant salary, which had risen less than 1 percent in the past four years; the annual incursion of mice beneath the basement vending machines near his office; the time and location of his sophomore seminar (Hesseldine's theory class met on Wednesday and Friday afternoons above a bowling alley); and the renewal of his intention to transfer, as soon as possible, to the Film Studies Program. He had received no response.

Ten more minutes until the start of the meeting. Hesseldine imagined he could sense, throughout the building's first and basement floors, the weight of a collective demoralization. Like chorus members in a poorly scripted bohemian opera, his colleagues, in their separate dressing rooms or offices, were engaged in last-minute preparations: a gathering of documents, a clicking of pens, a chewing of breath mints, a slamming of file drawers, a cursing at the state of ever-flickering overhead bulbs, a shaking of crumbs and other detritus from computer keyboards, and a searching for shoes discarded in the muggy heat beneath a desk.

In her windowless office across the hall from Zander Hesseldine, Jennifer Brown-Wilson (British Romanticism) also consulted the meeting's agenda, noting with a muffled cry of despair that she had been assigned to a committee with both Albert Tyne and Franklin Kentrell—a doubly punitive convergence. Tyne, it was said (Brown-Wilson had no reason to doubt the rumors), preserved his own urine as if it were wine, in a row of amber bottles in his office; and Kentrell had an innuendo-filled manner of speaking, and thick yellow fingernails that he wiggled in her direction when they met in the hall. At forty-two, Brown-Wilson was the youngest and most junior member of the English faculty, and she had spent the morning silently giving herself a pep talk: she had a tenure-track position, she had published two excerpts of her thesis (*On Ecstasy and Desire in William Blake*), and she had been invited to speak at an upcoming conference at Kansas U—i.e., she was fortunate, so much more fortunate than many of her graduate school colleagues, one of whom taught at a "liberal arts college" where it was no longer possible for students to major in English or, in fact, in literature of any kind. And yet: Albert Tyne (there were additional rumors about poorly taxidermied animals in his office) as well as Kentrell . . . Could she appeal to Fitger? No: she couldn't afford to seem uncooperative with her tenure vote only two years away. Dusting off the popsicle-stick-framed portrait of her eight-year-old twins, she wished she had availed herself of her husband's Xanax. She texted him quickly: *Please renew X prescription on your way home.*

Two doors away, near the basement elbow of the letter *E*, Franklin Kentrell (nineteenth-century American literature), who had printed but already lost the agenda, was searching through his trash can for an article about intestinal polyps, which he had last seen in the mailroom while making forty double-sided copies of Thoreau's "A Walk to Wachusett." Kentrell scratched his head. Might he have left the article, downloaded that morning, on the table next to the copy machine upstairs? In fact, he had. It was now in the hands of Helena Stang, who, it was rumored, bore a near-life-size tattoo of Alice B. Toklas on her left thigh. Stang, twentieth-century feminist literature, was at that moment perusing the article's scatological details and wondering whether someone had deliberately left it in the copy machine as a joke in poor taste, or—worse—was using it as a text in the classroom. (Tyne, she thought, was a distinct possibility.) Stang glanced at the faculty meeting agenda and the committee assignments, which she ignored. She did not serve on committees. She left the mailroom with the article—"Polypectomy Snare for Serrated Adenoma"—under her arm.

In Willard 106, opposite the mailroom, Martin Glenk, modernist poetry, saw Stang stride purposefully down the corridor (they had known each other for twenty-eight years but hadn't spoken for the last thirteen), and shut the door of his office with the tip of an old-fashioned pointer he kept near his desk. He picked up the phone to arrange for the purchase of a miniature donkey.

Albert Tyne, a Henry James–Edith Wharton specialist, was putting the finishing touches on a thirty-six-page rebuttal—it included a full page of citations—to the university's mandate requiring that he report for six weeks of sensitivity training. Meanwhile, in the women's restroom around the corner, Donna Lovejoy, medieval literature, carefully lowered herself onto a cracked porcelain horseshoe (it was broken and tended to slide out from under), noted the absence of toilet paper, and tried not to think about the pile of essays on her desk, the upcoming meeting, or the gradually increasing breadth of her thighs. She had dedicated most of the morning to a contemplation of her 401(k), estimating a possibility of retirement by the time she turned seventy-three—in twenty-one years.

A few minutes later, Virginia Beauchamp, modern drama, saw Lovejoy emerge in her unfortunate flat black shoes from the women's room (Beauchamp never used the restrooms in

Willard), a tampon wrapper glued to the bottom of a well-worn heel. Beauchamp tied her hair into a knot at the back of her head, removed the acupuncture needles from her left arm (though a productive scholar, she was working on a degree in herbology and alternative healing in her spare time), and walked down the hall to find the conference room dark. She rattled the knob. Why was the conference room locked? Coming up behind her were Helena Stang and director of composition and rhetoric Lance West, who as usual was wearing the knit slacks and matching shirt of a professional golfer. Stang jabbed at a sign on the door with her finger: *English faculty meeting to be held in room 102B.* She treated Beauchamp and then West to a frosty, condescending smile.

As a rule, West tried to be civil to every person he met, but Helena Stang made that commitment extremely hard.

Fitger had meant to get to campus at least an hour ahead of the meeting. Having woken at 4:50 a.m.—he suffered from prostate-induced insomnia—he had showered, read the paper, then cracked two eggs into a cast-iron pan and discovered a dollop of blood in both yolks. He was not in general a believer in omens, but the twin reddish blobs didn't foreshadow anything good, and he had nearly burned the eggs while considering whether to eat them. Ten minutes later, after fracturing a tooth on a slice of toast (the offending molar didn't fall out, but a segment of it was actively threatening to secede from the whole), he sensed the trajectory of the day already established. He might as well have quaffed eight ounces of gore in a drinking glass.

A hesitant phone call to the dentist (Fitger was squeamish

about dental work) was followed by the discovery that some-one had rear-ended his car in the night. The left taillight was gone, as if punched by a giant's fist, and the bumper dangled askew about an inch from the street. He tried hoisting and fixing the bumper in place with a rope, but after slicing his hand (would he need a tetanus shot on top of the trip to the dentist?), he kicked the bumper free of the car and tossed it, like a metal corpse, across the back seat.

Still, he managed to get to work with time to spare before the meeting, and entered Willard Hall through the lower floor. The building was stifling. Fist-sized dust balls hun-kered in the cobwebbed corners, and the smell of micro-waved vending-machine food seemed to have been pumped in through the vents, lending the low-ceilinged corridor a defeatist air. Fitger hustled up the steps, past the flyers offer-ing study-abroad opportunities, money for semen dona-tion, and clinical trials for individuals suffering from genital warts, acne, and hyperhidrosis. He sped past the conference room, empty and dark and presumably paid to remain so by Econ, his hand taped with gauze and his cracked tooth throbbing, an enamel iceberg ready to calve.

In the English office, he found not Fran but a needle-thin young person who introduced himself as Ashkir, the under-grad worker, who expressed such bounteous thanks for his employment that Fitger knew he had either misunderstood the salary (did they actually have money to pay him?) or the caliber of tasks—mainly opening mail and wrestling with the Stone Age copy machine—he would be asked to perform.

Glancing at the stack of boxes on the rug in his office, Fitger asked if any of the Tech-Help staff had happened by.

Ashkir said they had not. Was Professor Fitger expecting them?

Expecting? Ha ha! Realistically, no. He had left half a dozen messages and sent the director of the Tech-Help office a letter via U.S. certified mail, but so far his efforts had been unsuccessful. The "loaner laptop" Fran had provided failed to recognize the letter *S*. Fitger had been carefully composing e-mail and other documents to avoid this letter, steering clear of "is" and "was" and plurals, his correspondence beginning to sound as if it were translated from Quechua or Madurese.

He turned to Ashkir. Where was Fran?

Ah. Ms. Ignatieff regretted that she could not come in today; she had an emergency with her little girl.

"What little girl?"

Askhir held up his index finger as if testing the wind and consulted a pink slip of paper. "She says Gloria is not well and has to go to the clinic."

Who the hell was Gloria? Fitger scratched at his head, the stings from the wasps now faded to flat round patches of discolored skin.

"She left you this." Ashkir handed Fitger a personalized copy of the faculty meeting agenda:

1) Welcome back.
2) You are the chair.
3) Committee assignments. (Do not allow faculty to change assignments.)
4) The Statement of Vision.
5) Other/adjourn.

Fitger glanced at the clock; he still had time to catch his breath and collect his thoughts before the meeting. Tossing a pair of painkillers into his mouth (the broken tooth, the bandaged hand), he took a few minutes to review the university's new guidelines regarding Statements of Vision. After learning that "a department's identity and purpose are paramount in the cogent formation of a credible intellectual and pragmatic unity, this to be expressed in a planning document based upon disciplinary congruities," he put the guidelines down. The SOV was a formality, essentially meaningless—except for its link to the budget. Fitger's main job would be to keep the discussion moving, prohibiting speeches and vendettas, and then ask for a vote and disband.

With time still remaining before the meeting, he pulled a chair up next to the three-legged table that functioned as the department's reception area and Ashkir's workspace, its surface decorated, oddly, with a bowl of cheap plastic fruit. "So. Ashkir," he said. "What does Fran have you working on so far?"

Ashkir leaned away from the table so Fitger could see. On at least two hundred pieces of letterhead, *Payne University* in royal blue script across the top, Ashkir had crossed out *Mathematics* and, with a fine-point pen, written *English* instead.

Fitger examined the finished product. At least his penmanship was good. A matching set of envelopes waited nearby. "Ashkir, are you an English major?"

"Oh, no," Ashkir said. He laughed. He laughed harder than Fitger thought appropriate. "No, no, no, no. I am studying entrepreneurship."

"Really? That's an area of study? How does one learn to be an entrepreneur?"

Well, it was interesting. During the current semester—Ashkir was a junior—he was taking classes in marketing, leadership, and building sales teams. He was going to make *a lot* of money. Enough so that he could buy as many books as any of his English-major friends.

Did he like to read?

No, not really. Fortunately, most of his classes didn't involve a lot of reading; besides (he gestured to the earphones dangling from a cord around his neck), the lectures could be listened to online. And exams were taken via computer, sometimes at home. Entrepreneurship Studies, he said, was extremely well organized.

Fitger settled himself in for a lengthy discussion. "But Ashkir: entrepreneurship. Is that . . . intellectual in any way? Are you truly getting an education?" He probed at his broken tooth with his tongue. What about the in-person exchange of ideas? What about history, art, literature, philosophy, religion? Could any student, by sitting alone at a computer terminal in his apartment, truly claim to—

"Professor, excuse me." Ashkir held up his hand. "I am sorry to interrupt, but you are late for your meeting."

"No, I'm—" Fitger looked at the clock on the wall again; several dead wasps were trapped within it; its hands were still.

Dennis Cassovan, the first to arrive in room 102B for the meeting, nodded to his colleagues as they filtered in and tried to assess their respective attitudes toward Shakespeare at Payne. Helena Beauchamp was a scholar of theater (and had written half a dozen separate studies of Samuel Beckett); still, she and Hesseldine typically denigrated works of literature written prior to 1945 and could not be counted on for reasonable discourse; Tyne, "on principle," had abstained from every departmental initiative for the past thirty years. But what about Lovejoy or Brown-Wilson? Lovejoy's hair was flattened on one side as if she had recently risen from sleep, and one earpiece of her glasses was mended with tape. He remembered when she had been hired at Payne, a vivacious, energetic young scholar. Coming upon her soon after her hire in the faculty mailroom, he had mistaken her for a student. She seemed to have aged several decades in the past ten years.

Perhaps it was no longer possible to predict the intellectual or ideological camp within which a particular member of the department would fall. Each, it seemed to Cassovan, formed a prickly, obdurate focus group of his or her own.

Fitger, unsurprisingly, was ten minutes late to his own meeting. He found the faculty seated scattershot in the classroom's desk-and-chair contraptions, some facing east, some north or west—like frustrated drivers in a series of stalled bumper cars. In one corner of the room, Brown-Wilson, despairing of her committee assignments, was appealing—unsuccessfully—to Sandra Atherman (Victorian literature) and Lance West, neither of whom were willing to consider exchanging their own assignments for a yearlong series of meetings with the unhygienic Tyne and the reptilian Kentrell. In the opposite corner, Hesseldine was protesting the presence of vermin in the building: he claimed to have seen a rodent clutching a sandwich in the vending machine. Other conversations consisted of complaints about the temperature of the building, the broken fax machine, the dearth of research funds, the ever-increasing size of undergraduate classes, the autocracy of the university's administration, and now the loss—presumably Fitger's fault, because he was chair—of the conference room.

Cassovan bided his time during these first twenty chaotic minutes, taking stock of the classroom decor: a chalkboard, a set of small-print instructions regarding escape from fire or armed gunmen, and a series of crooked, laminated portraits of the seven presidents of Payne, all but Hoffman—the only woman—sporting muttonchops or Mephistophelian beards.

Finally, Fitger handed out copies of the Statement of Vision, revised and updated via e-mail during the previous spring. "Are we ready to vote?" he asked.

Sandra Atherman, dressed per usual as one of the Brontës (Atherman was popular with students because of the glass eye she sometimes removed and soaked in salt water, during her lectures), said, "If we're going to vote, we need a motion."

"I make a motion, then," said Fitger.

"But you have to say what the motion is for."

"The motion is . . . that we vote."

Virginia Beauchamp, removing from the back of her wrist a final acupuncture needle, said she didn't think the chair was entitled to make a motion. Someone else had to make it.

Fitger asked if anyone else would care to make—

Dennis Cassovan stood. "I call for discussion to precede any vote on this issue."

At the back of the room, someone groaned. Discussion was always an unpopular option, leading as it did to calumny, stalemate, lamentation, and wrath. Donna Lovejoy, perhaps because she had never heard Cassovan speak during a faculty meeting, struggled to turn around in the wooden tourniquet of her seat, perturbed. "Isn't the Statement of Vision a formality?" she asked. "I mean . . . We have to churn these things out every few years, and I assumed they were . . ."

"Irrelevant?" Hesseldine asked.

Cassovan acknowledged these questions and apologized for not taking part in the drafting or discussion of the SOV while he was on leave. The document's first paragraph, he said, with its mishmash of language regarding "literary as well as historical, social, political, and cultural aesthetics," might have been written about a dozen different departments. And while composition merited two or three sentences, the SOV—which his colleagues could criticize if they liked, but it was the means by which the administration would define their department—failed to mention crucial fields within English, and it specified only twenty-eight required credits for the undergraduate degree.

"We didn't have a choice about the credits," West said. He explained that almost every humanities department had been told to cut back, and that the more modest number of requirements was going to work in their favor. Not just at Payne but across the United States, students were defecting in droves from the traditional major in English to newer fields such as "business writing," "technical communications," and graphic design. The lower number of credits was an attempt to reverse those defections. It would make the department more attractive to students.

Cassovan's face was impassive. "And this is our object?" he asked. "To make the study of literature 'attractive'?"

"I don't understand your question," West said. He pointed out that English was competing for students, and for student tuition dollars, with other departments.

Jennifer Brown-Wilson swung her desk around in a half-circle to look at Cassovan. "What exactly are you objecting to?" she asked. "The smaller number of credits? Or something else more specifically?"

Cassovan thanked her for the opportunity to clarify. He was objecting, he said, to the absence in the Statement of Vision of any reference to Shakespeare, and to the attendant lack of clarity regarding the department's requiring of students to take at least one semester-long class in that field.

West caught his foot in the metal book rack under his desk. Shakespeare would obviously continue to be taught, he said. It was widely included in the curriculum: Helena Stang had just taught a class on the graphic novel that included a manga version of *Macbeth*.

Cassovan looked pained rather than pleased at this disclosure. A casual or passing reference or, even worse, a modern adaptation of the works of the dramatist, he said, could never—

Zander Hesseldine, combing the underside of his beard with his fingers, interrupted. Why should Cassovan's field be referenced in the SOV when others weren't? The document made no mention of Postcolonial Literature. Besides, suggesting that Shakespeare studies were in jeopardy was like treating the cockroach as an endangered species.

Stang, a heavy row of metal bracelets ringing her arm, swiftly agreed: her own field—feminist studies—was not represented in the SOV either; and requiring a semester-long class in the work of a single white male author was, in the twenty-first century, nothing less than absurd.

West explained that the SOV had deliberately been rewritten without reference to specific fields, because of the lower number of required credits. That said, students would certainly be able to study Shakespeare or medieval literature or poetry or—

"We have one Shakespearean in the department," Hesseldine murmured, in an audible aside to Stang. "And I assume that, sooner or later, he intends to retire."

Cassovan turned to his barbigerous colleague. An armchair Marxist who displayed a Cuban flag on the door of his office, Hesseldine was, in Cassovan's view, the worst sort of academician, encouraging in his students a smug, postmortem approach to literature and a view of the classics that stank of disdain. Cassovan had been a member of the department for forty-two years and he suspected that his retirement would elicit a yawn of indifference from most of his colleagues. He felt more of a kinship with his students—he had taught, by his estimation, some eight thousand undergraduates—who, though less widely read, were open-minded and intellectually alive. He was at present, on Tuesday and Thursday afternoons, leading a group of freshmen through *Othello,* and he had been struck during the most recent session to find

80

a young woman—the one who had helped him gather his books after Fitger assaulted him with a window screen—openly weeping over Desdemona's demise.

"A department of English," he said, "cannot exist without requiring, for its majors, at least one semester-long course in the study of Shakespeare. To require any less would be irresponsible; it is a dumbing down."

West said it was important that the Statement of Vision encompass the broad range of interests in the department; and because students majoring in English would now be required to complete only twenty-eight credits, greater flexibility in the curriculum—

"Shakespeare," Cassovan said, "is not an *interest.*"

Stang said that at least one class in feminist literature, and one in theory—

Atherman said that if the Brontës were not included—

Brown-Wilson suggested that the first paragraph of the Statement of Vision be entirely scrapped; and in the second paragraph, the word *requirement*—

Franklin Kentrell posed the idea of eliminating the dashes in paragraph three. He didn't care for the dash as a unit of punctuation. It was too breezy and too offhand. It was—

"We could *recommend* a semester of Shakespeare, instead of requiring it," Lovejoy said.

"A recommendation is insufficient," Cassovan said. "The English major—"

Kentrell explained that he was not alone in his aversion to the dash. He never permitted students to use it. He—

"The English major," Cassovan said, "is not a—"

Beauchamp said they obviously needed to rewrite the SOV, but fall, for her, was not a very propitious time. West moaned; they had just rewritten it, he said. Hesseldine also insisted on a thorough revision, but refused to participate himself; furthermore, he vehemently opposed the idea of the task being handled by a cabal of traditionalists. "And by 'traditionalists,'" he said, still grooming the underside of his beard, "I'm referring to people who haven't read any of the theoretical or Marxist literature in the past fifty years."

"Please don't say 'Marxist,'" Lovejoy said. The word was an open invitation to Albert Tyne's favorite diatribe regarding the vacuity of cultural studies, identity politics, political correctness, and "psychoanalytic hocus-pocus masquerading as legitimate inquiry"; Stang, as always, rose to the bait, following up with a mini-lecture on the subject of phallocentric hegemony and the necessary demise of the Anthropocene.

Martin Glenk, who had spent the past twenty minutes doing a crossword, said that if the meeting was going to be hijacked and sent downstream on a homemade raft of hackneyed rhetoric, they would have to excuse him, as he had more pressing things to do.

Fitger attempted to call them to order. "Do we have a motion?"

Atherman, her glass eye rolling toward the ceiling, moved that they vote.

Tyne asked if he would be speaking out of turn if he were to question the reputability of a department chaired not by a scholar but a "creative writer," a person whose publications consisted of B-grade coitive fantasies of various easily identifiable women on campus, including the author's ex-wife.

"The sensitivity training is going well, I see, Albert," Fitger said.

A student knocked and opened the door. He was sorry to interrupt, but he was part of a Bible as Literature study group whose members were meeting in room 102A. Would the professors be able, for the next fifteen minutes, to quiet down?

Brown-Wilson seconded the motion.

"Shakespeare," Cassovan said, "must always be the core of a department of English. We cannot allow—"

Glenk distributed ballots and the vote was taken: three were for the SOV as it stood and four were against; there were five abstentions.

"Goddammit," Fitger said. The room began to empty out. He stopped Dennis Cassovan at the door. "This is absurd," he said. "You know we could have tweaked the requirements later—or made some kind of in-house amendment to the SOV."

Cassovan had never liked Fitger—had never claimed to discern, as others had, a tenderhearted core within the churlish exterior. He was uninterested in "tweaking" or amendments, he said.

Fitger was tugging at a bandage on his hand. "We don't have a budget, Dennis. You might not appreciate the fact that I'm fighting here for the department's existence."

"Perhaps you should also fight for its soul."

"A noble sentiment," Fitger muttered, making a personal pledge: he would retire before in need of industrial hearing aids or orthopedic shoes. The bandage had tightened around his fingers. He gripped it with his teeth and pulled, then abruptly folded himself in half like a wallet and spit what appeared to be the bulk of a bloody molar into his hand.

He and Cassovan both stared at the tooth.

"You know I'm not anti-Shakespeare," Fitger said, a cascade of reddish saliva dribbling out of his mouth.

Cassovan pulled a linen handkerchief from his pocket; he gave it to Fitger, who was using the palm of his hand as a catchment for blood. "You should get that seen to," he said.

FIVE

On the butcher block in her kitchen, Janet Matthias (formerly Matthias-Fitger) chopped two small tomatoes, two cloves of garlic, an ovoid eggplant, and a handful of basil leaves and poured herself a glass of wine. Phil Hinckler was attending the soccer match of one of his sons (he was permitted to observe but not to cheer), so she was cooking for herself, which was more rewarding than cooking for two; she could eat standing up at the counter while watching one of the police shows she taped and hoarded for moments like these when she found herself contentedly alone.

The message button on her answering machine was blinking. She tapped it with a garlic-scented finger and heard the voice of her ex-husband, who ever since their act of postmarital misjudgment in August seemed to confuse her voicemail with a trip to the shrink, filling her in on crucial matters of business: he'd been stung by an insect; Fran had hired a student worker who didn't like books . . . Oh, the stressful existence of a tenured professor. And then of course there had been the call from the campus police, asking her to comment on the likelihood of one Jason T. Fitger wanting to burn down a building. She hit *delete* before he reached the end of his first sentence, and tossed the vegetables into a pan.

She drained the pasta and looked out the window over the sink. In the middle of the street, paying no attention whatsoever to oncoming cars, two little boys were jousting with hockey sticks while riding bicycles, their mother observing through a fog of cigarette smoke and a beer. Human beings, Janet thought, were a disappointment. She stirred the vegetables into the pasta and cued up an episode of *Undercover Lives,* which promised the usual addictive blend of mayhem, righteousness, corruption, and sin.

The phone rang. Janet checked the caller ID. Of course it was Fitger. She dropped the receiver back on its base. Her favorite detective, Lydia Burke, had entered a grim-looking apartment building alone. She'd requested backup but her partner was useless; Lydia often had to cover for his incompetence because of office politics and a lousy relationship with her misogynist boss. Janet speared a hunk of eggplant, watching Lydia Burke—still with no backup—chase a suspect onto a rusted fire escape, the camera zooming in on the sidewalk six floors below. The phone rang again. She glanced at the caller ID: MORADI DDS. Her *dentist?*

"Ms. Matthias? Hi, it's Cheryl here, calling from Dr. Moradi's office. I'm sorry to bother you at the dinner hour, but we have a bit of a situation."

"Let me guess." Janet put Lydia Burke on pause. "It has something to do with my ex-husband."

Well, yes, in fact it did. He'd had some dental work done— his bicuspids, on the left side in particular, were not in good shape—and because of the anesthesia (which they'd had a tussle about, to be honest), the professor wasn't in any condition to drive himself home. Would she mind coming to get him—and then picking up his pain prescription? They ordinarily closed the office at six, and he hadn't given them the name of anyone else they could call . . . "Hello? Ms. Matthias? Are you still there?"

"Unfortunately, yes, I am," Janet said. This was what she got for failing to move across state lines and adopt an unpronounceable alias, post-divorce. She should at least have found one of them a new dentist. Fitger had always been a coward about both medical and dental work, and during the years they were married she'd had to force him to get his flu shots and have his teeth cleaned. "Give me ten minutes," she said. She put on her shoes, put *Undercover Lives* on hold for another day, and threw the rest of her dinner into the trash.

In the passenger seat of her car, Fitger leaned back, drooling into a cloth and whimpering about his session in the dentist's chair. Dr. Moradi was ruthless, he said; his glabrous hands smelled of paint remover and his creepy eyepiece made him look like a moray eel. "They signed me up for four more appointments." His head lolled against the headrest. Four more appointments might be the end of him, he said; he knew that Janet had a soft spot for Dr. Moradi, but given the peerless state of her own gleaming enamel, she couldn't begin to imagine the torments that a— "Wait: Where are we going?"

"To the pharmacy," she said. "So we can get you some drugs that will make you stop talking."

"You don't understand. I've been traumatized." His voice was syrupy and slurred. "I had to pay extra for anesthesia. He wanted to drill below the gums without knocking me out; he likes seeing me suffer."

"I doubt he's the only one," Janet said. She parked between two mud-spattered trucks in front of the pharmacy; when Fitger didn't open his door, she got out and walked around to the passenger side.

"You didn't answer the phone when I called," he said.

"That's right; I didn't." She grabbed his arm and hauled him up and they entered the pharmacy, walking down an aisle that began with baby toys and pacifiers and ended with adult incontinence aids—an eloquent lifeline, Janet thought. They waited in a lengthy queue at the pharmacy window, Fitger holding a soggy cloth to his chin.

Janet leafed through a magazine while he launched into a woeful jeremiad about the state of English and Willard Hall, including a semi-coherent account of a Tech-Help employee who had spent an hour squatting in front of a pile of computer boxes, the frayed elastic of his underpants on display.

"Janet, listen. I'm beginning to think there's some sort of organized, you know . . ." He paused. "An organization working against me."

"An organization. Are you referring to the Mafia? The Knights Templar?"

No, not the Knights Templar. But had Fitger told her that English had been barred from its own conference room? And that his class had been scheduled in a fallout shelter? With Fran as second-in-command it was almost impossible to—

"Stop. I don't want to hear you try to pin your problems on Fran."

"I wouldn't dream of it," Fitger slurred. "I can't fairly blame a person who isn't tall enough to reach the doorknobs."

Janet put the magazine away. "Wait here." She walked to the next aisle and came back with a package of gauze. "We'll pay for this later." She tore the lid off the package, handed a few squares of the cotton to Fitger, and pointed to the trash can so he would throw his saliva-drenched bandage away.

They shuffled forward in line, Janet contemplating an array of nutritional supplements, which promised relief of everything from athlete's foot to zinc deficiency.

"Speaking of Fran," Fitger said. "She asked for two days off to attend a bird's funeral. How can it take two days to bury a bird?"

"God forbid she should have hobbies or a personal life," Janet said.

The woman in front of them in line was pushing a shopping cart full of wadded-up circulars and bottles of pills.

"You have to admit," Fitger said. "Fran is . . ."

"What?" Janet knew Fran; they had once served on a committee together.

"Well, right now she's not speaking to me. But the larger issue is that . . . I need better advice than she can give me. We're losing real estate in the building due to our flesh-eating neighbors upstairs. And Dennis Cassovan is making a stink about Shakespeare and the SOV."

"I thought you liked Dennis," Janet said. "Relatively speaking."

Fitger propped the sagging corner of his mouth with

gauze. "I don't dislike him. But he refuses to understand that every single humanities department at Payne is competing for students. They've all relaxed their requirements. Over in the Spanish Department all the undergrads need to do is say *adiós* and *buenos días* and then certify that they've had a burrito for lunch." They muddled forward, only the shopping cart woman in front of them. "I thought Cassovan was retiring," Fitger said. "I think he's been teaching since the Paleolithic Era."

Janet shrugged. Since the recession had cut their retirement accounts roughly in half, Payne was full of faculty like Dennis Cassovan who were well over seventy. During the summer, when the students were gone, she looked at the members of the professoriat muddling slowly across the quad and imagined she was working at a nursing home.

"It's almost like old times," Fitger said. "Talking about work together like this."

Janet agreed. "The similarity is that you're always talking."

The shopping cart woman, now at the window, was arguing with the pharmacist. She appeared to want to return— for cash in hand—her cartful of drugs to the store.

"What do you have there, ma'am?" Fitger asked. "If you have any Vicodin, I'll buy it from you."

Finally, a manager was summoned; following a brief altercation, he agreed to accept and dispose of the pills and offer cash for a possibly unopened bottle of milk of magnesia.

Fitger handed his prescription slip through the window. He wondered whether Janet had told Phil Hinckler about their lovely little slipup in August. If she had, it would make his upcoming request to the dean—for an emergency interim budget—a bit problematic. But Fitger didn't regret their liaison; it was the most pleasurable fifteen minutes he had spent in years. "You know what I mean about Fran," he said. "She's perfectly familiar with the ins and outs of the office. But I need someone who has a grasp of the larger picture. Someone with a more strategic attitude, and with tactical smarts."

The pharmacist handed over the drugs, and Fitger paid and followed Janet back to the car. She put her key in the ignition and said, "You haven't thanked me for picking you up."

"I'm sure I thanked you."

"No, you didn't."

"I must have. What were you doing when I called?"

"I was having dinner."

"What were you eating?"

She sighed. "Eggplant. With tomatoes and garlic."

"I remember your eggplant." Fitger was struggling to open the safety cap on his bottle of pills. "I'm going to be living on pureed vegetables for a month."

Janet opened the pills, then pulled out of the parking lot and onto the road. For a multitude of reasons, including her own health, it was not a good idea for her to give her ex-husband advice (he was a fuckup of the first order, his praise of her "tactical smarts" a pandering ploy)—but she had been a literature student herself, and she hated to see English founder at Payne. "Since this is your first semester as chair, and you're obviously lacking in common sense, I'm going to offer you some basic administrative suggestions."

"An insult as well as an offer," Fitger said. "I accept both."

"First," Janet said, "you need to apologize to Fran. If you can't get along with your admin assistant, you're totally sunk."

"Noted. But I don't think you—"

"Second: learn how to network. Did you go to the meeting of the assembly of chairs?"

"Yes: two hours of pointlessness," Fitger said. The number of ceremonial bodies to which he was supposed to belong was obscene. He was going to buy a departmental amphora that he could shake at the start of proceedings, like a voo-doo priest. "I don't think anything ever happens at those assemblies."

"That's because you're an idiot." Janet stopped at a light. "Everything happens off the agenda. It's all about private conversations."

He tried to swallow one of the pills but it bounced off his lip and rolled onto the floor.

"Third—and this is my last piece of advice for you—you need money."

"Don't we all. But, inconveniently, my budget is frozen. I may be drawing up a request for— Hang on a second." He found the pill under his shoe and dropped it into his mouth and washed it down with some cold coffee from a travel mug plucked from the console.

"You're not understanding me," Janet said. "I'm not talk-ing about your department budget, though I assume in that respect you're appealing to Phil. I'm talking about *raising* money. You need to find donors—people outside the univer-sity. Do you know anyone in the development office? Maybe Perrin Wilcox?"

Fitger frowned. "The name is familiar."

"Send her an e-mail. You need to prove to the administration that you know how to fund-raise. That's part of your job."

"I should think that would be Perrin Wilcox's job, if she works in development."

"Tell her I sent you," Janet said. "She doesn't like to meet face-to-face. She's somewhat . . . eccentric."

"Eccentric" within the context of Payne, Fitger thought, could mean "thoroughly unhinged" almost anywhere else.

Janet parked but left the car running. Fitger rented the right-hand side—both up- and downstairs—of a Victorian house, which the landlord had painted an unfortunate green, suggestive of bogs and algae and things of the swamp. Would she like to come in for a while and—

No, she would not. She watched him walk to the door, dropping his keys and then his pills on the sidewalk, and picking both of them up.

Walking into her own house ten minutes later, she heard the phone ring. Of course it was Fitger. She answered. "What?"

"I wanted to be sure you heard me thank you for the ride," he said.

"You didn't thank me."

"Also, I remembered that you'll be going to the reunion soon. And I wanted to tell you to have a good time."

Janet scrutinized the bottle of wine by the sink. Had she opened it only that afternoon? She filled up a glass. "You aren't . . . changing your mind about going?"

They'd both been invited to a retreat in Maine with half a dozen people with whom they had gone to graduate school, people who had known them when they were young and only mildly cynical, before they had made the mistake of getting married and intertwining their lives.

"No," he said. He wouldn't abuse her like that. He wanted her to let loose and have fun; perhaps his absence would persuade their former classmates that they had enjoyed his company, back in the day.

Janet wandered into her bedroom, massaging an oncoming headache at the base of her neck. She was relieved to know that Jay wasn't going. Among their graduate school colleagues, it would be too easy to slip back into what their marriage therapist had termed their "symbiotic disputes": Jay transgressed and Janet punished, each extracting psychic benefit from his or her role. During one of their final sessions, the therapist had asked Janet if the idea of getting divorced made her angry or sad. An easy question to answer: in the panoply of human emotions, Janet's default was anger. She was better at anger. At a moment's notice, she was primed and ready to be pissed off—that was how she was made.

She lay down on the bed and studied a network of cobwebs close to the ceiling. She remembered lying in bed with Jay two decades before, both of them reading the same book (an Irish novel; she didn't remember the author), turning the pages at the same time in order to synchronize the experience, each of them listening for the intake of breath that signaled, in the other, trepidation or delight or surprise. It was probably her most erotic memory.

"I suppose I should tell you," she said, opening the drawer in her bedside table to search for aspirin. "I'm going to be getting rid of the landline."

"What? Your house phone?" Fitger asked. "*This* landline? Why?"

"Because I don't need it anymore. I don't want to pay for it. You can find me at work or on my cell. Not that I'm recommending you call. In fact, please don't. You should give Dr. Moradi's office—and the police and the fire department and the local prison—someone else's number."

"You can't get rid of the landline," Fitger said.

"Why not?"

Because, he explained, that was their number—the number he had memorized and had once helped to pay for. It was the phone they had shared, the one on which some people might still try to reach him.

Janet found the aspirin and spilled a pair of white pills into the palm of her hand. Was she going to swallow them with wine? Apparently so. "Jay," she said. "No one has tried to reach you on this phone for years. You have a cell phone, don't you?"

Well, yes, he had a cell phone; he'd been forced to buy one because some tribe of tech-loving barbarians was systematically uprooting all the pay phones from L.A. to New York.

Janet asked if he was making plans to update his inkwell and his feather pen.

"Amuse yourself at my expense if you want to," he said, "but keep the landline. I'll pay twenty percent of it."

"You're not going to pay any of it; I'm getting rid of it." She noticed a size XL Payne T-shirt hanging on the bedpost. Though she had cleared out a drawer for him and made space in the closet, Phil Hinckler preferred to drape his semi-soiled clothes over the doorknobs and the backs of her chairs.

"Twenty-five percent, then," Fitger said. "And I promise to call you only once a week. Don't be hasty, Janet, because that's probably going to be my final—"

She unplugged the phone.

SIX

Arms on her hips so that she resembled a fleshy teapot, Fran stood in the doorway of Fitger's office. They had patched things up, to a certain extent, after he sent her a (belated) sympathy card on the death of Gloria. He had even copied out the poem "Hope is the thing with feathers" on a card with a picture of a robin eating a worm.

"I thought you were going to work on that Shakespeare business this week," she said.

Fitger didn't answer, but because he looked at her over the top of his reading glasses she knew he had heard her. This was the hallmark of their working relationship: she talked in his doorway while he ignored her; then he parked himself in her doorway while she did the same. This complementary pattern kept them from wearing on each other's nerves.

"If you don't submit a Statement of Vision, you won't get a budget."

Fitger thanked her for this nugget of wisdom, but explained that his efforts to convene a committee to revise the SOV had come to naught, because the faculty refused to approve of any subgroup that might take on the task. Therefore—no thanks to Dennis Cassovan, the old mossback—Fitger would have to rewrite this vaunted document himself. In preparation, he had decided to familiarize himself with previous SOVs and other absurd university protocol by studying the departmental records. This splendid set of documents consisted, in increasing order of volume, of files relating to:

website and PR (2 files)
technology (3 files)
events/lectures (8 files)
promotion and tenure (17 files)
committees/committee structure (21 files)
curriculum (26 files)
budget (32 files)
grievances (44 files)
misc/other (128 files)

A perusal of this final, intriguing category disclosed a thick wad of parking violations (unpaid—and belonging to the previous chair, Ted Boti); miscellaneous library fines; three police reports (one restraining order and two separate incidents of stalking—thankfully the faculty members in question had either died or moved on); some information regarding the care of a ficus; a petition requesting feminine hygiene product placement in the women's restrooms; the cover of a comic book; and one fecal occult blood test result, which Fitger deposited, wishing he were wearing medical gloves, into the trash.

He would get to Shakespeare and the SOV soon enough, but these weren't the only departmental priorities: he needed to argue for the reestablishment of the creative writing degree and for the literary magazine, *The Pride of Payne,* while making a case for two faculty hires.

"You might be too late on *The Pride of Payne,*" Fran said. "Or, at least, you'd have to find a different office."

"What do you mean? What about that office in the basement?"

"There's a new key-card lock on the door. I guess Econ is planning to use it for something."

"Piracy," Fitger said. "We turn our backs for a second and they capture our space. Soon they'll hit us with a surcharge for using the stairs."

"They have a budget," Fran said. "Which reminds me. I had to cancel an order for paper clips this week, and I'm about to send an e-mail to the faculty, telling them they need to buy their own paper for the copy machine."

Fitger stared at the mess of files spread across his desk. His stapler had a note taped to its spine: *Property of Department of Physics—Do Not Remove.* "There has to be a way of getting around these things. You keep telling me we don't have money, but somehow you managed to hire Ashkir."

Fran (re)explained that they were paying Ashkir with their maintenance funds, which included heat—so they would be hoping for a mild winter. "By the way, Althea Mulligan over in Accounting has called you three times to say that we're operating in the red. You might want to avoid running into her in person; she said something about wanting to display your head on a spike outside her cubicle."

Fitger suggested that Fran tell Althea Mulligan over in

Accounting that he had just submitted—to his ex-wife's boy-friend, the dean—a request for an emergency provisional budget.

"Yeah." Fran exhaled—a noisy whistle. "I saw what you sub-mitted. That shit's going to come right back with a long list of necessary supporting documents."

Yes, of course it would, Fitger said. Every transaction at Payne required an abundance of supporting documents, the simplest procedures requiring truckloads of paperwork accompanied by blood samples, DNA test results, finger-prints, and FBI files.

"Let me ask you something," he said, inserting a pencil into the electric sharpener, a growling receptacle that devoured all but about two inches of the tool in his hand. "Do you think it's possible that there's some sort of plot or plan at Payne whose object is to make our work life difficult, or at least pointlessly slow?"

"Are you asking me on or off the record?"

"There is no record. It's just a question."

"Then I'm not going to answer," Fran said. She paused and looked up. Through the ceiling, they could hear the manly locomotion of Roland Gladwell's rolling chair. "Will you be going to their party this afternoon?"

Fitger had no intention of going to the Econ celebration, the purpose of which was to extol the university's most rapa-cious department.

Fran returned to her portion of the office and promptly sent him a dozen e-mails, which quickly slid down his endless queue. An hour later, she announced that the workweek was done; she was going home. "But if you're planning to stick around for a while," she said, "you might want to return that phone call about Albert Tyne. He's refusing to finish his sensitivity training."

Fitger shrugged. He had no sympathy for Tyne, who had been slapped with a six-week sentence for making a remark about a fellow faculty member's vacation in "Sodomy Springs," but he didn't blame him for trying to avoid the training. The university's sensitivity sessions resembled Maoist reeducation camps: one was expected to recant, to weep, to offer up several bones to be broken, and to emerge gleaming with a proselyte's commitment to reform. There were other correctives for Tyne that Fitger would have prioritized and recommended, starting with a psychiatrist and a skilled barber.

Gingerly touching the left side of his face (just that morning he had endured another session of dental torment, the number of his natural teeth steadily dwindling), he wished Fran a good weekend.

"Your mouth is still bothering you?" she asked.

Fitger explained that his dentist was a tight-ass about pain pills, and had cut him off Vicodin in favor of Tylenol #3.

"I've got some Percocet if you need it," she said. "I had a cyst dug out of my armpit a year ago."

"Is Percocet similar to Vicodin?"

"Yeah, pretty much." She dug through her canvas bag and came up with an unlabeled bottle. "I don't think it's as strong, though, as Vicodin," she said. "So you should probably take two."

Fitger rolled the pills around in his hand—they looked a bit worn, their edges chipped—and then tossed them into his mouth. After Fran left the office, he gave up on the department's files and turned to his undergraduate students' essays, at least half of which, contrary to explicit instructions, included floral or multicolored paper or typeface, plastic cover-sheets, emoticons, and links to YouTube videos. Most of the essays, on the basis of faulty grammar alone, would earn well-deserved Cs—with the exception of a pithy little manuscript submitted by a student who evinced a startling ability to think clearly, express original ideas, and write. Angela Vackrey. Hmm. He made a mental note to review his seating chart: was she the rustic, knee-socked creature in the left-hand row?

He glanced at his watch: 5:35, and he had graded only a few of the essays. The left side of his mouth—a fleshy battlefield—still throbbed as if to the beat of a drum. He was probably suffering from periodontal PTSD: when he'd arrived that morning for his appointment at the House of Moradi, the hygienist had led him by the hand to room 4, where she tenderly scolded him for drinking coffee, tea, club soda, orange juice, and red wine, and for eating anything more durable than toast. Tears flooded his eyes when she tied on his bib and tipped him back in the chair, placing a stress ball into the sweating palm of his hand.

He heard a knock at the outer door of the office, which he ignored. A moment later a woman in a trim black dress was standing in front of him, a bottle of wine tucked cozily under her arm.

"This does not look like a very interesting party," she said.

Fitger stood up. Hello; was she looking for Econ? That

department's self-glorification ceremony had begun a short while ago, on the floor above.

The woman (she wore dark red polish on her nails; he could see her hip bones through the cloth of her dress) took in their surroundings: the matching fishbowl offices, the dust-colored carpet, the intermittent baseboard, and the tangle of extension cords that extended from Fitger's office into the hall. "This is very, very ugly," she said, her voice pitched low, with a polyglot European intonation. "It is much worse here than in my office. I am Marie Eland—languages. But you must have another place to do your work?"

"I used to," Fitger said. "But when I became chair my faculty office was . . . usurped." He mentioned Arnljot, the Norwegian, also in languages—perhaps she knew him? Arnljot kept a low profile, seeming to work ten-hour days without food or drink, and on the rare occasions when he did emerge from Fitger's faculty office, he slouched down the hall with the posture of a half-parenthesis. He was as pallid as a garden grub beneath a rock.

"No. I do not know this person." Marie Eland set her bottle of wine on Ashkir's table. Was Fitger planning to go to the party? They would go there together, she said; but first, a little drink to prepare themselves.

Fitger told her he would be happy to have a drink but he wasn't intending to go to the party. Having been forced to shelter-in-place during the yearlong construction project for the benefit of his colleagues upstairs, he was probably at risk for black lung, and didn't harbor in his breast a love of Econ.

"You are not thinking about this correctly." Marie Eland

took a corkscrew from her purse. "This is not about pin-the-wheels and enjoyment. We are at work. We and the other department chairs will all be gathering information. Do you have wineglasses?"

He offered her a choice between coffee mugs and paper cups. "So," he said. "You're the chair of Foreign Languages?"

She held a Payne ID in front of him for inspection; beneath her name was a very long title. "We were once the Department of French and Italian. But now, because the president favors consolidation, I am the chair of French, Italian, Spanish, German, Ojibwe, Arabic, and Linguistics. But we will be getting rid of Arabic and Linguistics soon." Expertly—"many years ago, I was a waitress in Paris"—she opened the wine and filled two paper cups.

Oh, the American university, she said. She was new to the campus. She had accepted the chairship and moved to Payne the year before in order to escape a previous position in Indiana—a reasonable school except that it was located in an impossible flat barren landscape devoid of literature, art, architecture, food, or music. In Indiana (perhaps Fitger understood this already), food was grown but could not—at least in restaurants—be eaten. But all over the American Midwest it was nearly the same: the diet was that of an alcoholic toddler, with beer and more beer and terrible yellow or bright orange cheese. "And your bookstores!" As if checking herself for fever, she put the back of her hand, theatrically, to her head.

Fitger lifted his cup and agreed. The campus bookstore at Payne was stocked primarily with electronics, novelties, lotion, jewelry, greeting cards, T-shirts (CAMPUS SADIST: I

LOVE PAYNE), and a smattering of textbooks interspersed with the ghostwritten memoirs of celebrities and billionaires. Books, a colleague had once informed him during a meeting, were "hegemonic learning devices" that could alienate students. Fitger had responded with a proposal that the university do away with scholarship altogether, and design an experiential curriculum beginning with a marijuana smoke-off, mild hallucinogens being delivered to one and all.

"À la vôtre." Marie Eland tapped her cup against his. "This is your first time being chair also, yes? Tell me how it is going."

Fitger pondered and drank. At the start of each week he tried to give himself a pep talk: still acquainting himself with the job, he was doing his best to stay on top of the workload and to avoid further interactions with the campus police. But the arc of the workweek inevitably tended downward, the end of each unproductive day like the lid of a coffin creaking shut. Crossing the parking lot on Monday mornings, he imagined a BBC-inflected voice narrating his progress across the asphalt: *There goes the chair of the department; step aside, here's the chair of English.* But by Friday afternoon the BBC anchor had been replaced by a scratchy Russian voice snarling in his ear: *Go home, you prick.* Even his teaching was enervating. In his Literature of Apocalypse class, moving from Saramago's *Blindness* to McCarthy's *The Road,* he'd begun to feel as if he were forcing a puppy's nose into shit, leading a fresh-faced group of eighteen-year-olds on a tour of mayhem and hopelessness one hour at a time.

On the plus side, his gums—he had just noticed—weren't throbbing as much. A comfortable buzzing began on the outskirts of his brain.

"You don't care to answer. Yes, it makes sense to be discreet," Marie Eland said. She rearranged the bowl of plastic fruit on Ashkir's work surface, leaving a clump of lint-covered grapes on top. "I have probably spoken too much."

"No, not at all," Fitger said. "I was collecting my thoughts. What about you? Do you like being chair?"

"Do I *like* it? No. This is not about liking or not liking." She touched his wrist. "It is about staying alive for the length of your term. Because this is a game for them—for the deans and the provost and the vice provosts: to cut us back and back and back and suppose what we will do. What do you name this? *A blood sport.* You will see when we go upstairs to the party: on the table with the food, they will give us spoons and forks, but no knives. This is so we do not slit each other's throats."

Fitger finished his wine. As alluring as she made the evening sound, he said, he wasn't convinced that he should attend. He had plenty of other work—he pointed toward the open door of his office—that still had to get done.

Marie Eland refilled their cups. "And what is this very important work?"

He ended up trailing behind her as she walked to his desk.

"Student papers?" She picked up the stack of undergraduate essays. "No. These go in your briefcase, to read later at home. You are printing out e-mails? No." She stuffed the essays into his satchel and dumped a handful of memos into the recycling bin. "You should read nothing unless it tells you 'confidential' or 'urgent.' This? This is nothing; no." She swept his pencil stubs and two of the department's "miscellaneous" files into the trash. "Your desk should send to every-one who sees it the message: *All is well; I am in control.*"

His mind pleasantly thawing, Fitger sat back and allowed her to rearrange. He asked about the health and status of Marie Eland's department: Consolidated Languages. ("Yes. Ugly. Like a corporation title," she said.) Were they also pressed for basic resources?

She tossed some more paper into the bin. "I used to teach literature," she said. "Céline, de Beauvoir, Duras, Robbe-Grillet . . ." She snapped her fingers. "But it is only the intro-ductory languages now. If we did not hold on to our courses in medical Spanish, we would be finished." She stood back from his desk. "Much better. Now I think you are ready to go to the party."

She pushed the cork into the wine and handed the bot-tle to Fitger, who, having forgotten about his teeth and his gums, as well as his decision to avoid any festivity sponsored by Econ, locked the office and followed her upstairs.

Lincoln Young stationed himself inside the Econ Depart-ment's new reception room, facing the entrance—a strategic vantage point that allowed him to see the university's elite as they filed in. He had infiltrated the celebration via the usual method: by wearing a black long-sleeved shirt ($1.29 at Goodwill) with the name FRANK above the breast pocket. One of a collection of similar shirts, it gave him a feeling of confidence he otherwise lacked, while simultaneously allowing him to pass for a waiter—a job which would have afforded him an hourly salary larger than what he earned as Cassovan's research assistant, with his PhD.

From the start of his graduate studies career, Lincoln had drawn up a weekly schedule of campus events that were likely to involve complimentary food: the business school, a prime provider, spared no expense; the social sciences could often be counted on for sandwiches; the arts and humanities usually furnished nothing other than crackers and lemonade. At first, this culinary surfing was a source of shame and a necessity: Lincoln was $86,000 in debt; he estimated an ability to pay off his student loans about a week before his own funeral. For almost two years he had benefitted from the larder of his roommate (Lincoln rented a bedroom—technically a closet—in Xiaowen's apartment); but Xiaowen had taken to locking his food in two sizeable coolers, which had impressed upon Lincoln the need to shake off his embarrassment and adopt the guise of a waiter. It actually felt good, though, to graze at least once a week at the university's table, usurping foodstuffs presumably purchased with tuition dollars but reserved for VIPs. It was politically subversive, an act of resistance. He was striking a blow against the regime.

At present, at the Econ reception, he was involved in dual acts of subterfuge: eating, and scouting out a potential piece of journalism he'd been trying to pitch to one of the student editors of the *Campus Scribe*. The editor had expressed a mild interest in an article about food waste at Payne— particularly about money lavished on donors during private events. Aware that an exposé might result in a reduction of his own food supply, Lincoln was nonetheless optimistic.

The *Scribe* didn't pay, but it provided bylines, and Lincoln needed something to add to his paltry CV.

He collected a few plates and cups, trying to keep a distance from the legitimate waitstaff, whose members—in some new catering fashion statement—were wearing white instead of black. He quickly snapped a clandestine photo: a pyramid of mini-quiche and a platter of salmon, denuded of all but a desolate eyeball and a ladder of bones. Pretending to tidy the buffet, he ate some stuffed mushrooms and tucked several pastries (he dressed in layers) into his shirt. He swiped an additional pastry for Xiaowen, which he would leave on the kitchen counter with fifteen dollars toward his rent. Xiaowen, a lowly undergrad when they met, was now completing a PhD in computer science, and Lincoln had spent countless hours trying to persuade him that they should collaborate on a project: a fan fiction video game based on an eleventh-century Arabic poem—which Lincoln would adapt and enhance by having the poem's protagonist travel through time, developing an S and M relationship with the heroine of a Japanese comic book. Lincoln knew there was money to be made in genre amalgamations, but Xiaowen, on track to earn a six-figure salary before his twenty-fifth birthday, would not yet commit.

But what was this? Sashaying into the room with a bottle of wine in his hand, here was Jason T. Fitger, local literary SOB and unexceptional novelist—and, of course, English Department chair. Lincoln had taken a class with him, years ago—a creative writing class for which Fitger, unbelievably, had given him a final grade of B, based on a sketch of the Arabic poem–comic book concept, under way even then. Why was Fitger here when everyone knew—based on his irate letters to the editor of the *Scribe* the year before—that he detested Econ? And who was the woman in the tight black dress? Could Lincoln possibly snap a few potentially compromising photos and—

Shit-on-a-brick: Fitger was headed toward him and toward the buffet. Would he recognize Lincoln, frozen now by the tray of bruschetta, a bulge of chocolate croissant in his shirt?

Apparently not. Fitger looked through him and asked, though he was standing next to a sizeable stack of white dinnerware, if Lincoln knew where he might find a plate.

Humiliated (though dressed like a waiter, he didn't want to be treated like one), Lincoln gave him a plate. Fitger's eyes were glassy, which was intriguing—was he high? There was a smile on his face that he seemed to have borrowed from someone else.

Lincoln watched him unwrap a fork and spoon, nested together in a linen napkin. Fitger held the silverware up for inspection. "No knives." He laughed, opening his mouth to emit a belated gust of sound.

In an alcove at one end of Econ's new reception room, a group of department chairs, Fitger included, had gathered in a gloomy, unsocialized cluster. Fitger had long wondered whether the primary qualification for chairing a department was a lack of attractiveness, and this hypothesis now seemed to have been confirmed. With a nod, he acknowledged Louisa Hatch, Biology, who sported remnants of lunch, and probably breakfast, tobogganing down the front of her dress; Dmitri Gusev, Classics, with his set of cauliflower ears; and the narcoleptic chair of Health Sciences, Marshall Scanlon, who even during his waking moments resembled a homunculus in a baggy brown suit.

But, breaking the trend, here came Marie Eland, striding toward him with two stemmed glasses from the bar. Gusev, with the air of a street thief, tried and failed to intercept one of them, then turned to Fitger and asked for his opinion of the reception room.

Privately thinking that Gusev's ears looked like pieces of dried fruit unevenly affixed to the sides of his head, Fitger said he wouldn't have used the term "reception room." It was more of a banquet hall or a titan's dream; he imagined a boar roasting on a spit at either end.

Marie Eland smiled and lightly trod on his foot. Was that an accident or a signal? Was there something he was supposed to know about Gusev? Having stocked his plate with dentally approved soft foods, Fitger ate a mini-quiche—delicious—which he washed down with wine. Fran's Percocet had definitely done its job: he felt as if his head were floating several feet above him, like a helium balloon attached by a slender string.

Someone dimmed the lights, quelling the burble of conversation. Louisa Hatch, a dollop of onion dip on one nipple, announced the start of the speeches. Was Fitger looking forward to hearing from the dean?

Who would look forward to hearing from Hinckler? His speeches were generally reminiscent of a pair of tennis shoes thumping around in a dryer. But if the dean was on duty, it was possible, even likely, Fitger thought, that Janet was with him. Hinckler certainly would have invited her. She had a sixth sense about social cues, and would immediately understand when "Allow me to introduce" was shorthand for *Help me talk this tightwad out of some cash.*

Fitger knocked back his wine and put another mini-quiche in his mouth. He scanned the audience—no sign of Janet so far—while the dean stepped to the podium and breathed into the mic. Hinckler had settled on the topic of "the Payne community." Unbelievable, Fitger thought, that a person could speak for fifteen minutes without saying a thing. "Community" was one of a number of terms he abhorred. *The snowblowing community. The tax evasion community. The argyle sweater community.* Unsteadily, he raised himself on tiptoes to examine the crowd, which was—apart from the faculty—very well-heeled: jewels on the women, virile pinky rings and hair plugs on the men. He tried to straighten his tie, then realized he had forgotten to wear one. Janet would have insisted that he wear a tie.

The dean exhausted his storehouse of platitudes and ceded the mic to Bill Fixx, one of Econ's multimillionaire donors, who *aw-shucksed* his way through an acknowledgment of the money he had already unloaded on Roland's department, entirely without expectations, of course (though he *had* recommended a few changes in favor of the free enterprise system). Gusev, of the cauliflower ears, made a satisfyingly obscene gesture.

"Now we will hear from your good friend Professor Gladwell," Marie Eland said, refilling his wine. "This is why we are here."

Fitger watched Roland step to the podium. A single vigorous nod, and a screen descended as if from the heavens behind him. Soon he was lifting his arm to summon Power-Point images with the air of Moses splitting the sea.

Marshall Scanlon, the narcoleptic, had fallen into a doze with his head against Fitger's shoulder.

"Do you know what they call him?" Marie Eland asked. "*The Gladiator.* Can you not imagine him with the breastplate? The silvery greaves? He will be in his chariot later, cracking his whip around campus."

Roland began with a series of genial anecdotes about the "annus horribilis" of the Willard Hall renovation, during which his faculty and their six-figure salaries had suffered an uncomfortable removal from the premises. Then, slowly and one by one, he introduced the "dramatis personae": a chorus line of architects, designers, university VIPs, and millionaires.

"A touch of dyslexia," Louisa Hatch said. "That's why he pronounces the names in that ponderous way."

"What's with the Latin, though?" Fitger asked, as the light-fingered Gusev lifted a lemon bar from his plate.

"It tells you how learned he is." Marie Eland put a cigarette in her mouth: every building on campus was nonsmoking. "And it is also a message: *Hannibal ad portas.* Don't worry; I will translate for you when he speaks."

Fitger blinked. His vision was blurring, and his skin had begun to feel strange—as if every hair on his body were standing at attention and getting ready to belt out a song. Was that Janet, on the opposite side of the podium?

"First he is telling us how very powerful he is," Marie

Eland said. "He wants us to be his tiny friends so that he can crush us."

"Did you hear him use the word 'quality'?" Louisa Hatch asked. She shared a rumor about Roland bathing once a week in red wine.

Fitger was trying to disentangle himself from Scanlon, who was snoring gently against his shoulder. Perhaps he should have taken only one of Fran's Percocets?

"*Quality* is everyone's favorite new word." Marie Eland tried to light her cigarette from a battery-operated votive candle. "Look at his colorful pie-shapes and pretty pictures. These are intended to distract us. He is saying, 'I am not here to fuck around.'"

Gusev whispered something to Hatch, who now wore onion dip on both nipples. "Are you certain?" Hatch asked.

Gusev was certain. It was going to move forward.

"What's going to move forward?" Fitger asked.

Scanlon woke with a snort and said, "QUAP!"

There was a round of applause, Roland ceding the mic to one of the donors, an elderly woman whose adenoidal speech reminded Fitger of water leaking from a soiled rag.

He asked if QUAP was the mythical beast of a committee that the faculty had been threatened with for years. It couldn't be that much of a danger, could it?

Gusev suggested that he familiarize himself with the Stalinist purges.

Marie Eland touched Fitger's chin, gently turning his head an inch to the right. "Over there," she said. "There is your danger. Your gladiatorial friend has the dean in his pocket."

On the opposite side of the room, Roland Gladwell and Philip Hinckler, eager smiles on both of their faces, had sandwiched between them a woman whose emerald necklace trickled into the crevasse of her décolletage.

Fitger pointed out that he had his own reasons for not being particularly fond of the dean, but Hinckler was, after all, a musician and a professor of music. He would hardly endorse an annihilative program capable of sweeping through the arts and humanities and—

"Their friend is watching you," Marie Eland said, wiping a fragment of quiche from his lip.

To Phil Hinckler's left, looking directly but expressionlessly at Fitger, was Janet Matthias, his ex.

Janet had agreed to attend the reception only because Phil had promised to take her to dinner immediately after (a reward for services rendered; she was so good with the non-university civilians) at Le Creuset. She had changed into the dark blue dress she kept in her office for these sorts of occasions, met Phil on the second floor of Willard, and allowed him to steer her, via several rudder-like fingers at the small of her back, into the glittering crowd.

During the previous weekend Phil had surprised her by suggesting that they consider combining their households. Perhaps not yet (he must have noticed the astonishment on her face); but they had been together now for eight months, and it was something he had begun to think about, and he hoped they could keep it in mind. Phil's sons spent most of their time at their mother's, and Janet (who had seen but not met them) would, he assured her, hit it off with the two uncommunicative teens very well. If she wasn't ready yet for this next step, that was fine too; he understood. But he wanted her to know that she made him feel good, and their relationship was, well, comfortable, for lack of a better word. He couldn't help thinking about how comfortable it would be if he could come home to her every day. Janet began to wonder whether he thought of her as a couch, or a convenient spot in a parking garage.

Of course that was unfair. Unlike some people she had been married to or involved with, Phil was generous, he was solicitous . . . Had they really been going out for eight months? She had meant to tell him about that fornicatory misstep back in August, but either it had felt like a minor breach (she and Jay had shared a bed for a dozen years) or she had lost track of the amount of time she had spent with Phil. Maybe she *should* move in with him. She took stock of the Econ partygoers. Almost everyone was paired up— including (apparently) Jay, who was canoodling with a bony little creature in black on the other side of the room. It was time to go. Having momentarily misplaced Phil, Janet found him at the buffet, a plate of mini-quiche and shrimp in his hand.

"You must have forgotten," she said. "We're going out." She took the plate away from him and gave it to a waiter— FRANK, according to the embroidered lettering on his shirt— who ate the shrimp before setting the plate on a tray.

"I need five more minutes—maybe ten," Phil said, his cheek bulging with food. He had to finish making the rounds. Did Janet want to come with him? He nodded in the direction of

"Big Bill" Fixx, a corporate kingpin known for his opposition to clean air and water.

"A nice offer, but no," Janet said. She would meet him in eight minutes—a compromise—in the hall. At the seven-minute mark (Janet had a gift for keeping time), someone lurched out of the conference room in her direction.

It was Fitger, not Phil.

Though her ex-husband often looked disheveled, in need of a lint brush and a comb, there was now a Quasimodo quality to his posture, Janet thought, his shoulders canted to the left as if he were dragging a ball and chain in his wake. "Good work," she said. "The chair of English, getting drunk at a university function."

"I'm not drunk." He waggled his index finger in front of her. "I've been drugged."

"Who would bother to drug you? The woman who was feeding and petting you, in the corner? I wonder if that little dress she was wearing comes in her size."

"No. It was Fran," he said. "Fran gave me dugs. Drugs."

Two women emerged from the restroom, briefly stared at them, and moved on.

Janet started to walk away, but Fitger circled her wrist with his fingers—a familiar and therefore intimate gesture. Everyone at the party was talking about her boyfriend, he said, Phil's name cropping up in relation to QUAP. What could she tell him? Janet was known for keeping one if not both ears pressed close to the ground; she played tennis with a vice provost and slept with a dean. Of course she had slept with a department chair, too—speaking of which, Fitger hoped she hadn't told Hinckler about their nostalgic little conclave in August, because he needed to squeeze some money and a few work-a-day privileges out of—

In the doorway to the reception room, wearing the dark blue suit she had persuaded him to purchase (after forbidding him, in future, from wearing khaki), was Hinckler, the dean. He didn't want to intrude, he said, but if Janet needed any assistance . . .

"Thanks. I'm taking care of it," she said.

Fitger noted her use of the word "it." She freed her wrist from his fingers.

"Let me go over a few things," she said. "You and I are divorced."

Fitger nodded. *Yes, understood.* He had been meaning to schedule an appointment with Hinckler to discuss emergency provisional funds for English, but that struck him as problematic, now.

"And I don't work for you," Janet said. "Or with you."

True, but—

"I gave you some advice a while back—a mistake on my part—which I assume you ignored. Now I'm telling you to take your job seriously, for god's sake, and sober up."

"I'm not drunk," Fitger said, "I—"

She walked away, then turned and pointed an accusing finger. "And do *not* get behind the wheel of a car."

He tried to adopt an abstemious expression. Not knowing how long it would take for Fran's pills to wear off, he considered asking for a ride, but this brought to mind an unfortunate image—of Janet and Phil in the front of Phil's minivan, with Fitger, like an irresponsible teen, throwing up across the seats in the rear.

He watched Janet walk toward the stairwell, arm in arm with the dean. And the thought occurred to him: she had made a comment, somewhat cutting, about Marie Eland. That was intriguing; he tucked that observation away for another time.

Ten minutes later, Fitger was rinsing his head in the men's room sink. His thoughts proceeded in cyclical fashion: to defend his department against Econ and other incursions, aka QUAP, he needed a budget; to get a budget (without assistance from Hinckler) he needed a Statement of Vision; to gain faculty approval of a Statement of Vision (via a three-quarters majority vote) he needed his faculty to decide whether a full semester of Shakespeare—he silently cursed Dennis Cassovan—would or would not be required.

The water cascaded around the nape of his neck. He tried to remember the last time he had been this high. It might have been just before his divorce: a regrettable evening culminating in Janet nearly killing him in a FreshWay store by knocking him into a frozen food case with a grocery cart.

Turning the water off at last—he felt like his brain had been replaced with foam insulation—he raised his head. The restroom, unlike its counterpart on the English floor, was stocked with functional soap dispensers and a wicker basket full of fluffy white towels. It appeared not to be a breeding ground for hepatitis A or E. coli, and was free of X-rated graffiti. Roland was probably planning a steam-room addition, he thought, with a pedicure station and a eucalyptus-wielding masseur.

To his left, he heard the cheery, functional flush of a urinal. He shut his eyes, dispatching a quick secular prayer: *Don't let it be an economist. Please, at least don't let it be—*

"Jason Fitger. You seem to have found the evening enjoyable."

Fitger opened his eyes, gazing deeply into the drain of the sink. There was no mistaking the rumbling bass of Roland Gladwell, the self-satisfied growl of a papa bear in its den. Fitger groped for a towel and found one pressed into his outstretched hand.

"I think it went well," Roland said. "An excellent turnout. Some of our philanthropic heavy hitters were there. They like to meet faculty—to see exactly where their hard-earned dollars are going. To know who they can trust."

"Whom," Fitger said, mopping his head with the towel.

"Most of our donors"—Roland washed his hands at a neighboring sink, pretending not to have heard—"are interested in only one thing. *Quality.* That's their only criterion, and it makes my job very simple." He dried his hands and then buffed his nails with a cloth. "Some people imagine that running a department or a university is hard. But I tell them it's not."

Fitger tried to avoid the sight of his own waterlogged face in the mirror. "You aren't running a university."

"Quality," Roland went on, "is such a basic concept, and yet many people—including some here at Payne—have no idea how to achieve it. On every level, the object should be to separate the wheat from the chaff."

Tossing his towel into a bin, Fitger noted Roland's habit of speaking to a vacant spot in the distance, as if—even within the confines of the men's room—he were addressing an eagle in flight. He suggested that Roland's sifting of wheat versus chaff would be opposed by anyone deemed to be chaff. And if all his chitchat about quality was a not-so-subtle reference to QUAP, that committee—like most—would be pointless: Payne's forests of red tape would bring any new initiative to a terminal halt.

Roland chuckled, then rested his arm, as heavy as the limb of a sequoia, across Fitger's shoulders. He certainly shared Fitger's frustration with some of Payne's administrative machinery. But QUAP (of which—had he heard?—Roland had recently been appointed chair) was going to be different. The committee would be small, and it wouldn't concern itself with documents and charters. Which was all to the good. As a fellow head-of-department, Fitger surely agreed that, during a time of scarce resources, there was no room for underperforming academic units. No one wanted to pay for mediocrity when there were methods of ensuring excellence instead.

"Methods," Fitger repeated.

Roland nodded. Yes, the one common denominator across the span of the university had to be quality, and the QUAP committee would study each academic discipline with that goal in mind. The logical place to begin, of course, was with an examination of the Statements of Vision. Roland had a bit of an inside track and was already beginning to review them, but he found it startling that some departments had incomplete or missing Statements. Did Fitger know of any such departments? If so, Roland would be happy to lend him an ear.

About twenty years earlier, in Venice, Fitger had spent several long moments contemplating a slot into which seventeenth-century accusers could anonymously slip the names of heretics and dissenters, who would soon enjoy a visit from a robed employee of the Inquisition; that memory returned to him now.

He lifted the sequoia arm from his shoulders. The Statements of Vision were token documents, he said; no one cared about them or read them.

Roland begged to differ. An academic unit that had no vision and no coherence would surely lack . . . *quality*—and would therefore be reviewed with particular care. And— one additional administrative detail, in case it was relevant: departments submitting after the due date, which of course was long past, would from now on be required to submit their SOVs with evidence of faculty consensus: that is, unanimous approval of the Statement rather than majority vote.

"Unanimous?" Fitger had started for the door but turned around. Unanimity in English—it was akin to a rainbow over a field of unicorns.

Would that be a problem? Roland asked. Perhaps there were schisms or difficulties within his unit that—

No. Definitely not, Fitger said. In English, all was happiness, harmony, and intellectual light.

SEVEN

Halfway through her first semester at Payne, Angela Vackrey was trying to look at the bright side of being at college and away from home. She liked her classes, which weren't—as she had feared they might be—too hard; she had found a Bible study group (though she had skipped its last two devotions); and she had already learned, although alone in her room, the words to Payne's official song. (She had never sung "Payne, Our Payne" with other students. She knew it was sung at football games, which she had thought would be free but, when she was turned away at the gate, had learned they were not. To charge admission to students seemed strange: the stadium was huge and at least half empty and, according to the *Campus Scribe*, the team hadn't won a game all year.)

On the not-so-bright side, there were things about her first semester of college that she wished she could change. She wished she had a roommate, even though a couple of the girls on her hall repeatedly told her how lucky she was to have a room of her own. Paxia had sent another postcard in mid-September (with a picture of an erotic statue in a museum; finding it in her mailbox, Angela had blushed), saying she was still coming, so Angela had reserved half the

123

room, untouched, for her. But by October ("Having too much fun out here in the fucking real world"), Paxia had changed her mind. For a while, Angela had done her homework with her door open as a gesture of friendliness, in case any of her dorm-mates wanted to wander in. Soon, though, she felt awkward and wondered if they were pitying her or even averting their eyes so as not to see her sitting alone at her desk, so she had begun to shut the door.

Now, with only ten days left until Thanksgiving break, Angela was almost dreading the trip back to Vellmar, because she would have to lie to her mother about how happy she was at Payne. If she wasn't happy, her mother would want her to move back home—which Angela sometimes wanted to do as well, especially at night, and especially when she thought about the Bible study group (one of the girls in the group had stopped Angela in the mailroom and asked her why she'd missed the most recent devotion), and also during dinner in the dining hall. Angela particularly dreaded the moment when, sliding her tray along the silver track, she would be funneled as if via the mouth of a river into the ocean of the cafeteria, her hands sweating, her eyes often blurring as she scanned the chaos of the room for an empty seat at a table, a place where—even if she was reading while she ate—she would not appear to be conspicuously alone.

Oh, what was wrong with her, that she had come to a place with thousands of people her own age and not made any friends? The resident adviser in her dorm—a rugby player named Brandi who was fond of nicknames and asked that everyone call her "Shazam"—had stopped in her doorway one morning and suggested that Angela not spend so much time in her room. The change was painful at first: she forced herself to take long walks every day around campus, stopping in at department offices and reading their informational pamphlets (*Study in Bulgaria!*); and then, if anyone noticed her, consulting her watch to give the impression that she was urgently needed somewhere else.

But then, in the English Department office, she had met Fran. Fran had seen her reading the *Discover English* pamphlet—for the third or fourth time—and caught on. "First semester?" she'd asked. "It can definitely be a tough adjustment."

Angela had glanced at her watch, then realized she'd forgotten to wear it. Fran asked her where she was from (Fran had never been to Vellmar but she knew where it was) and soon Angela was helping to peel the labels from a stack of old files. Fran had told her to come back whenever she liked, and Angela did. She helped Fran tidy the supply closet and she met Ashkir (which made her nervous at first, because she had never met a Muslim), and later she met Ashkir's two older sisters, who came by to visit him sometimes, in their dark cloaks and hijabs. They argued and fussed over Ashkir; their bodies swayed like cloth bells.

On his way into or out of the office, Professor Fitger occasionally nodded in her direction. She was in his apocalypse class, wasn't she? Was she waiting to see him?

Angela felt her face flush. Yes, she was in his class, but no, she wasn't waiting to see him; she was fine.

Fran and Ashkir had gently scolded her about this later.

She should make time to talk to her professors, who were regular flesh-and-blood people, even if some of them, despite their PhDs, Fran said, were not very bright. Professor Fitger was her adviser, for heaven's sake! But Angela wasn't sure what sort of advice she needed; she could see how busy he was, and she didn't want to take up his time.

But now, only ten days before Thanksgiving, Professor Fitger and Fran were arguing about her. Professor Fitger seemed to be angry about Angela cleaning and refilling the coffee pot. (Fran always told her to refill it in the nicer bathroom, upstairs.) Angela wanted to run out of the office and never return—she wanted to die—but Fran had pointed to Ashkir's chair and told her to *wait in that spot and don't move.* Angela put on her jacket and took it off and thought about going home for Thanksgiving (her mother's green beans with onions, the breast of turkey, her grandmother's tablecloth and napkins, ironed with starch) and having to tell her mother that she'd been expelled. Impossible. She couldn't do it. She would have to lie. She would tell her mother that Paxia's family had invited her to stay with them for the holiday, and then she could hide for the weekend in the dorm.

"Ahem." Professor Fitger was standing in front of her. "Fran and I are finished with our little chat," he said. "Thank you for waiting."

Angela stood up. Professor Fitger was not as tall as he seemed in class.

He said that Fran had explained that Angela enjoyed lending a hand in the department, but her generosity, however laudable, would unfortunately have to be declined. "We're discouraged from the active exploitation of students," he said. "Askhir, as far as I know—but Fran will correct me if I'm wrong—is being paid."

Fran muttered something about professors not having much of a talent for humor.

"Have you looked for work-study jobs on campus? Or paid internships?"

Angela shook her head.

"You might want to do that. It's often a way to make money and friends at the same time." He paused; perhaps he was waiting for her to say something. "There are no hard feelings, I hope. It was kind of you to assist Fran, but we can't allow rampant volunteerism or unpaid labor here in the office."

He steered her to the door. They shook hands. She was halfway to the stairs when he shouted after her. "Ms. Vackrey!"

She turned around.

"I meant to tell you in person: your essays are very impressive. You write very well. Exceptionally well, for a first-year student."

Angela repeated those words—*exceptionally well; exceptionally*—all the way across campus to her physics class in Glasgow Hall.

Dennis Cassovan had spent the long Thanksgiving weekend at home, tinkering (again) with his opening chapter. The desire to rewrite and rewrite the first twenty pages, removing a paragraph here and inserting it there, was not, in his experience, a very good sign. It indicated a logical misstep that was probably lurking under the surface; but no matter how many times he combed through the prose—sometimes awakening in the middle of the night, pencil in hand—he could not find it out.

He wasn't sleeping well, and his thinking felt muddled. Twice during the break he had experienced the odd sensation of someone standing just out of his line of sight. Both times he had turned and seen no one. A premonition? A ghost? *This bodes some strange eruption to our state . . .* Perhaps he was coming down with something, or was simply unsettled by the department's shortsighted stupidity regarding the Shakespeare requirement. Fitger had circulated several inadequate suggestions (perhaps *half* a semester of Shakespeare?) and dusted off a few punctuation marks in the Statement of Vision; but each of these feeble efforts, Cassovan was gratified to see, had been quickly shot down.

On Monday after the break he had been invited to guest-lecture ("On Structure and Staging in *King Lear*") at a small private college two hours away. So it wasn't until Tuesday that he returned to the Payne campus, still discouraged and not feeling well rested. In the mailroom he picked up the handful of irrelevant notices and flyers that constituted his campus correspondence, dropped them into the recycling bin, and then headed down the hall to his office. The building was quiet. (Many of the faculty, he had noticed, avoided their offices, asking students to "meet" them via e-mail or Skype, but Cassovan understood that regular and reliable habits were the underpinnings of a productive academic career.) He paused outside the conference room—which, given the ladder and the cans of paint in the entry, seemed to be undergoing some sort of renovation—and noted the faint strip of light under the visiting Norwegian's door.

For a few hours he wrestled, still dissatisfied, with his chapter, occasionally distracted by the sound of footsteps and conversation outside his office. After lunch, his research assistant knocked and came in, his threadbare scalp gleaming under the lights. How was Professor Cassovan's holiday? Relaxing? Lincoln Young had only briefly left town, he'd had papers to grade and of course the work that Professor Cassovan had assigned him, but because of the travel and the time off, he was slightly behind.

Cassovan wondered whether he would be better off with a different RA; but hiring someone else would involve a search and an interview, and Lincoln Young, judging from his appearance, would find it a hardship not to be rehired.

Lincoln sat down and patted his hair. He wanted Professor Cassovan to know that the students—both graduates and undergrads—were following the Shakespeare issue closely via social media. "We made a Facebook page," he said. "Campus opinion is definitely going to be in your favor."

"Campus opinion?"

Lincoln nodded and perused the books and journals— neatly alphabetized by author—on the shelves. On more than one occasion Cassovan had bequeathed to his RA duplicate or review copies of books he no longer needed, which was probably a mistake: Lincoln was examining the shelves with the covetous air of a legatee. "Payne has a code of ethics about this kind of thing," Lincoln said. "It's harassment, you know—the creation of a hostile work environment."

Cassovan frowned. He didn't consider curricular disputes harassment, but most faculty meetings, in English, were certainly hostile. It was obviously time for a change of topic. He cleared his throat and opened a folder. So: where were they? Had Lincoln checked the citations he had given him?

Citations? Yes, he had checked them. Or, at least, some of them. As he'd already said, he was running behind, but he would have them done by the following week.

Cassovan reminded him, sternly, of the deadline for the conference in the spring. If they didn't have the paper revised and submitted by—

Yes, yes, Lincoln knew all about the deadline; he was well aware. And he hoped Professor Cassovan knew how much he appreciated the opportunity to collaborate and to showcase even his minor contributions. He was so looking forward to the conference, never having scored an invitation before. In fact—now that they were talking about the conference— Lincoln had a thought about the informal, open sessions in the evening. Ironically, it was the contempt for Shakespeare at Payne that inspired the idea.

"The open sessions?" Cassovan disapproved of the free-wheeling portions of the annual conference, which consisted of amateur readings and other juvenilia scheduled after 8:00 p.m., when many participants had already spent several sodden hours at one of the hotel bars. Cassovan attended only the refereed portions of the proceedings and was indifferent—if not actively opposed—to costume balls, ribald sixteenth-century pun-offs, debates with anti-Stratfordians, Shakespeare look-alike contests, Bardolatry, and overflowing glasses of mead. "I don't want to discuss the open sessions. For now, I'd simply like to make sure that—"

"Wait: let me show you," Lincoln said. He removed an object from his pocket. "This one's a prototype, but you'll get the idea." In his hand was a button, about an inch in diameter, attached on the back to a sharp metal pin. On the front of the button was a black-and-white drawing of Shakespeare with the bars of a jail cell over his face, the bars tightly clutched in two cartoon fists. In bold red writing beneath the bars of the cell were three capital letters: *SOS*.

"I don't understand," Cassovan said. "What is it? What is it for?"

Lincoln indulged in a brief, oleaginous grin. " 'Save Our Shakespeare.' We can distribute them at the conference." He brought a second button, attached to a fleck of lint, from his pocket. This one, in bright red letters, said simply, "SAVE WILL." Lincoln explained that other universities and other Shakespeare scholars would be interested in what was happening at Payne; they might be experiencing similar struggles, and the buttons would provide a valuable point of contact.

Cassovan, dumbfounded, was unable to answer.

"You can keep this one," Lincoln said. "I'm making more." He pinned the SOS button to Cassovan's gray wool scarf, which hung with his coat on a hook by the shelves. Then, perhaps noticing that Cassovan was struck silent, he said that plenty of others on campus—and not only students— had taken notice, and frankly they were outraged, because vandalism was essentially bullying. In sum, the issue was not just Cassovan's anymore. When an esteemed professor was targeted, his life's work demeaned, no one on campus could be considered safe. Had the campus police offered any idea about who was involved?

They stared at each other over the desk. "I have no idea what you're talking about," Cassovan said.

"Your door," Lincoln said. He gestured behind him. "You haven't . . . seen it?"

They stood up. Cassovan followed his RA into the hall and turned around and looked at his office. There was his nameplate—*Professor D. Cassovan, English*—with his office hours and e-mail address and phone number listed underneath, and there was his—

For multiple decades, a black-and-white poster of William Shakespeare—bought by his wife in a Stratford-upon-Avon gift shop—had graced the glass-front portion of the door to his office. Someone had removed the poster from its protective plastic sleeve (how? the paper was brittle and faded now in the corners) and before reinserting it, had circled the dramatist's face and bluntly X-ed out his eyes. In a cartoon dialogue bubble next to Shakespeare's mouth, in all caps and in bloodred marker, the words "KILL WILL" occupied most of the poster's right side.

EIGHT

PAYNE-FUL DRAMA UNFOLDS
IN ENGLISH DEPARTMENT

—*by L. R. Young*

The Campus Scribe (November 30, 2010): To be, or not to be: that is the question that Payne's Department of English is currently debating in regard to the teaching of Shakespeare. Should the study of the playwright's works be required of students majoring in English?

Department chair and creative writing professor Jason Fitger (above, left) did not return calls and was unavailable to comment on this question, but Professor Dennis Cassovan (right), reached in his office, argued strongly for continued study of the Bard. "Students should certainly have choices and electives and the opportunity to study contemporary and theoretical literature," Cassovan said. "But Shakespeare's plays are fundamental. Those who would cheapen our discipline and pander to fashion or expediency will obviously begin by trying to extinguish this essential work."

Cassovan further suggested that the elimination

133

of Shakespeare at Payne is "intellectual theft," and that students majoring in English are being cheated by shortsighted budget cuts as well as changes to the curriculum.

An indication of the heatedness of the debate: a poster of William Shakespeare on Professor Cassovan's door has been vandalized.

Any questions or comments about the proposed shift in policy or the harassment of Professor Cassovan and the affront to his office should be directed, Cassovan says, to Fitger, the chair.

What kind of jackass—Janet posed this question to herself—would allow a photo like that to appear on the front page of the paper, even a student publication like the *Campus Scribe*? On the right, Professor Cassovan, all ninety-six pounds of him, looked appropriately fusty and indignant against a backdrop of books, while on the left, Professor Fitger, local madman, sported a weird gray smokestack of hair and a depraved expression.

Well, it was none of her concern. Fitger had caused her enough trouble already: following the party for Econ, she'd had an awkward conversation with Phil, who had retreated to his own apartment for two or three days before picking their relationship up where it was before. If Fitger was determined to blame the mob or, godforbid, Fran for his own stupidity, so be it. At work, Janet muted the volume on her phone: Fitger's extension—0729—continued showing up on her caller ID.

Midweek, the phone calls ceased, and at three o'clock on Wednesday afternoon a thin young man—dressed like a law or business student—appeared in her doorway and introduced himself as Ashkir. Did he have the pleasure of speaking to Ms. Janet Matthias?

Yes. How could she help him?

Ah! Excellent. He was delighted to meet her. Might he sit down?

Janet offered him a chair and, from a bowl on her desk, a leftover chocolate from Halloween. Every office at Payne had given out candy for the holiday, which had transitioned, on campus, from an occasion for little children to play with costumes into an R-rated brawl.

Tucking the chocolate into his pocket, Ashkir spoke about his experience at Payne. His family was from Somalia, he was an immigrant and a child of refugees, and as a junior majoring in entrepreneurship, he appreciated the sense of community and the willingness of staff, faculty, and students to assist one another and to help one another succeed. It was *so* important. He had heard others complain about their experiences at the university, and certainly no institution was perfect—but he had always found Payne to be a place where cooperation and kindness could be expected, where respect and the mutual furtherance of academic and personal and professional goals could—

"Let me cut in for a moment," Janet said. "Did someone send you here to my office? Perhaps someone from English?"

Ashkir looked surprised, then disappointed.

"I'll take another stab in the dark. Could that person possibly be Jason Fitger?"

Yes, she was correct. Professor Fitger had been trying to reach her. He would like to meet her that afternoon—in town at the Flagon, at five-fifteen.

"Interesting," Janet said. "But I'm afraid that's not going to work with my schedule."

Ashkir seemed to regain his self-assuredness. He accepted a second chocolate. "Professor Fitger understands that you may be reluctant, and he told me to assure you that he is proposing a meeting that is purely professional. He has no intention of discussing personal matters."

"I don't suppose he mentioned any plans to apologize?"

"I am not sure . . . I don't . . ." Ashkir glanced at her copy of the *Scribe*. "He asked me to say that he found your previous assistance very valuable; and he finds himself in dire need of additional advice. He wants to discuss the problem of *quality* in his department. He says you will understand what that means."

"Quality," Janet said. "I see." She sipped from a bottle of flavored water. "Ashkir, I'm sorry you had to come all the way over here to—"

"And if today isn't convenient," Ashkir said, "I believe you will see me again tomorrow. I work on Tuesday, Wednesday, and Thursday from one o'clock until four-fifteen. Professor Fitger says you will not want to see English flushed down the toilet."

She screwed the cap back onto the bottle of water, having paid four dollars for a sprinkle of orange food coloring and a bullshit marketing campaign. "Are you majoring in English, Ashkir?"

"No." He held up his hands like side-by-side stop signs.

He did have some sympathy for the discipline, but—no. He might have a future interest in law school, however. Did Ms. Matthias have information about student scholarships?

Janet directed him to a website and they talked about funding and the LSAT. Ashkir thanked her and stood. She was very kind to have spent so much time with him; she was very generous. Professor Fitger would be waiting for her, he said, at the Flagon at five-fifteen.

Fitger had planned to station himself in the Flagon's hind-most booth by 5:00 p.m. at the latest (Janet had a Swiss watch for a brain, and one of the sources of her ever-replenishing well of anger was the lateness of others), but due to no fault of his own (he had forgotten, again, that the clock in the English office was broken), he was running behind.

"Sorry," he said. "Have you been waiting?"

What did it look like? Janet asked. She was sipping a half-finished drink and cracking a peanut shell in two fingers—a trick she had perfected at the Flagon years before.

She had ordered a double, god bless her. Fitger had always enjoyed drinking with Janet. Booze was a mutual, frequently practiced activity; they did it well. He signaled the barkeep, a bearded man with a ring in his nose and with crescents of dirt forever embedded under his nails.

"I got here ten minutes late, counting on your inability to be on time," Janet said, "and still I waited for another ten minutes." She watched. Fitger take in their surroundings; he had an inexplicable fondness for the Flagon's Neander-thal furniture and permanently disagreeable waitstaff. The imprint of his buttocks, she thought, had probably shaped the cushion on which he sat. He had told her once that, postmortem, he wanted his ashes scattered over the Flagon's sticky wood floor.

"So." She splintered another peanut. "I spoke to your charming entrepreneurial assistant. And I read the article in the *Scribe*. Did you really refuse to return a reporter's phone calls?"

"I don't think I got any reporter's phone calls. But I guess it's possible that—"

The bartender trundled over with Fitger's drink, his thumb inserted up to the knuckle inside the glass. It was the Flagon's unstated public-spirited mission to expose everyone who walked through the door to a spectrum of germs.

"That what?" Janet asked.

"I'm not good with voicemails. I might have deleted them accidentally." Lifting his glass and noticing the gnat-like insect hugging its rim, he updated and summarized for her benefit (because he knew that, secretly, she wished she were running it) the administrative nightmare that was the Department of English: in short, (a) Roland and a team of like-minded marauders (aka QUAP) were going to keep English from obtaining its budget by insisting on unanimity on the Statement of Vision; (b) Fitger had already rewritten the SOV several times (one iteration was so vague that no one could possibly dispute it), but the English faculty would not, at this point, agree with one another that the earth was round; and (c) without resources, Fitger was forced to stand helplessly by while the portions of Willard Hall that had once been the province of English were cannibalized by the number-crunching assassins upstairs. The remainder of the academic year would resemble an eternity in hell, each day spent in crossing and recrossing the river Styx with a hundred versions of the Statement of Vision in hand. He had thought about quitting, but the second he forfeited the chairship, Roland Gladwell, jeweled scabbard at his hip, would plant an Econ flag on the English floor.

Phil Hinckler, perhaps understandably, had not responded to Fitger's e-mail. Absent the interest or protection of the dean, where might Fitger turn?

Because a broad knowledge of university politics was important to the law school and therefore her job, Janet had made it her business to learn a few things about QUAP. Roland was a controversial choice to lead the committee: already chair of a powerful department and capable of pulling strings when it came to the university's budget, he was known for a ruthless promotion of Econ's interests above everything else. But Phil had claimed that he had no option other than Roland. Besides, he said, QUAP was an advisory body. Its recommendations would have to be approved by his own office (and Janet knew how Phil felt about the arts and humanities) as well as the provost's, after which President Hoffman would give them a cursory glance and probably bury them the bottom of a bottomless drawer. Still, Janet thought, it was good to be cautious.

Fitger watched while she drummed her fingers—long and elegant and well-kept—amid the peanut shells on the table. She was thinking; Janet loved strategy. This gave him hope.

"I told you that you need to raise money," she said. "Did you e-mail Perrin Wilcox in the development office?"

Yes, he had e-mailed Wilcox but gotten nowhere. Like almost everyone who worked in development, she was weirdly secretive, her correspondence elliptical, seeming at times to require the use of a decoder ring. Her response to Fitger's request for donor information had hinted at a *possible person of interest* who had once been an English major at Payne but *eventually graduated from W*sc*ns*n*. This unidentified individual had founded a successful manufacturing firm, Wilcox cagily informed him, *in the east*—which might have been Pennsylvania, Maine, or Beijing.

"It's easy for you to talk about money," he said. "We don't have millionaire alumni. I can't sell advertising space on my syllabus. 'Today's discussion sponsored by Glenwood Plumbing and Septic.' Maybe I should auction off naming rights to our diminishing half of the building: The Janet Matthias Janitorial Closet. The Jason T. Fitger Limited Edition Urinal Puck."

Janet said he should put her name down for a dozen of the urinal pucks, particularly if they were emblazoned with Fitger's likeness. She drummed her fingers for another minute. Phil wasn't the type to hold a grudge, she said; still, Fitger had at least temporarily set that bridge aflame during the Econ celebration. What about moving up a level and asking for an appointment with Rutledge, the provost?

He had already tried. Twice he had entered the hushed terrain of the administration building (thickly carpeted to muffle the sound of petitioners' feet), only to learn that the provost was "not available"—this according to his administrative assistant, Harvey Wu, who reported, without glancing up from the three computer screens on his desk (given the rate at which he was typing, he appeared to have more than a dozen fingers), that he had "no idea" when his boss might be in. This was not surprising: Rutledge was famously elusive, to the point of being almost mythical.

Fitger looked down at the detritus of peanuts and shells that littered the table. "You're opening these things but not eating them?"

"That's right." She was prehypertensive, and she was trying to cut down on salt.

Fitger wanted to know what her blood pressure was. A hundred and forty? That was bad; his was 125 over 80. Was she taking meds? Or was she going to be stubborn and opt for a heart attack instead? What about that New Age meditation class she had talked about signing up for?

Janet didn't remember telling him about the class; actually, she had tried it but it hadn't gone well. During the first session, instructed to concentrate on her breath, she had spent fifteen minutes contemplating the state of her toenails, one of them wrinkled due to some kind of fungus, and the remainder of the hour deciding that if the dry cleaner didn't get that spot out of her blouse, which hadn't been there when she brought it in to be cleaned, she was going to sue.

Fitger was glad to see, he said, that she hadn't cut back on her drinking: she was fifty pounds lighter than he was but had twice his tolerance for booze.

Janet cracked another peanut. It was possible, she said, that Roland would use QUAP to target English. But Fitger— in failing to sort out the Shakespeare business and the Statement of Vision—had left his department vulnerable to attack. It was time to unite and defend. "You have to talk to your faculty," she said. "Go door-to-door if you have to. Find out what they want, and what they're willing to compromise for. Every single one of them is going to want something. They'll all have their own price points."

"You want me to behave like a racketeer," Fitger said.

"Yes. And try to be charming," Janet said. "Start with Cassovan. Find out what it will take for every single member of your department to sign on to the same SOV." She swished the liquid around in her glass. Fitger realized this was something he liked watching her do.

"Should we have another round? I wanted to ask you something else," he said. "I have an undergrad who needs a job. Even an internship would suffice."

"Are you referring to the undergrad you sent to my office, as a personal courier?"

"Ashkir? No, he'll be running a Fortune 500 business in a few short years. I'm talking about a freshman, first semester. Her name is Angela. She's bright and unsocialized and afraid of her own shadow—just the sort of person you would enjoy whipping into shape."

Janet reached for her wallet. "I can't find jobs for your undergrads, Jay."

"Of course you can. You're sitting on tuffets of money over there. And Angela is terrific. How about I send her to your office so you can meet her?"

"No." She put a few wrinkled bills on the table.

"Will you be here over the winter break?" Fitger asked.

"Why does that matter?"

It mattered because he hoped she would hire Angela before then. Besides, it was a polite question. If Janet was in town over the break, maybe they could have another drink. As for his own plans: he would be catching up on some dental work, and probably dining on prunes and a pudding cup.

"No to the drink. And no, I won't be here."

"Really? Where are you going?"

Janet leaned toward him, the tendons in her neck like a bridge's suspension cables. "Not that it's any of your business," she said, "but I'll be with Phil, in the Caribbean. Is there anything else you'd like to know?"

Fitger imagined Janet dozing faceup on a white sand beach, her freckled breasts within groping distance of the dean. "You and I should have gone to the Caribbean. We meant to do that."

"We were never going to do that. You hate the beach. You don't like sand or salt water."

This was true. In general, Fitger didn't like the outdoors; it was always too windy or too bright—or rain or snow were falling from the sky. He tossed a peanut into his mouth and it lodged itself, with pinpoint accuracy, into the back of his throat. He coughed into his fist and then tried to inhale. It was as if someone had turned the spigot on a pipe—he was without air.

Janet was rifling through her wallet. "I need to go to the bank," she said. "I thought I had more cash in here."

Man chokes on nut in presence of ex-wife. Fitger wanted to laugh, but laughing would require breathing. He rapped his knuckles on the table to win her attention, but she was examining, one by one, a series of receipts. He surged to his feet.

"I guess I ate out during the past few days," Janet said.

I'm going to die in the Flagon, Fitger thought. He tried to pound, Godzilla-like, at his own chest, then looked around for an appropriate surface against which to self-Heimlich. For lack of a better idea, he ended up diving, breastbone first, onto the tableful of peanut shells.

"Jay, what are you doing?" Janet asked.

Pinpricks of silvery light trickled into the periphery of his vision. He prepared himself for another walrus-like assault on the table, but found himself hefted off his feet by a colossal pair of arms that encircled his ribs, a fist forming an iron knot beneath his diaphragm and a bearded mouth exhaling onions next to his cheek.

He raised a hand as if to say, *Caution!* but the fist crashed like a battering ram into his sternum, and the peanut, accompanied by a gobbet of saliva, was quickly expelled.

He leaned over the table, catching his breath and wondering how many of his broken ribs might be perforating one of his lungs. He wheezed out his thanks.

"Yeah, that happens in here about once a month, I guess," the bartender said. "It's always the peanuts." He ambled back to his post.

"And yet they still serve peanuts here," Fitger said. "Wait. Are you leaving?"

Yes, Janet said. She had seen enough. She zipped up her coat and asked Fitger to send her regards to Dr. Moradi, and to enjoy eating pudding cup during the break.

For QUAP to function as fully and efficiently as it should—that is, for the committee to avoid the usual roadblocks and preconditions—it would need, Roland knew, some friendly administrative grease for its wheels. Which was why he was in attendance at one of the university's "listening sessions"— twice-yearly gatherings during which President Hoffman and her adjutants pretended to consider the opinions of a small and carefully vetted group of faculty, students, and staff. Hoffman, as most everyone knew, was mainly a figurehead at Payne, but Provost Rutledge was scheduled to be at the evening's session, and Rutledge, notoriously difficult to locate, was clearly the power behind the throne.

So: Roland had arrived early, noted the thirty place-cards around the horseshoe-shaped table, and switched his card with that of a student. Ten minutes next to Rutledge would be all he needed to gain a green light for QUAP's operations; if time remained, he could discuss the need for more space in Willard Hall for his department, as well as the problem of the humanities (particularly English)—freeloading bastions of political correctness whose students were encouraged to be afraid of real-world ideas. But after ducking out of the room and returning several minutes ahead of the introductions, he found that his place-card, which appeared to have been clasped in soiled hands, had been moved. The seat next to Rutledge's was now occupied by the ever-jocular Coach Klapp, who winked across the table at Roland. In his sweatpants and matching jacket, Klapp had the physique of a boiled potato with legs. Rutledge, Roland noticed, hadn't yet shown.

For seventy-five minutes, seated next to an undergraduate who took notes on his forearm during the meeting, Roland listened to burning questions about sweatshop clothing in the bookstore, university sanctioning of various sexual inclinations, and the need for a Bikram (and *not* Iyengar) yoga instructor on campus. President Hoffman, as expressive as a department store mannequin, blinked robotically throughout. Roland stared at Rutledge's empty seat while the student beside him wolfed down the entire assortment of cookies at their end of the table. Someone raised the usual complaint about the cost of tuition, which received—from Hoffman—a noncommittal response.

With ten minutes left, Coach Klapp, who always spoke as if accepting a major award, aired a request for a "greater commitment"—despite an 0–9 record—to football at Payne. The recent construction of a multimillion-dollar stadium, it turned out, only increased the need for financial investment. The coach stood up and blew a whistle, causing the double doors to open, and in walked L. J. Portman, Payne's quarterback, in full uniform, along with the left tackle, Miles Quinn. Quinn had recently been released from jail (for the second time) for aggravated assault. Following Quinn were half a dozen grinning cheerleaders in their sparkling blue-and-white harem suits, and, at the end of the parade, none other than Pup-Dog himself, pileous head bobbing, oversized front teeth chomping away. Roland shuddered. The repulsive creature tunneled at the air with its tufted hands.

Coach Klapp insisted on a photograph, so they were all shooed from their chairs and arranged against the wall, Roland—given the continued absence of Rutledge—taking a position on the president's left. If he might have a moment of her time to discuss something that—

"Say 'Payne,' everybody! Smile!"

Roland formed his lips into an arc, and then—good god,

could it be the same absurd student in costume?—felt a furry, lascivious hand cupping his buttocks. Pup-Dog, behind him, erupted in a series of chittering barks.

The entire evening was a waste and a humiliation, with Rutledge truant and Hoffman exhibiting the insights and opinions of a telephone pole. Leaving the session feeling snappish and chafed, he walked through the center of campus, past the statue of Cyril Payne, whose sartorial preferences currently tended toward the Hawaiian, with a hula skirt and yellow bra.

Roland had left his briefcase in his office in Willard and, because the sidewalks were slick, he cut through the student center on his way there. The main area on the center's first floor was a carpeted playground; it was brightly lit and full of energetic noise. A group of fifteen or twenty students were lying on the floor and decorating some sort of banner. Roland strode past. He didn't generally work with the undergraduates, whom he found to be undisciplined and unprepared for education. They could be ferocious on the one hand, ready to burn their higher-ups in effigy for the slightest misstep; and on the other hand they claimed to be terribly sensitive, ever dreaming up new ways in which they believed themselves to have been harmed. It was the era, Roland thought, of the student-as-victim: one's social status increased according to the extent to which one imagined oneself damaged and wronged. Here was a group of the oppressed right now, playing foosball and eating junk food in a corner. They wanted trigger warnings and petting and coddling—when what they needed, Roland thought, was a kick in the ass.

In Willard Hall, on the way to his office, Roland checked on the conference room formerly used by English. He was having it recarpeted and painted as an overflow meeting space for his own department, which would soon be expanding and required the room. So far it looked adequate, he thought. He strolled down the hall, noting the English faculty's predilection for decorating their doors with clippings and cartoons and other retrograde paraphernalia: postcard images of leftist writers (Gertrude Stein was popular, perhaps because she was so unattractive) and Che Guevara, in his ratty beret. Roland paused to read a poem about trees, which he didn't care for, and then noticed a poster on the office next door. It included the words "KILL WILL," and the figure's eyes—Shakespeare's, he believed—were thickly crossed out. *Interesting,* Roland thought. He stepped back from the door. Of course: Dennis Cassovan's office. Roland didn't know Cassovan (he didn't need to know him), but had read, with full attention, the article about the Shakespeare fracas in the *Campus Scribe.* Mind gently abuzz, he went upstairs to collect his things.

On his way out of the building a few minutes later, he took a tour through the basement, having put in a bid—and won dominion of—the modest space in which Payne's literary journal (now defunct) had once had its home. English had no current use for it, or for the adjoining room to the south, for that matter—a room alternately described as a weeping station or a breastfeeding lounge. It was absurd that a department resembling a ragtag army of misfit toys should have two floors to the Economics Department's one. True, the faculty in English taught three times as many courses, given the prevalence of freshman comp; and its cavelike basement-level was thoroughly crosshatched with dribbling pipes—still, half of the building, not a third, should logically belong to Roland's department.

If the English faculty were persuaded to double up and share offices . . . Roland did a quick head count, reading the names on the basement doors. Zander Hesseldine (was that a poster of the *Communist Manifesto*?), Franklin Kentrell, Jennifer Brown-Wilson . . . Toward the end of the corridor, which resembled the backdrop for a Hollywood murder scene, a single door was ajar, the office lit. Roland slowed his steps and approached and noted the placard: TA/GRA UATE STU ENTS/IN TRUCTORS. He heard swearing, quietly pushed the door open, and walked in.

A slump-shouldered man stood at a table, struggling with a machine. This was the Department of English; was he building weaponry of some kind? Making counterfeit coins?

"Shit! You scared me." The man leapt away from the table, spilling a handful of medallions onto the floor.

"Apologies," Roland said. "I was on my way out of the building and saw the light on." He introduced himself.

The poor-postured man wiped the sweat from his forehead before shaking hands. "Lincoln Young," he said. "I'm a temporary instructor. And a research assistant. I'm doing some work for Professor Cassovan."

"Ah." Roland pulled out a chair. He hadn't been in this part of the basement before and needed a moment to acclimatize. The room was hideous, with three filthy, barred windows and an asbestos-tile ceiling pockmarked with stains. Beyond the table at the front of the room were a dozen cubicles, a sort of academic sweatshop, the squalid fabric dividers between them so low they provided no privacy of any kind. The space would require much more than carpet and paint.

Instructor Young had scooped up the items on the floor and was clearly waiting for Roland to leave.

"You look familiar," Roland said.

The instructor shrugged. Why did he seem nervous, as if he'd been caught doing something wrong?

"I'm good at faces. It'll probably come to me." Roland folded his hands in his lap in the attitude of a person patiently waiting for the evening train. He addressed a series of rambling remarks to the ceiling in an effort to put Mr. Nervous at ease.

After three or four minutes, this strategy bore fruit, and Cassovan's little helper returned to his work, which appeared to be the manufacturing of medallions or buttons. Roland quickly saw the source of Lincoln's previous frustrated swearing: the handle on the machine was sticky, and on every third or fourth effort, it jammed.

"Mind if I give it a try?" He stood up. On the table next to Lincoln Young's machine (which bore a PROPERTY OF ART DEPARTMENT label) were a box of metal disks, a circle punch, and a series of round plastic coverlets and similarly sized paper. He turned one of the finished buttons over. The illustration was off-center but legible: a drawing—of Shakespeare, like the poster on Cassovan's door—but this bard was behind the bars of a prison cell. Underneath him, in bold red letters, were the words "SAVE WILL." Lincoln ceded his place, and Roland fiddled with the lever. He extracted a wrinkled bit of plastic from the turntable bed and, using the penknife on his keychain, gave the screw on the handle a few firm right turns. "It needed a bit of persuasion, I think." He worked the machine, producing half a dozen well-centered buttons. "How much are you selling them for?" he asked.

What? Well, Mr. Nervous wasn't *selling* them, exactly. At least, not yet. The buttons were . . . an experiment. A way of showing his support for Professor Cassovan.

"Admirable," Roland said. He was getting into a rhythm with the machine: pop the button into the metal bed, cover with a Shakespeare illustration (of which there were several) and a Mylar disk, turn the dial, and pull. He noted the fraying cuffs of Lincoln's shirt (signifying loneliness, debt, and a PhD that had led to a rotisserie of underpaid jobs) and remembered where he had seen him—at the celebration. Holding a tray. "I'm sure Professor Cassovan appreciates the support."

Lincoln Young didn't answer. A grayish-brown rodent skirted the baseboard.

"University politics," Roland said, shaking his head. It was hard to keep up with all the various issues. He had heard or read about the schism in English—though perhaps "schism" was too strong a word.

Lincoln Young thought the word was appropriate.

"Out of curiosity," Roland said. "How is the department leadership handling the conflict? You have a new chair this year, don't you? Fitger?"

Lincoln Young looked carefully at Roland; his suit was beautifully pressed, with neat, pointed lapels. There was something here, he thought. Something deserving of his attention. "Some people in the department don't care for Professor Fitger," he said. "At least, that's what I've heard."

"Interesting," Roland said. He picked up a button. "May I?"

Of course.

Roland dropped the "SAVE WILL" medallion into his pocket. "How much is Cassovan paying you?"

"Twenty-five an hour," Lincoln said.

Roland knew this was a lie, but he didn't care. He picked up his briefcase. By the by, he said, his own department—Economics—occasionally hired PhDs in other fields to work on short-term discretionary projects. Nothing permanent, but if Lincoln was available, the pay was thirty dollars an hour.

Lincoln was settling another metal disk into the machine. "What kind of work?"

"Communications. You might call yourself a consultant," Roland said. "Come to my office next week. I'll see if I can find something for you to do."

NINE

It was all very peculiar and unsettling, Cassovan thought, the vandalized poster sparking a hum of unrest that began at the door to his office and vibrated throughout Willard Hall. In the following days, he felt himself to be observed. Through the semitransparent (and now vandalized) poster he could see people standing in the hall in whispered clusters. Students were intrigued by the "KILL WILL," and colleagues—some of them coming from other departments—appeared to view his office as a sort of black spot, as if the poster were a notice regarding the plague. Lincoln's remarks about harassment and the campus police were clearly extreme but, on the other hand, someone had carefully unscrewed the tiny fasteners on the plastic covering, lifted the poster out without tearing it, then defiled it and returned it to its home. Cassovan had originally assumed that this was the childish but annoying act of an undergraduate, but Willard Hall had been locked over the Thanksgiving weekend, when virtually every student on campus was away.

Could the vandal have been one of his colleagues? It had to be someone with weekend access and keys to the building. Zander Hesseldine often taught in the evenings and was probably a night owl. Helena Stang? Cassovan had heard her refer to Shakespeare as "the king of dead white irrelevant men." But of course Virginia Beauchamp had once argued—and not facetiously—for the possibility of "problematizing" Shakespeare by including him in a survey on writers of color.

Cassovan looked at his watch—noon. Another morning had gone by, and he had done almost nothing, and the night before he had torn the opening chapter of his monograph apart again. Wondering whether this lack of concentration was a harbinger of dementia, he spread out his lunch: half a sandwich, an orange (peeled), and a serving of raisins from the cardboard container he kept on his shelf. The poster of Shakespeare with his extinguished black eyes seemed to examine him, and the "ꟿⱭ ꟿⱭ" did seem threatening, even shining through in reverse from the other side.

After he had eaten, he used the restroom and returned to find the English Department chairman outside his door.

"Dennis," Fitger said. "Do you have time to talk?"

No, actually, he didn't. Noticing that Fitger had a sizeable bruise on his cheek, as if he had fallen, face-first, onto a table or floor, he said, "I have a class in twenty-five minutes."

Fitger said he would take whatever was offered; he simply wanted to open the conversational channel and reestablish a civil dialogue. "By the way," he said, "I was sorry to see this." He gestured toward the poster. "I could probably scare up enough funds to buy you a replacement. Perhaps not the same visage, with that lovely ruff around the neck, but—"

"That isn't necessary." Fitger, Cassovan thought, was as likely a culprit as any other colleague to have defaced the poster and, as chair, he had keys to the building.

"You intend to leave it there?" Fitger asked.

Cassovan had been gathering notes for his lecture. "Are you asking me to take it down?"

No, he wasn't—though he wondered what the point of leaving it was.

Cassovan snapped the clasp on his briefcase. He hadn't taken the poster down because he needed a small screwdriver in order to do so; but now, he thought, he might let it be. Not wanting to be accused of histrionics, he had made light of the defacement with one or two other colleagues— it was a poster and not a person, and the writing, thankfully, was not obscene—but he would not minimize the affront with Fitger.

He put on his gloves and his scarf and his hat. The first floor was cold and seemed almost unheated; he had been wearing his coat most of the week.

Fitger noticed the button pinned to his colleague's scarf. "SOS. Is that for 'Shakespeare Our Savior'?"

Cassovan looked down at his scarf, annoyed. He had forgotten about the button. He had meant to remove it, but now that Fitger had ridiculed it, he would allow it—like the poster—to stay. "I'm leaving for class now," he said. "I teach in Buford."

"I'll keep you company," Fitger said. "I'll walk you there."

Cassovan preferred to walk alone; it allowed him to ruminate on his lecture. He understood that most faculty had forsaken this traditional format, spending class time on a multimedia assemblage of PowerPoint, soundtrack, student caucus groups, clickers, and dramatizations, but Cassovan lectured. His long-established habit was to review his notes at the lectern in the final minutes before class and, when the second hand reached the top of the hour, to clear his throat and begin. He paused every ten minutes for students' questions, and ended each session with a quotation or a poetic reading, despite the tremolo of his voice, which had once been strong. But here—annoyingly—was Fitger, trotting alongside.

Outdoors, the wind had kicked up. Thick wet snow from the day before was dripping from rooftops; it had formed a slushy white hedge on both sides of the walk.

Fitger shivered; he wasn't wearing a jacket. "Listen, Dennis," he said. "We haven't gotten off on the right foot this semester. But I think we can try to find a compromise. I've been working on some new language for the Statement of Vision that—" He pulled some mangled scraps of paper from his pocket. "Hold on; I need to find the most recent version . . ."

They were moving slowly. Cassovan stuck to the middle of the walk to avoid the ice—following the window screen incident, he was wary of falls—leaving Fitger to hopscotch through the puddles and avoid oncoming students, who were staggering in their carbohydrate comas away from the main dining hall.

"I want both of us to be candid," Fitger said, still sifting through scraps and odds and ends in his pocket. "I assume you know that, as a scholar and a colleague, I respect you. And I certainly hope you return that respect. You were on the committee that invited me to Payne and hired me, nearly twenty-four years ago."

Cassovan nodded hello to a passing student. "To be

candid—because you asked for candor," he said, "I voted against your hire. It wasn't personal. I didn't care for your work."

"My novel?" Fitger looked stunned. "*Stain*? It got terrific reviews."

"I found it pretentious and discursive."

"Really? But— How many people voted against me?"

"I don't remember the exact number." Cassovan greeted another student, who gave him a thumbs-up and hefted her backpack—many of the students carried packs the size of steamer trunks—to show him a button: "SAVE WILL."

"Were there more than two votes against me?" Fitger asked.

"I believe there were three of us. Perhaps four."

"Well, I suppose that's in the past," Fitger said. "So we can put it aside, though I do think— Fuck!"

They had been walking next to the library, the sloping overhang of which seemed specifically engineered to funnel precipitation onto pedestrians on the walk below. A frigid cascade of slush had slipped down the roof and landed with a slap against Fitger's neck, and was now melting and trickling into his shirt. "Whoever designed this goddamn building must have graduated from a clown academy instead of architecture school."

Cassovan waited under the overhang while Fitger, doglike, shook the snow from his shirt.

"It seems I don't have the current version of the SOV with me," he said, "but that can wait for another time. The gist of the thing is, I need to hammer out a compromise, and in order to do that I'm going to talk to every member of the English faculty and find out what they need. And, Dennis,

I'm talking to you first. I want you to let me know what it might be in my power to do, to make your position in the department more agreeable. In return, I'll work with you directly, to propose a solution: something along the lines of a semester of Shakespeare being required for honors students, or a requirement that all majors enroll in a semester of Chaucer *or* Milton *or* Shakespeare—or perhaps any pre-eighteenth-century survey. What do you think?"

Cassovan stopped walking. Here was one of the reasons why, years ago, he had voted not to hire Fitger. It wasn't simply that he had found his novel pompous; he had also sensed in the then young man a cocksure certainty about the influence he could wield over others. "No," he said.

"No, what?" They were out of range of the library's treacherous overhang; still, Fitger looked up, wary of hazards from above. "Do you mean no, you won't work with me? Or no, you don't like the solutions I've proposed?"

"Both," Cassovan said. "And, in addition, I'm not interested in 'whatever it might be in your power' to do for me. The idea is insulting; it smacks of graft."

Fitger laughed—what were academic politics without graft?—then looked perturbed. "You're categorically rejecting the idea of compromise?"

"On this issue, yes," Cassovan said. "We either have a Shakespeare requirement written into the document, or we don't."

They climbed the steps of Buford Hall, where Cassovan's class was due to start in ten minutes. Fitger paused by the door. "It's curious," he said. "You want everyone to believe that some anti-Shakespeare hooligan scribbled on your precious poster . . ." He tapped his index finger—*tick tack tick*—on the SOS button on his colleague's scarf. "But maybe that's not really what happened."

"What are you suggesting?" Cassovan asked.

"I think you know what I'm suggesting."

"Excuse me—Professors?" A student was trying to make her way into the building.

"Excuse *us*, Ms. Vackrey." Cassovan stepped to the side.

"Angela," Fitger said. "Hello. You have a class in Buford?"

"With Professor Cassovan." She bobbed her head. As always, she wore a skirt that made her look like a Mennonite, her knee socks slipping down her legs and into her shoes.

"Two English classes during your first semester—that's unusual." Fitger opened the door. Angela said nothing, and they watched her fumble her ungainly way down the hall.

"An excellent student," Cassovan murmured.

Fitger held the door for his colleague. He said he hoped that Cassovan would understand his earlier remark as something blurted out in the heat of the moment and not to be seriously considered.

"Be assured that I do not and will continue not to take you seriously," Cassovan said.

Fitger headed back down the stairs the way he had come.

Letters to the editor—on the topic of Shakespeare—began to appear with regularity in the *Campus Scribe*. Some offered support of Professor Cassovan, who was a "good professor even if his classes were pretty hard"; a few suggested that Fitger be severely castigated and, preferably, fired. One letter made an unusual claim about censorship, enjoining other members of the Payne campus to "stick up for Shakespeare and other blacklisted writers."

Fitger skimmed the latest group of letters and shoved the *Scribe* in the trash. Noting the layer of ice covering the interior of his office window, he tested the radiator with the palm of his hand. Nothing. In some portions of campus, steam heat churned through the buildings; on the first floor of Willard, the metal accordion-like structures mainly served as abstract art, remaining cool to the touch while occasionally emitting a few clanking sounds.

It was December, the season of personal crises and exhaustion, and there were only two weeks left until the end of the term. Some sort of virus was on the loose, turning classrooms into sick wards. During his Literature of Apocalypse class, irriguous coughs erupting from every corner, Fitger had snapped in response to a student's question: *Why would any writer bother to make stuff up?* Because, Fitger answered, reality was bleak and often unbearable, their puny lives a meaningless trudge toward the blank vault of death. One of the students named Sam—Fitger had trouble, still, distinguishing one from the others—gathered his books and his coat and walked out of the room.

In the wake of his ineffectual conversation with Cassovan, Fitger found it difficult to motivate himself for additional tête-à-têtes with the faculty; but remembering with a certain wistfulness Janet's suggestion that he journey door-to-door through the building, charming his colleagues, he knocked at the office of Helena Stang.

Stang was obviously surprised to see him: he didn't remember ever having entered her office, which—with its stark metal-topped desk and barbed-wire artwork on the wall, brought to mind a modernist abattoir.

She listened calmly while he referred to the department's "unfortunate curricular challenge" regarding the requirement—or lack of requirement—of the work of Shakespeare. Compromise would be difficult, he said, and he understood that faculty had principles from which he would never attempt to dissuade them; but he hoped, eventually, to find common ground. Might Helena Stang be flexible regarding some of the Statement of Vision's finer points? How might he persuade her to be so, if she was not?

While he talked, Stang toyed with her necklace, a heavy, industrial design composed of ball bearings and roofing nails, and stared at him flatly, fixedly, without blinking, across the desk. Fitger had seen her employ this technique on students: after four or five minutes even the most cynical were apt to succumb to her mesmeric gaze, confessing to plagiarism, unexcused absences, sexual errors and misjudgments, and childhood cruelty to siblings and pets. Stang lifted the necklace—he guessed that it must have weighed fifteen pounds—and let it fall with a clank against her chest. "Do you know how long I've been a member of this department, Jay?"

He heard a squeak of despair escape his throat. He was going to have to listen to a Personal History, including a roster of indignities suffered, against a backdrop of his colleague's sterling intellectual capabilities, her exemplary research and publication, and the collegial virtues that had surely served as inspiration to one and all. "You were hired before I was," he said.

"Correct." Without turning around, Stang pushed the button on an espresso machine, the scent of French roast filling the room. Fitger dialed up a facial expression—something between "alert" and "concerned"—while Stang, continuously talking, steamed a cup of vanilla froth and sprinkled on top of it, via a doll-sized spoon, a few motes of cinnamon. She hadn't offered him a coffee, and its intoxicating smell was a torment. "Nevertheless," she said, finally bringing her self-congratulatory remarks to a close, "I don't delude myself by imagining that you've come to talk to me about the value of my participation in the department, or that this conversation is taking place for my benefit."

Fitger protested. She was wrong. That was precisely why he wanted to talk to her. He wanted to ask whether there were ways in which her contributions might be recognized or acknowledged, so that perhaps . . .

"Ah." Stang indulged in a moment of reflection. Fitger tried not to imagine the dwindling sand in the hourglass of his life.

"I'm sure you know I have always been—more than anyone else in this department—collaborative and open-minded."

Fitger forced himself to nod.

"And I am prepared to be so again," she said. "Depending."

"Depending." He swam up through several levels of consciousness. "Depending . . . on what?"

Well, she was merely thinking aloud right now rather than making promises, but as he appeared to be inquiring about things that would lighten her load and make it easier for her to be fully productive and therefore open-minded—

"Yes, exactly," he said, digging a small pad of paper (courtesy of Dr. Moradi and the *American Academy of Periodontology*) from his pocket. "Go ahead. What?"

Stang pushed her coffee cup aside. "I haven't been entirely happy this semester with my teaching schedule. I didn't want to mention it earlier, but you're raising the subject . . ."

Fitger clicked the tip of his pen. For the past dozen years, via some obscure and unwritten agreement, Stang had taught only on Tuesdays and Thursdays, while most of the other professors taught three, if not five, days per week. "What about the schedule?"

"My Women in Literature class isn't over this semester until four-fifteen," she said. "As you probably know, I'm a single parent. I don't want to teach after three-thirty." It was only reasonable, Stang said, that the department adopt a family-friendly attitude and give scheduling precedence to professors with children.

Fitger had started making a note on his pad of paper, but paused to look up. "Isn't your son at least in high school?" He remembered running into Helena Stang at the grocery store over the summer, and seeing her arguing with a sullen, heavily tattooed young man among the frozen foods.

"Rudy is sixteen," she said. But a child was a child, and as a mother she had particular duties and responsibilities that made it difficult for her to be on campus, whether for class or for a meeting, after 3:00 p.m.

He nodded and scribbled: *Stang—childcare?!?—not after 3*. In order to give her an even more preferential schedule, he would have to nudge some of the other faculty into the most inconvenient teaching slots—an arrangement to which Fran would undoubtedly raise some objection—but he could deal with that at another time.

He thanked Stang and stood—the blood had pooled in his lower legs—and then let himself out. On the way back to his own office, he walked past Cassovan's Shakespeare poster, now accompanied by twenty or thirty SOS buttons (where were the absurd things coming from?) taped to the door.

Buoyed by his tentative success with Helena Stang, Fitger continued to seek out his colleagues. He tracked Sandra Atherman through a parking lot (though dressed in character as one of the Brontës, she darted across a street and was nearly hit by a truck in an effort to evade him), and subsequently discussed with Jennifer Brown-Wilson the possibility of her removal, in perpetuity, from any committee assignment or task involving Albert Tyne or Franklin Kentrell.

When he knocked and presented himself at Donna Lovejoy's basement office—he noticed the rusted space heater, an obvious fire code violation—she addressed him without looking up. "I don't have time, Jay. I'm grading."

He offered what he hoped was a sympathetic nod and took a seat across from her in one of the chairs reserved for students. On the desk between them were several thick stacks of essays. On top of one of them, Lovejoy's hand was a scribbling autonomous creature holding a pen. She had taken on an additional class for extra pay, and, between the yearlong survey and her *Beowulf* seminar and two sections of comp, was probably evaluating the work, each week, of 125 students.

"Sorry to intrude," he said, stretching one foot in the direction of the unauthorized heater. "I waited until your office hours began before I came by." The index card on Lovejoy's door said *You may find me here on Wednesdays and Fridays, 3–4:30; DO NOT text me or attempt to find me at home.*

"Office hours are for students, not faculty." Lovejoy briefly glanced up, so that he saw the dark crescents of fatigue beneath her eyes. Watching her return to the stack of papers, Fitger suspected that she could grade essays while she slept or bathed or had sex. Her hand would keep moving, circling subject/verb disagreements and flawed logic, scrawling *awk* and *cite!* down the length of each page.

He repeated the speech he had delivered to Stang and Brown-Wilson: Now near the end of his first semester as chair, he wanted to check in with the faculty on a one-to-one basis, finding out what particular concerns they might have and discussing the ways in which—despite a nonexistent budget and no real power or leverage of any kind—he might be able to ease their respective burdens so that they, in turn, might become more flexible in outlook regarding the Shakespeare requirement and the SOV. "It looks like you could use some additional bookshelves." He gestured toward a precarious tower of books on the floor.

Lovejoy—her name grimly incongruous, Fitger reflected—didn't respond.

"And maybe some paint on that wall behind you; it looks like it's peeling." He tried to envision himself, later, explaining to Fran that, in addition to foraging through other departments' closets for office supplies, she would need to be on the lookout for drop cloths, brushes, paint, and a set of old clothes.

Lovejoy set her pen down. "My wall isn't peeling," she said. "That's mold—from water leaking through the ceiling from the bathroom upstairs." She grabbed a wooden ruler and, leaning back, used it to scrape a crooked six-inch scar in the plaster. She set the ruler—now tipped with a fringe of black fungus—close to Fitger, at the edge of the desk. "I don't seem to be allergic to it, at least not yet. If I get a fatal lung disease from inhaling the spores later on, I figure I can sue, and leave some money behind for my kids."

Fitger studied the tip of the ruler, trying to ascertain whether the fungus was moving or breathing; it looked almost alive. "Good lord, that's appalling," he said. "Have you complained to—"

"Buildings and grounds? Yes. They brought me some poster board to cover the worst of it, under the window, but my son needed poster board for a school assignment so I brought it home."

There was a knock at the door. Lovejoy leaned forward and shouted, it seemed, directly into Fitger's ear. "Come in!"

It was an undergrad. "Professor Lovejoy? Um, hi. On my last assignment you said that I should try to—"

"We're in the middle of a conversation here." Fitger held his hand up in front of the student. "Give us ten minutes."

"Five minutes," Lovejoy said, head bent over the essays again. The undergrad left.

"Listen, Donna." Fitger couldn't keep his eyes away from

the mold on the ruler. The stuff of nightmares, it might or might not have been exuding a faint treacly smell. "You probably know why I'm here. If there's anything reasonable I can offer that might—"

"I don't care about bookshelves and I don't want my office painted," Lovejoy said. "Well, I do want it painted, but if you're trying to buy my vote on the SOV or on a Shakespeare plan, that won't be enough." She started massaging the palm of her hand.

Fitger noted the callus on her middle finger, from gripping the pen. He wasn't talking about buying or selling votes, he said—what a silly idea—but if she wanted to talk to him about—

"I have a problem student," she said.

"Oh?" Fitger sat back, relieved. Students he could handle. He jerked his thumb toward the hall. "Is it that one?"

"No. Other than a lack of organizational skills, he's fine. The student I'm talking about is a—" She shook her head. "I would have let it go at this point, with only a few classes left, but I'm teaching the yearlong survey, and he's enrolled in the second half of it, in the spring. I can't deal with this for another fifteen weeks. It's just . . . I'm not—"

"Jesus," Fitger said. "What the hell is he doing?" Lovejoy was no stranger to confrontation. Like most of the English faculty, she had dealt with suicidal and homicidal students, students with eating disorders who fainted in class, students with depression, cancer, learning disabilities, dead or dying parents, autism, schizophrenia, gender identity issues, romantic heartbreak, and various syndromes involving the inability to sit quietly and read. She usually seemed to be in desperate need of sleep, but he had never seen her visibly perturbed. "Can you tell me if the student is—"

Another knock at the door.

"Come in!" Lovejoy roared.

The first undergraduate had been joined by two others; they had formed a small posse. One of them spoke up. "Professor Lovejoy, I have band practice at four-thirty, and Brian says that on our last paper you wanted us to—"

"Five minutes," said Fitger.

"Two minutes," said Lovejoy. She had already picked up her pen and gone back to her grading.

Probably what Lovejoy needed most, Fitger thought, was two weeks with her hand in a splint and a prescription for sleeping pills. Taking his periodontal notebook from his pants pocket, he inadvertently brushed against the moldy ruler. Should he wipe the poisonous spores on his jacket or—

"Here." Lovejoy reached behind her for an economy-sized container of hand sanitizer, which she set on the desk in front of him with a plop. She nudged the ruler into the trash. "I have a masturbator," she said.

"Excuse me?" Fitger pumped a liberal quantity of the gel-like substance into his hand. "Are you saying that—"

"I didn't notice it until a week or two ago," Lovejoy said. "I think it started during our discussion of Samuel Pepys. I was telling them about Cromwell and the Anglo-Dutch war and at the end of the class one of the other students brought it to my attention. She'd taken pictures on her phone. I suppose it might have violated a privacy clause, but I looked them over."

"I'm not sure I fully understand," Fitger said, availing himself of another squirt from the dispenser. "You're saying that during class, while you were lecturing—"

"Professor Lovejoy?" The students in the hall were knocking again. Fitger pushed the door shut with his shoe and then locked it.

"Yes, that's what I'm saying," Lovejoy said. "I've seen it myself. Each . . . iteration is more overt. Other than that, I'm not going into any detail." She wrote down the student's name and ID number and passed them on a slip of paper to Fitger.

"So . . . you want me to talk to him?" he asked.

"I don't care what you do." Lovejoy stood up to unlock her door. "I want him out of my class, and I don't want to see him next semester. He apparently needs the survey to graduate, but I'm done, I won't teach him." She put her hand on the doorknob and got ready to let the undergrads in. "You're the chair," she told Fitger. "I want him gone."

In the basement men's room, nose-to-knees on the toilet in the leftmost stall, Franklin Kentrell was suffering from what, in his own mind and prior to his diagnosis, he preferred to call "the old trouble." How old was old? Professor Franklin Kentrell was fifty-six, and he had endured a smorgasbord of gastrointestinal maladies since the seventh grade. For days or even weeks at a time, he would dose himself with Pepto-Bismol, his pants pocket a mini-storehouse of the chalky pink pills; then, abruptly, his symptoms would shift, and he would replace the antidiarrheals with a roundhouse of laxa-

169

tives, his symptoms reeling, pendulum-like, between the two extremes.

Kentrell heard the creak of the bathroom door. To announce his presence and his location, he harrumphed and rattled the pages of the student paper. He had already skimmed its few articles (a mysterious virus had prevented the chess club from competition; Kottuolo and his elongated chin had won a philosophy award) and was wishing he had brought something longer to read. A spasm shook him. The pain was hideously familiar: first the lightning-bolt cramps, as if he had swallowed a rotating spear, and then the brutal, convulsive pressure. Shifting his feet to keep the cuffs of his pants off the floor, he began his usual recitation of the things he would no longer consume: ice cream and Indian food and cheese and beans and chocolate and tomatoes and spices of any kind, along with coffee and alcohol and citrus, though he did love his orange juice first thing in the morning. He would make obeisance to the digestive gods and subsist for the remainder of his life on white rice and vegetable broth if only the old trouble—evident now from a splatter of blood in the bowl—would leave him alone.

"Franklin?"

Kentrell froze. "Yes?"

"Your office door across the hall was open. I was hoping we might have a talk."

"Now?" Kentrell asked. The rotating spear began its torturous work again, carving a propeller-like path through his entrails. His gastroenterologist, Dr. Syme, had insisted on surgery after the most recent round of tests: Crohn's and diverticulitis, with a chaser of irritable bowel. They were going to remove a foot or two of his small intestine, which Dr. Syme claimed, with a cheerfulness Kentrell found unbecoming, he would never miss.

"I thought we could chat about your request for a medical leave," Fitger said. His shoes were just visible beneath the stall door. "You said you need six to eight weeks?"

Kentrell batted weakly at the toilet paper dispenser. To have to plead his case with Fitger! Unfair. Life was unfair. Kentrell had taught the American Literature Survey for twenty-two years, and what sort of recognition had he been afforded? He hadn't once won an award or a fellowship, even the consolation prizes of academe passing him by. Fitger, meanwhile, had been elected chair—though he had a lousy master's degree instead of a doctorate, having spent two years airing unfounded opinions around a seminar table. Kentrell had read one of his novels, *Stain,* but didn't think much of it. Any idiot could write a novel. Kentrell had written part of one once.

What was particularly galling: a few years before, someone had gotten hold of, and systematically distributed, a confidential spreadsheet showing the salaries of every faculty member in English, and Kentrell had found his name near the bottom. He hadn't expected to find himself on top—Hesseldine regularly pimped himself out at international conferences, and Beauchamp seemed to publish a newly unreadable book every year—but he had been hired prior to both of them. Even worse: Fitger's annual salary was higher than his. Not by much (seven hundred and fifty-three dollars and twenty-six cents, to be exact) but the discrepancy irked.

"I don't want to pry," Fitger said. (The sick-leave documen-

171

tation Kentrell had submitted was heavily redacted; Fitger had been tempted to send it back with a FOIA request.) "But you know that, technically, you can only have two weeks of paid leave."

Kentrell's bony thighs shivered. He had lost weight: he had to cinch his corduroy pants at the waist with his belt. But had anyone asked how he was feeling? "I've been told I'll need at least six," he said.

"But you applied for a leave over the winter break. You don't need to count that part," Fitger said.

Kentrell reached behind him and flushed in order to mask an unpleasant noise.

"What I'm proposing"—Kentrell could hear Fitger opening the window—"is that we change the request so that your leave doesn't begin until the first teaching day of the second semester. Then you'll be asking for only three weeks—with two of them paid."

Kentrell leaned his head against the wall, the vulgar graffiti scrawled across it as familiar now as his own last name.

"Franklin? We'll still need to find someone to sub for your classes."

The hinge on the restroom door announced the entry of another visitor. If Franklin wanted to talk more later, Fitger said—about his request, or about the need for faculty consensus on the SOV—he could find Fitger in his office, upstairs.

When he wasn't knocking on doors like Little Red Riding Hood with his basket of unfulfillable promises, Fitger was responding to endless requests for credentials, affidavits, and documentation. (*Explain why the writing classes listed below fulfill the university's writing requirement.* "Because they are writing classes," he wrote; the form was returned to him. *You must fill out and complete the answers in full.*) He also tinkered, almost daily, with the Statement of Vision. He had written one version of the document that was twelve pages long; others were as short as a single paragraph. He was tempted to pen an SOV haiku:

English at Payne is
About reading and writing
And things in between.

During lulls he graded, taught, answered e-mail (Fran sent him, he estimated, fifty e-mails a day), and made multiple efforts to appeal to the provost. But he had found that an appointment with Rutledge was as easily obtained as an audience with the Wizard of Oz. Each time he penetrated the inner sanctum of Lefferts Hall, he was told that Rutledge's office hours had just ended, or had not yet begun, or had been canceled altogether due to urgent, unspecified matters out of town.

Finally, with only one week left until the winter break, to which he was looking forward with something akin to desperation, Fitger set out early and full of purpose, a satchel of student essays in hand. Crossing the ice sheets that passed as sidewalks at Payne in December, he considered the anomalous appearance of the university's administration building: on a campus dominated by colorless squat rectangular structures, Lefferts was a strangely rounded edifice resembling a reddish, ominous planet—a place from which, through one of the numerous darkly tinted windows, the rest of campus could be covertly observed.

He arrived at Rutledge's office at 9:30 a.m., eschewing coffee and other liquids in case a twenty-two-second visit to the restroom should result in missing the provost's sole appearance of the day. As usual, Rutledge's door was tightly closed; but in the anteroom, Harvey Wu, provostial assistant, was racketing away on the keyboard attached to three different screens. He barely glanced in Fitger's direction. "He isn't in right now," he said.

Fitger said he would wait.

"I wouldn't advise that."

"It's fine. I brought work with me." Indicating his briefcase, he sat down.

Wu's typing slowed briefly. "You might as well have brought a sleeping bag. He'll be out all day."

"It's the final week of the semester. I've been trying to meet him since October," Fitger said. "Will he be in tomorrow?"

"No."

"Later this week, before the break?"

Wu sighed and appeared to summon a calendar on one of his screens. "Late January, I'd say, is probably soonest. February would be safer."

"Jesus," Fitger said. "Can I reach him by phone?"

Wu stopped typing entirely, closing his eyes. "The provost is in Suriname," he said.

"Suriname." Fitger paused. "Would that be on . . . business?"

"Partly. He's following the business portion of the trip with two weeks of vacation, followed by several weeks of discretionary leave."

"All of that in Suriname."

"Yes. He's pursuing a hobby there. An interest."

"And the hobby or interest," Fitger said, wondering if they were playing Twenty Questions. "May I ask . . ."

"The provost collects tarantulas," Wu said. "He's a member of the American Tarantula Society. *Theraphosa blondi.* In fact, he's an officer."

"An officer in the tarantula society." Fitger immediately envisioned Rutledge wearing a fuzzy gray tunic and an eight-legged cap.

"He brings the tarantulas back to the U.S. in Styrofoam coolers," Wu said. "He's had some difficulty in the past, getting through customs."

"How surprising," Fitger said. He had been interrogated for nearly an hour once, at customs, for an unlabeled bottle of shampoo. "The tarantulas don't attempt to escape?"

"No." Wu explained that the giant spiders—their legs, the provost had once explained, could overhang the edges of a dinner plate—would be carefully enclosed in individual Tupperware containers; otherwise, they would devour one another in transit.

The conversation seemed to have come to an end. Fitger stood and buttoned his coat, then asked if, between daily forays to collect his woolly specimens, Rutledge might, for example via e-mail, entertain a few brief but important requests regarding—

"All e-mail and other correspondence is being held here."

Wu returned to his screens. "Try again in February," he said. "He should be in then."

"That looks like a scorecard." Fran had stationed herself, once again, in the open doorway of Fitger's office.

"I guess you could call it that," he said. On his desk on a piece of cardboard, he had written the word "Shakespeare" and, beneath it, on the left in a column, the names of the faculty. On the right, he had left space for yeses, nos, bargaining chips, opinions, incentives, bribes.

Fran studied the cardboard. "It looks like you're at only about fifty percent—and you've done the easier ones first. I thought you were going to talk to every member of the department before winter break."

"I've been busy." Fitger gestured toward the mayhem that was his desk. "I spent nearly two days chasing Donna Lovejoy's wanker. If someone had told me that being chair was going to involve the apprehending of onanists . . ."

"Privilege of the office. What did you do with him?"

"I arranged to have him finish the term as well as his next semester's credits via independent study—with me. We'll meet in my office once a week. I'll have to stipulate that his hands remain in view at all times."

"Good idea." Fran rubbed her own hands together. She was wearing fingerless gloves because of the plummeting temperature in the office. "By the way," she said. "Your student Angela came by to tell you that she got an internship at the law school—which is pretty unusual for a first-year student. She brought you a gift to show her appreciation." She ambled around the divider between their two offices and came back with a tissue-wrapped package.

Janet, Fitger thought. *Janet pulling some strings.* "I don't think students should be giving me presents."

"Agreed," Fran said. "It probably doesn't happen to you often. If it turns out to be underwear, you should give it back."

He unwrapped the package, which contained a decorative white hand towel embroidered with the words *Thank You* in slightly crooked blue letters.

"I think you can keep that," Fran said, "but I wouldn't put it in the washer or dryer. Okay, a few items of business while I have your attention. First, Dennis Cassovan claims that someone broke into his office."

Fitger frowned. "Did they take anything? His computer?"

"Nothing was stolen. Or damaged. But he says someone got in even though he left the office locked, and some of the things on his desk—a stapler and a tape dispenser, I think— were rearranged."

"No comment," Fitger said. "What else have you got?"

"Next up: hate mail. I had Ashkir make you a file."

What? They were getting hate mail? Was she referring to those asinine letters in the *Campus Scribe?*

No. She was talking about e-mail and letters through the U.S. post. "And let me clarify: *we* are not getting hate mail; it's directed to you." She handed him a yellow folder, explaining that department chairs often got hate mail; when she worked for the Department of Studio Art's Fiamatu, he had received a series of voodoo-style sculptures from a former student who was offended by his critique of Howard Pyle.

Fitger leafed through the folder and skimmed the letters.

The first was generic, blaming the department and the university for the problems of drug abuse, poverty, and latchkey children; the second accused Fitger specifically of contributing to "a nation of unemployables" who were graduating from college with "degrees in pseudo-academic claptrap such as Tie-dyeing Studies and Peruvian Film."

"Who are these idiots?" he asked.

"Concerned members of the public," Fran said. "Cassovan seems to be getting the word out; apparently there have been a couple of articles about our Shakespeare kerfuffle in the national press." As for the hate mail: the best approach, Fran could tell him from experience, was not to respond. As he could probably imagine, she had occasionally been a target herself. Even members of her own family, when she was younger, had invented insults and embarrassing nicknames, calling her Thumbelina, or even Hop-o'-my-Thumb.

Fitger stared at her over the rim of his black glasses. "They shortened 'Fran' to 'Hop-o'-my-Thumb'?"

"Being short isn't a joke," she said.

"Obviously not." He shivered and buttoned his jacket because of the cold. "Do we have to save these? Can't we throw them away?"

"We save them in case things . . . escalate. You know, blackmail, arson, threats, felonies. It's always important to keep a record."

He gave her the folder.

"All right, then, moving along. Let's see." She consulted a pad of paper. "Althea Mulligan over in Accounting still wants to drive a stake through your heart and tie your body to an anthill; and Marie Eland over in Languages called. She left a

178

message about QUAP making test runs, sharpening its claws, she said, over in Theater. And then she asked if you were up for a drink sometime over the break. I looked up her photo in the faculty directory and said you probably were." Fran added that, if or when QUAP directed its turret guns toward English, Fitger would need to keep an eye on his most vulnerable colleagues—the ones who might not look good under review.

Where to start, Fitger thought. The department was a fun-house of dysfunctional characters. Academia was, tradition-ally, a refuge for the poorly socialized and the obsessive; but English, at Payne, had a higher percentage of crackpots than most.

Fran picked up his Shakespeare scorecard. Who was he planning to talk to next? Glenk? West? Just FYI: he should not, under any circumstances, release Albert Tyne from sensitivity training. Maybe, instead, he could arrange to clear some of the hazardous debris, collected over a period of decades, from Tyne's corner office.

"Not an appetizing thought," Fitger muttered.

"Speaking of appetizing," Fran said, "Franklin Kentrell revised the dates on his request for a medical leave. Was that your work?"

Fitger spared her an account of their dialogue in the base-ment men's room. Kentrell, who had a ferret-like physique and a sidewinding way of traversing the halls, had taken to nodding to him, almost cordially, ever since. "Hand it over, I'll sign it," he said.

Fran produced the request, which had been submitted, Fit-ger noticed, on personal letterhead, with Kentrell's initials—*FCK*—at the top. "Hm. Interesting monogram." Fitger signed.

In the outer office, the phone rang. Fran answered. "Okay," she said. "Yup. Yup, I hear you. And you think it's just one? Or more than one? Hang on a second." She put her hand over the receiver. "It's Zander Hesseldine, in the basement. He has a mouse in his office. Possibly two mice. And judging from the tone of his voice, we're dealing with some kind of phobia. He says it's unreasonable that he should have to work among vermin."

"I hope he's not talking about me," Fitger said. It was almost four-thirty. Would Marie Eland still be in her office?

On the phone, Fran asked how big the mouse was. Uh-huh. Was it gray or brownish? Tail ridged or smooth? Thick or thin? Putting her hand over the receiver again, she turned to Fitger. "He doesn't want to think about its tail. But the tails of rats are much thicker. That's why I asked." She told Hesseldine that she and Fitger were coming down to take a look.

"Why do we both need to go?" Fitger asked. Perhaps, given Fran's proficiency with the zoological world, it would make more sense for her to tend to this somewhat specialized issue while he made use of the time by returning some phone calls . . .

She pointed to the Shakespeare scorecard at the edge of his desk.

Ten minutes later, after peering behind Hesseldine's bookcase and concluding that mice (some of the planet's most reproductive creatures) had probably established a rodent base camp, Fitger promised—in the spirit of departmental comradeship, which he was certain Hesseldine shared—to find a solution to the problem soon.

TEN

Winter break at Payne began with a snowstorm. In the center of campus, wearing a size eighteen sundress and a military cartridge belt over one granite shoulder, Cyril Payne, founder and first president of his eponymous university, presided over the fleecy accumulation, directing his resolute stare down the frosted slope that led from the administration building all the way to the Soviet-style dorms. Only a few international students remained in their rooms during the vacation. A single, antiquated cafeteria offered these castaways once-a-day soup-line service, featuring a steam table of chicken parts, overboiled vegetables, and sugared fruit in plastic cups.

Two and a half hours away, in Vellmar, Angela Vackrey was in her bedroom, having told her mother she didn't feel well and needed a nap. "It must be all the studying you've done," her mother said. "It's made your brain tired." She tucked Angela's hair behind her ear. Ever since Angela had gotten home, her mother was always touching her. She was hugging her, clasping her shoulder, stroking her hair. Angela tried to stand still and not flinch. Her mother had written to her all semester—actual letters, in envelopes with stamps, that arrived in Angela's cubbyhole mailbox once a week. The letters didn't say much—they were short and chatty—but each one thrummed with a subtext (Angela had learned about subtext in Professor Fitger's apocalypse class) of desperation and need. Angela felt terribly guilty: her mother had sacrificed herself for Angela and now Angela was repaying her by discarding her like an old glove, going off to college and leaving her alone in the house with nothing to look forward to (her mother was almost fifty) but retirement and old age. But the more affection her mother showed her, the more fervently Angela wanted to return to school, to get away.

There was a gulf between them, and being at Payne had helped to cause it—which was exactly what her mother had feared, that Angela would turn into a stranger and not fit back into the life they had always shared. Going home had felt awkward and stressful over Thanksgiving, and Angela had told herself that it would be better at Christmas; but she was wrong. It was exhausting, every day waking up and pretending to fit into the costume of her former self.

She had lied to her mother all semester. She hadn't told her that she had dropped chemistry for a second English class, or that her roommate, Paxia, had never showed up. At first she had lied because she didn't want her mother to nag or to worry: yes, she was fine, and yes of course she had made friends, all of whom were responsible, hardworking students, and yes, Angela would remember to put her education, not her social life, first. Angela had intended these lies to be temporary, a bridge leading to the moment when her life would assume its expected shape; but eventually they took on a life of their own, and she found that she had created a shadow existence. She began to respond to her mother's letters with more detailed information about Paxia, who was majoring in neuroscience (she was *so* bright!) and had a funny habit of talking about her homework in her sleep. Paxia and Angela had become close; Paxia thanked Angela's mother for the birthday wishes in December; she and Angela had celebrated by going out for pizza and root beer with a group of friends.

Angela stared out the window. It was true, at least, that she didn't feel well. She was queasy and tired, and in the bathroom mirror her reflection looked alien or somehow inaccurate. Angela knew what this meant on the one hand, but on the other hand she still couldn't believe it. It seemed impossible; it had to be happening to some other person—maybe to Paxia, who, if she had actually enrolled at Payne, might have woken from uneasy dreams in the middle of the night and come to sit on the edge of Angela's mattress so that the two of them could confide in each other, Paxia promising to stand by her, both of them in tears. Angela had thought about writing to Paxia about her trouble, but what would she say? *We haven't met but I have been talking to you all semester and now I need to tell you that I am six weeks late and please help me, Paxia, because I think I am pregnant?*

Paxia would know what to do. Technically, Angela knew what to do also: during orientation she had watched, embarrassed, with everyone else as two sophomores unrolled a purple condom onto a banana; and she had practically memorized the phone number of the campus health center, which was featured prominently on bright blue posters throughout her dorm. But the days went by and she never called or made an appointment. She should take a pregnancy test, to make sure, but she had put this off while studying for finals, and she couldn't possibly ask for a test at the drugstore in Vellmar. She felt dazed, waking up a hundred times each day to this new, unwelcome knowledge, then gliding back to sleepy ignorance again.

Her mother would be so upset and so disappointed. She would flatten her lips into a thin, straight line so as not to say all the things both of them knew she would be thinking: that Angela shouldn't have gone away; that she obviously hadn't been able to handle being off on her own and had proven herself irresponsible and immature. She was a slut. Well, her mother would never use that word—Angela had never heard her mother swear—but that was the word both of them would be silently thinking. She was cheap. Immoral. Gullible. Careless. Sleazy. She was a whore.

But that was all wrong! Angela wiped her face on the flowered hem of her bedsheet. It hadn't happened the way her mother might think. While it was true that Angela had had a beer (there was a party at the end of her hall, and someone had kept handing out red plastic cups), she wasn't drunk; and when she saw Trevor, a member of her Bible study group, with his own cup in hand, she had been so relieved: here was a person she knew and might talk to, a person with values similar to hers. Trevor, who had been brought to the party by his roommate, looked uncomfortable and almost afraid. He was at least as shy as Angela—he stared at the carpet when he spoke—and she had invited him into her room in order to hear him over the sound of her dorm mates' joyful screams and the insistent, thumping music in the hall. They talked about school and told each other about their families: Trevor had grown up as an only child without a father, too. Angela watched his Adam's apple bobbing up and down while he spoke: it looked like a blade that was trying to work its way out of his neck, especially when he talked about his mother, who wanted the best for him but who got so angry sometimes; she had made Trevor change high schools twice, and—

At first Angela had thought he was going to sneeze, but he was trying not to cry, so she had reached for his hand and held it, and because his face was still contorted she had moved from the wooden chair by her desk and sat beside him, putting her arm around his shoulders, on the bed. Was this who she was? A girl who invited a boy she barely knew into her bedroom? But it had felt so good to talk to someone else who felt lost, so she leaned her head against Trevor's shoulder and lay down with him on the bedspread; and because it was cold they got under the blankets, and while the party continued raging in the hall they held on to each other and started to take off their clothes.

She had smelled the plastic, medicinal scent of the condom when he tore a corner from the little package, and while she debated within herself whether it was too late to suggest that they stop (she had invited him into her bed; wasn't that permission?), Trevor juddered, fixed her with a look of horror and hostility, and it was done. At least no one in the hall had heard them, Angela thought. Then she noticed that the condom had rolled itself up and slipped off somehow. She hadn't been the one to secure it; perhaps it wasn't as firmly attached as the demonstration model had been to the banana. Could it have been the wrong size?

Blowing her nose and peering around the eyelet curtains in her bedroom window in Vellmar, Angela saw her grandmother's car threading its way down the snowbound two-lane, coming from town. Her mother and grandmother would make a pot of weak coffee in the kitchen and sit facing each other, sipping and doing the crossword and waiting for Angela to get up from her nap and come downstairs. If she told them the truth, they would never let her go back to Payne for her second semester. They would tell her she'd had her chance and made poor use of it, and now she'd have to drop out and stay home. Angela remembered reading somewhere that a lot of pregnant women had miscarriages in the first couple of months. It would be foolish to confide in her mother if that were to happen. She might have a stomachache for a day—even before it was time to go back to school—and it would be over. What a relief that would be. She would be able, then, to tell her mother that Paxia had transferred to another school, erasing the lies that had intruded between them. And, having learned her lesson, Angela would be happy and studious and confident; she wouldn't need to tell Trevor what had happened and, dropping the Bible study group for choir or Pilates, she would learn to be outgoing at last.

But what if the stomachache didn't come? She would have to go to the sexual health center and confess, to talk to a stranger. Maybe she could go at an odd hour or in the middle of the night when no one would see her. She could pretend she was asking questions for a friend. Angela studied her calendar. How much longer could she wait? A week would be safe. Probably two or three weeks. Outdoors, on the driveway, Angela's grandmother, still recovering from a knee replacement, slowly removed herself from her car. A few days earlier, she had given Angela a card containing a fifty-dollar bill and a scribbled message: *Happy Christmas and remember I am always here for you and so is Jesus!*

Angela loved her grandmother and appreciated the money as well as the sentiment, but she needed someone to talk to who wouldn't take her failure personally—and someone who had more up-to-date information about pregnancy than Jesus. She had considered talking to Brandi, her resident adviser, but that didn't feel right, either. Brandi had a thick, whooping laugh and assigned every girl on their hall a different nickname. She had called Angela "Glowworm" more than once.

The only person who came to mind as a possible confidant was her adviser, Professor Fitger—which was strange, because he was a man. Angela hadn't spoken up much in his class, but he had given her an A on her final paper and twice he had told her that she wrote well and that she was smart. He had arranged for her to get an internship, which clearly showed that he cared. It would be horribly embarrassing to talk to him—Angela's heart beat double-time at the thought—but he could definitely be trusted. She heard the clank of the kettle on the kitchen stove and the *whump whump* of her grandmother's boots, which she always took off to keep the floors clean, putting on a pair of fuzzy blue slippers instead. Her mother and grandmother would soon begin talking about Angela—wondering aloud whether she was sick or just tired—if she didn't appear. She put a saltine cracker into her mouth—she had hidden a sleeve of them in her dresser—and brushed her hair. She would keep her secret to herself for now, and make an appointment with Professor Fitger when she got back to school.

Twenty-two hundred miles southeast, on an island in the Caribbean, Janet Matthias was standing in waist-deep water, holding a thick green leaf full of sand above the rocking sea. Because Phil had left to her the selection of the resort where they would vacation, Janet had chosen a cluster of oceanside *palapas* run by a trio of retired Californians. *De Luz* emphasized relaxation and wellness and offered optional sessions like "Spirit Bath" and "Attentive Calm." Hokey, yes; but Janet (blood pressure 135 over 100) had decided to force herself to learn to be calm and attentive, which is why she was listening to one of the owners gently scold her (he scolded several other guests as well) for her tendency to measure life according to a series of tasks scratched off a list—according to progress and to getting things done. *How the fuck do you think I paid for this?* she thought; but, with the others in her group—two mother-daughter pairs and an older man who was wearing short, ill-fitting trunks that periodically revealed one low-hanging testicle—she breathed in and then out, attempting to be tranquil and at rest.

The idea was to imagine that she was holding her entire existence on the surface of the thick green leaf, her life and all its incidents and its trillions of moments, good and bad, as distinct grains of sand. Cradling these innumerable elements, she should walk slowly, breathing deeply, into the ocean. Relaxed and powerful, she would relinquish herself to the water. Breathing in again, breathing out . . . Calm and attentive and—

Something slimy—a massive water slug or worse— dragged itself across the top of her foot. Plunging her existence, wholesale, into the ocean, she fled for shore and tried not to scream.

"Okay, so don't sign up for things," Phil said, when she told him about the muculent underwater creature, that night in their room. He had spent the day with his laptop on his knees, beneath an umbrella. "Come and sit." He patted the duvet. "Look: there's plenty of space." Without referring directly to the idea of combining their households, they had recently been debating the merits of a king-sized mattress versus a queen. Phil said that a king was more comfortable. Janet said that two non-obese human beings, in a world where most people were sleeping on mud or straw and had no concept of dual controls and foam toppers, should not require a bed the size of a pontoon.

She ignored the bed-patting, annoyed at him for spending the day working, and for his lack of interest in the manhole-cover-sized slug. "There's something strange about vacations. They give you a false sense of reality."

"I think that's the attraction," Phil said, his laptop still perched against his knees.

"They're supposed to make us feel relaxed," she went on, "but the entire experience is artificial. The people who work here are being paid to create a fantasy. Just by being here, we're probably contributing to sewage problems and erosion and overfishing. You might have eaten something nearly extinct today with your lunch."

"It was delicious, whatever it was," Phil said. "So I hope there are enough of them to last through the end of the week. Do you want to visit that turtle farm tomorrow?"

The words "turtle" and "farm" didn't belong in the same sentence, Janet said. She had browsed the resort's website before they arrived and sent Phil a link to the turtle farm as well as to a "forest adventure," but both now struck her as factitious. She suggested that they walk into town instead.

Phil pointed out that it was ninety degrees in the shade and they would have to walk along the highway. "I'm beginning to think that vacations don't agree with you," he said. "Maybe you prefer stress to sun and salt water."

"Don't be ridiculous," Janet said. Had she accused Jay, a few weeks before, of the very same thing? She went into the bathroom to brush her teeth. "You're the one who's sitting there typing," she said, her mouth full of foam. "What have you been working on?"

"Nothing. Just . . . e-mail."

She spit into the sink, then stood in the doorway, watching, while he typed and squinted at the screen. He was leaning against the headboard, surrounded by pillows. There were at least a dozen pillows on the bed, many of them large and oddly shaped; they seemed to migrate around the room of their own volition.

"Working in bed can give you curvature of the spine," she said.

"I think I'm too old for curvature of the spine. Or not old

enough." He shut the computer and, grabbing her hand, reeled her in and kissed her.

"You smell like beer and crustaceans," she said.

He kissed her again, his lips salty and chapped. He took her place in the bathroom, and she heard the clank of the toilet lid, then the rattling shriek of the rings on the shower rod.

"Janet?" he asked. "Would you bring me my soap?"

She found the aloe vera bar he had packed in his suitcase; he had sensitive skin. She unwrapped it. "Here." Phil's nipples were large and surrounded by hair—two pinkish islands ringed by trees.

"Maybe if we took more vacations you'd feel better about them," he said. "We could find a place where you'd be poorly treated. Let's go to a ranch for spring break. And maybe we can spend the whole summer at a prison camp."

"Funny," Janet said. "But I get fourteen days' vacation. And I thought deans were tied to campus during the summer."

Phil soaped his chest and turned around in the water. "That might change. I have a chance to go back to the Department of Music."

"How would that happen?" Janet stared at his gleaming backside. "I thought they eliminated your position."

"Looks like they're going to reinstate it."

She walked out of the bathroom and picked up a column-like pillow. Then she walked into the bathroom again. "Why would they reinstate your position?"

Phil lifted his arm and soaped underneath it. "Because I asked them to," he said. "I don't know what you mean."

"What I mean," Janet said, holding the pillow against her sternum, "is that a lot of departments are being cut back.

Margulies just got pushed off a cliff, over in Theater. Why would Payne create a new position in Music? There's no way they're giving that position back to you for free."

Phil turned off the water. Enough talk about work for a while, he said; they were on vacation. Besides, the appointment in Music wasn't yet certain; he shouldn't have mentioned it until it was, and he hoped Janet would keep the news, at least for now, to herself.

Fitger's winter holiday began with an e-mail from President Hoffman's office: the media coverage of his department's "Shakespeare problem" was not the PR the university needed; that sort of news could stir up alumni and frighten donors. What was going on, over in English? And when did Fitger plan to reverse the tide of bad press? Hoffman wanted to see his department's image improved, and soon; she wanted things *clean.*

Thinking that "clean" had a sinister and unfortunate tone, Fitger mentally drafted a reply (something about "vigorous debate enlivening the discipline") while on the way to Fran's house for a Christmas Eve dinner. He had tried, unsuccessfully, to refuse her invitation, and now found himself knocking at the door of her one-story home with (as requested) a large brick of cheese. Hoping to be one of a number of guests (he assumed Fran had invited a collection of the reclusive and friendless), and therefore able to depart undetected after only an hour, he saw, while removing his boots in the entry, a table set for two people. *Damn.*

A few friends who lived out of town, Fran told him, had in

fact canceled that afternoon: the roads were bad, the snow almost a foot deep and continuing to fall from a lead-colored sky. Fitger lived only a mile away and had been able to walk.

He shook the snow from his clothes and was quickly put to work, slicing potatoes. When he told Fran about President Hoffman's ominous message, she turned toward him with a knife in her hand. She had been thinking about this, she said, the blade grazing his sleeve, and what they needed was a visiting writer or speaker. Lots of departments hosted events to sanitize or boost their reputations; events were good for showing off, for creating a razzle-dazzle that the administration enjoyed. Couldn't Fitger round up a playwright or a fellow author, someone semifamous or impressive, whose face they could put on a poster so they could leave the Shakespeare controversy behind?

And what would they pay this visiting luminary? Fitger asked. Would the semifamous writer pay his or her way, and be compensated with sincere appreciation and an IOU?

Fran said her job was to offer suggestions; Fitger was paid the big money to wrestle problems to the ground.

He finished slicing the potatoes. Next to the sink, a radio emitted tinkly versions of holiday tunes.

Fran asked him if he usually celebrated Christmas.

No, not usually. To the soundtrack of "Frosty the Snowman," sung by the threadlike voices of a preschool choir, he explained that he respected others' interest in ritual, myth, and religious and spiritual festivity, but had not been a celebrant of any stripe for many years. Mainly, he said, he marked the passage of seasons via the beginnings and ends of semesters. He had recently finished grading his students' essays, successfully resisting the temptation to soak the majority in gasoline and, in a nod to the holiday season, set them alight.

Fran excused herself and left the kitchen. Thinking that he heard her talking to someone, he turned the radio down; but she turned it up again when she came back. "President Hoffman's not going to let this go," she said, putting his potatoes into the oven and stirring up a mixture of grains and dried fruit—the meal appeared to be vegetarian. "She made a whole speech last month about the university's image. I guess you won't be taking any time off during the break."

"What do you mean? We have almost three weeks off," Fitger said. He had been planning to spend the next few days on the couch with a book in his hand.

Fran pursed her lips in disapprobation. "The break is for students. In addition to keeping Hoffman at bay, you have to write teaching and service reviews for every member of the department, as well as a self-assessment as chair—that'll make for interesting reading. And then there's admissions, which is obviously no picnic, and you need to finish your heart-to-hearts with your colleagues, who are probably eager to discuss a compromise solution to the Shakespeare plan."

"None of the faculty will be in their offices over the break," Fitger said. "They were wearing hats and gloves in the basement all through December."

"You can make house calls," Fran said. "I hear Martin Glenk has a hobby farm."

On the radio, "Frosty the Snowman" was followed by a baritone paean to Mr. Grinch.

"Can we turn this music off?" Fitger asked. "Or find a station with a higher IQ?"

Fran switched the radio off and filled two jelly glasses with wine—it was white and sweet and would definitely give Fitger a headache. He tossed it back anyway, refilling his glass before following Fran to the living room, where the furniture consisted of a short-legged sofa and two short-legged chairs. He sat with his knees jacked up close to his chest, sipping the migraine-inducing beverage and mentally subtracting vacation days from his winter break, which also—he now remembered—would include an appointment to have his gums rearranged by a psychopath in latex gloves. Conversation flagged. Fran asked if Fitger had any updates about the provost, and he reported that Rutledge was probably hanging upside down in a giant web, in Suriname. He heard a shuffling sound, then a whimper. "Fran? Is there . . . someone else here?"

Fran rustled back and forth in her chair like a hen on its nest. "He's not thoroughly socialized yet. I wasn't planning to show him to you, but now that you've asked—"

Fitger imagined a vertically challenged inamorato, trussed up in a closet.

She left the room and soon she was coaxing toward him the ugliest creature Fitger had ever seen: a nearly hairless dog with a torn flap for one ear and with patches of rough pink skin on which it seemed he'd been gnawing. The dog snapped in Fitger's general direction, showing its teeth. Fran clipped its collar to a leash and tied the leash to the leg of a chair.

"Is this . . . a new pet?" Fitger asked.

No. Fran didn't keep "pets." As she believed she had already explained more than once, she was—in her spare time because she had to make a living—an animal rehabili-tationist. The shelter had wanted her to accept a blind and pregnant cat, too, but Fran was, in general, a one-at-a-time kind of gal.

The dog lay down and licked its crotch.

"His fur will grow back," Fran said. "I have a cream that should do the trick. He just needs some TLC and some train-ing. And he needs a name."

Privately thinking that what the dog needed was a syringe full of something lethal, Fitger suggested—given the hairlessness—that she call the dog Rogaine.

With the dog tethered nearby, they ate. Fitger noticed that while the food on his own plate was vegetarian, the dog was allowed to enjoy a poached chicken breast.

"I didn't make dessert," Fran said. She opened a package of marshmallows and spilled a dozen of them into a bowl. Fitger ate two and put a third in his coffee. When Fran wasn't looking, he tossed a fourth to the dog, which lifted the cor-ner of a black rubbery lip before wolfing it down.

They cleared the dishes. Fitger thanked Fran for dinner, then put on his coat and boots at the door.

Was he going to spend Christmas alone? she asked.

Yes. He was going to spend at least three days pretending *not* to be the chair of a department, or even an employee of a university. He would answer President Hoffman after New Year's; and in the meantime, he was not going to look at his e-mail or check in at the office and, as a personal gesture toward the holiday, he might unplug his phone.

"You shouldn't unplug your phone," Fran said. "I'm sure

they won't call you, but I had to provide an emergency contact."

"To whom?"

"The hospital. Franklin Kentrell is having his surgery. You signed off on his medical leave, remember?"

"Yes, I signed off, but—"

"Crohn's disease," Fran said. "It sounds pretty unpleasant. They're going to take out part of his lower intestine and reattach it to—"

"I don't need the details." Fitger had already endured a mailroom conversation in which Kentrell had compared his struggles on the toilet with those of Santiago and his marlin in *The Old Man and the Sea*. Unable to turn the discourse toward the subject of the English curriculum, Fitger had mentally canceled any plans to reread, assign, or mention Hemingway's novella for the rest of his life.

"No one at the hospital is going to call me," he said to Fran. "I'm not next of kin."

Fran shrugged. "Franklin doesn't have family, and I had to provide an emergency contact." She had let the dog off its leash, and it bared its teeth in Fitger's direction. "Look. He likes you," she said. "Anyway, they probably won't call you—but don't unplug your phone."

On the 25th, Fitger ate Chinese food and slept and read and shoveled and took himself for a walk around the block. On the 26th, he dismantled a closet shelf, intending to fix it, after which (leaving the hardware scattered over the floor) he purchased and ate—in a single sitting—a pint of ice cream. On the 27th, feeling a bit forlorn and hoping to avoid work a little longer, he sent Marie Eland an e-mail. Was she still interested in a holiday drink?

Yes a good idea, she responded. *Where and when?*

They agreed to meet that night, in town at six-thirty. At noon, throwing some laundry into the washer in an effort to locate a shirt without stains, Fitger heard the phone ring. Was this Mr. Finger? Yes? He was speaking to Darla, a social worker from the hospital. Mr. Franklin Kentrell was ready to be released; would his friend Mr. Finger be available to collect him at the west entrance at four-fifteen?

"I'm sorry. Four-fifteen? I'm not sure that—"

The east entrance (Darla seemed to be reading from a script) was currently undergoing renovation, so he should be sure to arrive at the *west* entrance, the one off Sixth Street, with the circular drive. He could not leave his car there or leave it running to go into the building, so it was important to arrive on time. If, in fact, he could arrive a few minutes early, at the *west entrance,* that would be optimum.

"Optimal," Fitger said. "But I wonder if—"

Darla wished him a wonderful holiday season and hung up the phone.

At ten minutes past four, Fitger was slowly cruising (windows fogging, engine running) through the patient-retrieval queue at the hospital's west entrance; his car's thermometer registered minus-six degrees. Two volunteers—one dressed as a Santa, the other, oddly, as a multicolored dinosaur—

were ineffectually managing traffic, waving the same dozen cars around the merry-go-round of the circular drive-through, though no patients had emerged from the hospital's pneumatic door.

Fitger rolled down his passenger's-side window and beckoned the dinosaur forward. "Why don't you let us turn off our cars and wait? There's no sense in our continuing to circle around."

The dinosaur—an unshaven man with a smoker's cough—picked up his tie-dyed tail and snarled at Fitger through the open window. "This is a no-parking zone," he said. "You can't park here."

"But this is pointless," Fitger said. "You're just filling the entry to the hospital with exhaust."

The dinosaur leaned through the car's window, gripping the passenger door with tie-dyed mittens shaped like claws. "What's your problem? You think you're the only person waiting?"

Fitger wanted to remind the dinosaur that he and his ilk had been extinct for fifty or sixty million years, but he put the car in gear and circled around, again, to the back of the line.

Forty minutes later—Fitger looked at his watch; he still had plenty of time before meeting Marie Eland—the Santa hailed him. "Are you Finger?" he asked.

Fitger said that he was. The Santa directed him to the top of the drive and told him to pop his trunk and get out of the car. Fitger stood shivering on the sidewalk—he caught a glimpse of the dinosaur on a smoke break around the corner—until at last an orderly approached, pushing a person in a wheelchair. Was it Kentrell? The person was bundled up and resembled a piece of driftwood wrapped in a blanket.

The orderly buckled the patient into the car while Fitger blew on his hands and uselessly held the passenger door open; he avoided looking at his shriveled colleague. Fitger's trunk was summarily filled with a collapsible walker and what appeared to be a shower stool, an overnight bag, a thick manila envelope ("post-op instructions," the orderly said, "to review at home"), and several plastic bags full of miscellaneous hospital souvenirs. The orderly made a short speech (the windchill had to be twenty below) about pain relief and potentially troubling symptoms that would warrant a call to the twenty-four-hour nurse line. "He's a little dopey with drugs, but I'm sure he's ready for the comforts of home." He knocked on the passenger's-side window. "Isn't that right, Mr. Kentrell?"

From the passenger seat, no response.

"You take good care of him. He's a real sweetheart." The orderly shook Fitger's hand, patted the Santa on the shoulder, and hustled back through the hospital door.

Fitger sprinted around to the driver's side and cranked the heater. "So," he said. "Franklin. We're headed to 2217 Goodwell, am I right?"

A faint nod from the passenger side of the car, where Kentrell wore the uncomprehending expression of a slaughter-bound sheep.

Detesting himself, Fitger chattered about the weather. Cold, wasn't it? Perhaps by the end of the week it would be warmer. Or perhaps it would not.

Soon they arrived at a redbrick row house: 2217. Kentrell was asleep. Fitger turned off the car. "Franklin?" Kentrell's face was thin. He had clearly lost weight, and pain had impressed itself on his features. "Franklin. Do you have your keys?"

Kentrell roused himself and gestured toward a canvas bag by his feet.

"Sit tight, I'll get them." Fitger rummaged through the canvas bag, located the keys, and then managed with the help of the collapsible walker to convey his colleague from the car, up the frozen, unshoveled sidewalk and the three short steps to the door. Once inside, Kentrell deposited himself in a dark blue armchair—clearly a favorite, based on the soiled spot for his head—his eyes fluttering closed.

Hardly a medical expert, Fitger didn't think his colleague's face was a healthful color. Hospitals were wont to release patients, he thought, while the surgeons were still busy stitching them up. He looked at his watch. Five-twenty—an hour left until he needed to leave for his drink with Marie Eland. "Is there something I can get for you, Franklin?" he asked.

Kentrell shook his head.

"Something to eat? I could probably manage an egg or a piece of burnt toast."

No answer.

"Maybe a glass of water?" Fitger headed into the kitchen. The house, surprisingly, he thought, was modern and spare. The walls were a muted, indefinite color, the floors were dark wood, and over the couch near the gas fireplace was a framed Picasso poster that, Fitger noticed, had been hung upside down. He decided to unpack some of the hospital paraphernalia, setting the pills and the medical instructions on the kitchen counter next to the stove. Would Kentrell want some soup or some crackers later? Fitger looked through the cabinets (which held a vast selection of tuna but not much else) and the refrigerator, where he found a jar of tomato sauce, some mustard and mayonnaise, a stale-looking dinner roll, and half a gallon of expired milk.

Well, all right. He could fit in a quick trip to the store. He returned to the living room to find out if there was something Kentrell might want to add to a grocery list, but his colleague had fallen asleep again.

The house, Fitger realized, was cold. He turned the gas fireplace on and found the thermostat and cranked up the heat. He put on his coat and his gloves and went outside and shoveled the walk. Kentrell was snoring when he came in. It was five thirty-five—still enough time for Fitger to pick up some groceries and go home and shave and change his clothes. *Should* he change his clothes? Perhaps he had read too much into Marie Eland's interest in having a drink. His shirts, in any case, had probably tied themselves into a wrinkled knot in the dryer.

He decided to set Kentrell's hospital bath chair in the shower or tub. Tucking the contraption under his arm, he mounted the stairs, which were steep and uncarpeted and would probably be difficult if not impossible for someone in Kentrell's condition (the poor bastard) to—

Fitger stopped. Shower chair under his arm, he descended the stairs and walked slowly, room by room, through the house. There was no bedroom or bathroom on the first floor.

"Franklin," he said. Kentrell barely stirred. Fitger switched the gas fireplace off, turned off the thermostat, and went into the kitchen and poured the expired milk down the drain. He packed up the bottles of pills with their instructions and gathered up the overnight bag and put everything back into the trunk of his car. He called Marie Eland; then he touched Kentrell's shoulder. "Wake up, Franklin. I'm taking you home."

ELEVEN

Momentarily stymied by his lack of access to the provost, Roland Gladwell—never thwarted or disappointed for long—was pursuing a number of strategies vis-à-vis the removal of English from Willard Hall. First, he had purchased Hinckler's noninterference with the promise of a paltry position in Music. Second, he was close to securing a multimillion-dollar donation from two benefactors. (He had recently led Manuela Pratt and Big Bill Fixx on a tour of the building, pointing out the benefits of a newly refashioned, and rechristened, Pratt-Fixx Hall.) Third, he had used Theater, a hopelessly inept department, as a test case for shrinkage and subjugation; he would soon turn QUAP's attention to English, steering the committee toward recommendations such as a 50 percent reduction in the size of the faculty (to be achieved by moving West into administration, denying tenure to Brown-Wilson, and pushing Tyne, Glenk, and Cassovan into retirement) after which the remainder of Fitger's department could be compressed onto the basement floor.

But: because of the attention—and sympathy—Cassovan had lately received in the press, Roland thought it prudent to proceed with caution where the Shakespearean was concerned. Three times since the middle of the fall semester, Roland had made overtures, suggesting an after-work drink or a midmorning coffee; Cassovan had declined. After refusing Roland's first invitation, he had ignored all the others, which was why, in early January, during the doldrums of winter break, Roland made inquiries and learned that, driven out of his office like the Little Match Girl in the cold, Cassovan was laboring away in a study carrel toward the back of the library's fourth (and top) floor.

Roland hadn't been in the Payne library for years. Known as a place where undergraduates went to nap (and, some said, to engage in intercourse in the group study rooms), the building was sadly in need of modernization. Its towering metal rows of floor-to-ceiling shelves created a catacomb-like effect, and the overhead lights, cued to old-fashioned timers, had a way of clicking off all at once, leaving patrons stranded in the airless dark. Roland exited the clangorous elevator, which opened its doors several inches above its stop, and—spinning the timers on the lights as he went—began an exploratory tour of the modest carrels that hugged the outer rim of the fourth floor. In a pinched little cubby (consisting of a wooden slab of a desk, a small metal overhead locker, a gooseneck lamp, and a worn, uncomfortable-looking chair) he found Dennis Cassovan taking notes on a series of index cards in a cramped but immaculate hand.

Roland stood by the side of the carrel and waited. Cassovan must have been at least eighty, he thought; and in his black suit, white shirt, and black tie, and with a fountain pen in his fist, he looked like a tonsured monk in his cell.

Cassovan capped his pen and set it neatly down on the desk. "Is there something I can help you with?" he asked.

Roland stepped into his line of sight. He introduced himself—a gesture typically unnecessary at Payne, because everyone knew who he was, but there was no telling what shape the old man's mind might be in. "You aren't easy to find," he said. "This is a gloomy little hideaway; the library is fairly empty during winter term."

"I chose it because I'm not usually disturbed here," Cassovan said. He wouldn't have been disturbed in his office, either, especially with the students still enjoying their winter break, but the cold (due to Fitger's mismanagement, Cassovan assumed, of the budget) had driven him out. In truth, the vandalism of his poster and its aftermath had driven him out also. His door was now pockmarked with SOS buttons interspersed with clippings from the papers: *Shakespeare in Danger at Universities? No Room for the Bard in Higher Ed?* While at first he had found the attention justified and affirming (Lincoln Young assured him that it would help), the publicity began to feel distasteful. That other literature scholars would have a stake in the issue made sense; but the larger brouhaha was peculiar, as was—at Payne—the undergraduates' continuing interest. Something strange was afoot. Late in the fall, Cassovan had entered his office and found the items on his desk rearranged: the tape dispenser had been moved to the place where the clock usually rested, and the letter opener (always kept on the left, parallel to the stapler) protruded, weapon-like, from a drawer. A threat? Or was he losing his mind? Picking up the ersatz weapon (the letter opener was, in fact, sharp), Cassovan remembered the board game his son, Ben, had liked to play when he was small, the object being to identify a murderer: the colleague with the letter opener in the office; the department chair with the window screen on the sidewalk; and now, perhaps, the economist, with a sharpened pencil, amid the library's shelves.

Roland dragged a chair to the edge of the carrel, hemming Cassovan in. Through the narrow window by the desk, a gunmetal sky was threatening snow. "I won't take up much of your time," Roland said. "You may have heard about the quality assessment program, of which I am chair. I understand that you have some frustrations—some dissatisfaction—with your department."

Cassovan didn't answer. He didn't care for Gladwell's ambitions or for his pedagogical philosophy, which seemed to have been developed from a North Korean model, each student to be hewn and fashioned into a cog in the grinding wheel. Their two pairs of knees (Roland's three times the size) were uncomfortably close. An expensive watch gleamed from within the hair on Roland's wrist.

"You might suppose that it's none of my business, what transpires in English," Roland said. "But QUAP has made it my business. And while some may be needlessly cautious or timid about the assessment process, I think you might find it could work to your benefit."

The overhead lights began to click off one row at a time, a tide of darkness approaching. Roland stood up and spun the two nearest dials. Cassovan might not know, he said, that he had studied Shakespeare in college and had once taken the part of Claudius in a classroom play.

Cassovan cleaned his glasses with a handkerchief. His eyes

were bloodshot, rheumy, set deep in his face like matching fires in two ancient caves.

"In any case, the point I'm getting to," Roland said, "is that I applaud what you're doing: you're defending *quality* and upholding standards. But I wonder if it's occurred to you that English—as a department—isn't the best way to do that. Why entrust your legacy at Payne to a poorly functioning unit and its powerless chair?"

Cassovan finished cleaning his glasses and put them back on. *What an implacable buzzard,* Roland thought: he might as well have been chatting with one of the statues on Easter Island. That twerp of an assistant, Lincoln Young, hadn't adequately briefed him. Never mind: Roland laid out his plan. In order for any curricular initiative to survive, he explained, it would have to be funded; to think otherwise was to believe in fairy tales. English didn't have funding. If Cassovan was angling for a permanent, or close to permanent, place for Shakespeare at Payne, he would need to think and to work beyond English. He would need to—

The lights began to extinguish themselves again. Roland stood up, nearly knocking his chair over, and strode from one metal bookshelf to the next, spinning the dials.

"*'Upon the world dim darkness doth display,'*" Cassovan murmured.

Roland sat down again, releasing a subtle whiff of cologne. "Excuse me?"

"A poem. Go on."

Roland's proposal, he assured his older colleague, was innovative and cross-disciplinary. Payne would offer Shakespeare instruction across the curriculum, rather than in

English. English was bankrupt anyway, having turned its back on traditional literatures. What did Cassovan think about the idea of an annual Shakespeare lecture, perhaps bearing his name? They would have to fund-raise and gather the money, of course, but Roland had contacts. "And if you were to retire next fall"—he paused to allow this proposition time to sink in—"we could arrange to kick-start the fund with a semester's worth of your salary."

With the tip of a finger, Cassovan straightened his stack of index cards. He found the smell of the library—the quiet, musty scent of books—oddly reassuring. It reminded him of the impermanence of his work: how deeply invested in it he was, and how little it meant to almost anyone else—which was as it should be. Men like Roland Gladwell imagined themselves with each completed project to be hewing their likenesses in bronze; but all scholarly endeavor was eventually reduced to these codified symbols tucked into endless paper beds, then bound between tombstone covers and seldom disturbed.

Still, the economist's proposition was somewhat intriguing: a lecture series in exchange for retirement. Cassovan cleared his throat. In his experience, he said, few students attended campus-wide lectures. Could undergraduates majoring in biology or Spanish or—he gestured in the direction of his robust colleague—economics be expected to rush off to hear an analysis of *Twelfth Night*? Occasional lectures were for those who had already cultivated an interest in a given topic; in the absence of a Shakespeare curriculum, there would be no audience for a series such as the one he described.

Roland planted his fists on his monumental knees. "You're saying a lecture isn't enough for you?"

In the darkness beyond the columns of books, they heard a clanking, jangling noise, as of chains being dragged along a prison floor.

"Ghosts." Cassovan smiled. A few seconds later, a custodian emerged from the gloom, pushing a bucket and mop contraption.

"Hello, Henry," Cassovan said.

The custodian nodded, depositing a clump of grime on Roland's pants with the edge of his cart.

"Whether it is or isn't enough *for me* is irrelevant," Cassovan said. Roland brought to mind one of Cassovan's undergraduates: a handsome soccer player, quick to anger, who took every editorial comment and correction as a personal slight, his pride a trophy he carried with him everywhere. "I'm interested only in what benefits the students. An annual lecture delivered by an overpaid visiting scholar is not the same as a recognition of Shakespeare's place in the curriculum."

Roland examined his polished wingtips. He respected a colleague who knew how to bargain. Cassovan was one of the few well-regarded scholars in English. If Roland couldn't persuade him to retire, he could perhaps pluck him from the bosom of his department. "You want a class, then," he said. "Presumably a class the undergrads have no choice but to take."

Cassovan didn't care for the phrasing—"no choice" had a punitive ring—but he shrugged his assent.

"Such a class," Roland said, "wouldn't have to be offered by English. Might another academic department absorb it?"

Another department? Through the slice of window on his left, Cassovan saw the snow begin again, oversized flakes spinning down from a flat gray sky. What other department would regularly offer a class on Shakespeare? Roland was probably thinking of Theater—whose chair, Margulies, was about to be coerced into retirement—or, god forbid, Film. So many of Cassovan's students already showed up in his Shakespeare seminar talking about Claire Danes and Leonardo DiCaprio. One student had wanted, for "extra credit" (a phenomenon, akin to raffles and lottery tickets, in which Cassovan had never indulged), to screen an animated barbarity called *Gnomeo and Juliet*. Turning back from the window, he said, "I'm afraid the Film Studies Program is not equipped to—"

Roland held up a meaty hand. "It wouldn't have to be Film. It could be funded by the president or the provost, as part of a 'Great Works' experience. The faculty member in charge"—he was thinking now on his feet—"could be a member of any department. He could be a Shakespeare scholar-at-large. In light of the protests here on campus, we could easily sell the idea to donors: 'Payne reestablishing rigorous standards in undergraduate education.' Remove it from English, and every student on campus—not just the literature majors—could be required to study Shakespeare."

Every student? Cassovan felt the tug of a fishing line—and there was Roland Gladwell sitting on the riverbank with a rod and a reel. "We've never had a required course that crosses departments," he said. "And I imagine the chairs of Sociology and History and Physics would want their disciplines represented."

Roland erased this petty concern from the airspace between them. QUAP had been authorized to make curricular recommendations; and, as the committee's chair, he had access to donors and to clout.

The snowflakes were falling faster now, pressing themselves like tiny, desperate hands against the glass. It had been snowing on the afternoon that Cassovan's son had died at the age of fourteen. The vivid memory of that day, though decades old, occasionally rose up in Cassovan's mind to assail him. Ben would be middle-aged now. Year by year, his brief, graceful life grew more distant, like that of a character in a novel his father had dearly loved but would never read again.

He gathered his things. He wanted to leave before the snow made walking difficult; falling, at his age, might mean a permanent change of address, to a nursing home.

"You're leaving?" Roland asked. "We'll walk out together." He spun the timer, and a runway of light illuminated their path through the shelves. As they reached the elevator, Roland put his hand—it felt more like a lion's paw—on Cassovan's shoulder. "You'll give some thought to our conversation?"

Cassovan was tired; the daily fog of exhaustion had begun to roll in. *Wisely and slow,* he thought; *they stumble that run fast.* "I'll consider it," he said.

Roland patted his shoulder again, sending Cassovan almost tripping through the elevator doors. By the time he righted himself and pushed the button for the ground floor, Roland—feeling no need to end their tête-à-tête with formalities—had turned and begun to walk down the stairs.

In the middle of the night, sleep a distant country to which he had once again been denied a visa, Fitger lay in bed and stared at the ceiling, listening to Franklin Kentrell's shambling progress down the hall to the bathroom, his hourly voyage announced via the squeaking wheel on his walker on the floor below. Kentrell had been oystered away in Fitger's first-floor study since his return from the hospital five days before, Fitger having moved his own computer and most of the contents of his desk to his bedroom upstairs. He had equipped what was now Kentrell's sick bay with a pullout guest bed, extra pillows, blankets, beverages, a side table stocked with magazines, and a small TV. The TV—its provision, in retrospect, a significant error—was on at all hours, tuned to talk shows and mindless midday dramas whose soundtracks floated freely (the downstairs study had no door), along with the sound of Kentrell's intermittent snoring, through every room.

Impossible, Fitger thought, to endure even another hour of his colleague's presence. Twice, shutting himself in his bedroom closet so Kentrell wouldn't hear, he had called the hospital's patient helpline to ask if his invalid friend might be transferred to an aftercare facility—perhaps a day care center or a pet motel. But he was told that Kentrell had not requested aftercare, which, in any case, was not available under his insurance plan.

He heard the toilet flush downstairs—Kentrell typically left the bathroom door open during use—and discerned the sound of his corduroy slippers (they were in fact Fitger's slippers) as they began their shuffling journey down the hall. He lay perfectly still, lest he be summoned. The daily reality of Kentrell's sojourn was painful enough (the bottles of pills on the kitchen counter, the incessant TV, the compromised cleanliness of the toilet); but at night, to hear his colleague whimpering in dreams . . . appalling, appalling. Each morning, Fitger rose and dressed in disbelief that Kentrell was still there.

Fran called him at home one icy January afternoon. "I thought you were coming in today," she said. "You were going to write those performance reviews."

Fitger stood at the sink, rinsing the remains of Kentrell's lunch—a nauseating mix of applesauce, yogurt, and bananas—into the drain. He lowered his voice. "I had to take him in today—for a checkup." He had not only driven Kentrell to the clinic but accompanied him into the examination room and watched him struggle into a polka-dotted gown. The female physician who eventually knocked and came into the room looked young enough to have a jump rope rather than a stethoscope in her white coat pocket.

"Are you his partner?" she'd asked, after shaking hands with Kentrell.

"No, I'm his department chair."

The doctor had ended up scolding Fitger for neglecting to bring his colleague in sooner. Hadn't he noticed the patient's lethargy? His fever? After ordering antibiotics, she had charged Fitger with the responsibility of taking Kentrell's temperature every four hours and, after administering the drug, making sure it "stayed down."

"Wait: Kentrell is still living with you?" Fran asked.

Yes, because a member of the staff had apparently listed him as an emergency contact. But perhaps that member of the staff would now be interested in setting aside a room in her own home and taking a turn with—

"Nope." It would be inappropriate, Fran said, for a female member of the administration to take care of the faculty.

"It must be equally against some rule for me to be stuck with him," Fitger said. He squeezed out a sponge. He had accomplished none of the reading or writing he had intended to tackle during the break, and his attempts to placate President Hoffman had failed: she had sent him the latest round of clippings (*Shakespeare a Payne in the Neck at Midwestern University*) and insisted that he put a stop to the unfavorable publicity ASAP. And Fran was right about Hoffman's desire for an event or a speaker. In her latest e-mail she had suggested that the damage to his department might be assuaged if English were to host someone prestigious: a scholar or author who had won a major award. How Fitger would pay for such an event without a budget, she didn't say. Meanwhile, Kentrell—beginning day six of his convalescence in Fitger's study—was turning into an oversized foster child.

"Well, Franklin will owe you one," Fran said. She asked if Fitger intended, all week, to work from home.

"I wouldn't call this working," he said. "It's more like telecommuting from hell." Was there anything interesting happening up at the office?

No, not much. What with the lack of heat, Fran was dressing in layers, but it was quiet, with the students gone. The conference room had gotten a new coat of paint and looked very good. English still couldn't use it, but Fran had managed to get a look at it through the locked door. Also—maybe this was of interest—Roland had toured a few bigwigs through the first floor of Willard with his accomplice, Marilyn Hoopes. And he seemed to be pursuing friendships with faculty in English. Fran had overheard something about Roland paying a visit to Martin Glenk, at Glenk's hobby farm.

"Why would he visit Glenk?" Fitger asked. "And what the hell is a hobby farm?"

Kentrell trundled past, the front of his bathrobe open.

Fran said she didn't know, but if Fitger was restless and looking for an outing, he could give Glenk a call and visit the hobby farm himself.

During the forty-minute drive through frozen pastureland, a wrinkled map on the passenger seat by his side, Fitger wondered about the mental well-being of the sort of person who would consider farming—one of the most precarious and physically dangerous ways to make a living—a weekend hobby or source of fun. Did other citizens relax on the weekends by spending their free time working at miniature construction sites? Did they dabble in restaurant work or podiatry? What had happened to reading on the weekends, or playing cards? Turning left as Glenk had instructed at the skeleton of a VFW hall, he traversed a final stretch of veld (broken cornstalks jutting unevenly up through the snow) that led to a vinyl-sided rambler, tenuously connected, via a sort of breezeway, to a matching barn. He parked at the top of a gravel drive. The thermometer on his dashboard registered eight degrees, so he put on his hat before giving a cordial tap to the horn. On the phone, Glenk had sounded surprised that he was coming and had told him to honk when he arrived. Getting out of the car, Fitger hoped his visit might occasion something hot to drink. A coffee with whiskey would be perfect, perhaps accompanied by a leather footstool in front of a fire.

Before he could make his way to the door, he heard a shout and saw Martin Glenk, T. S. Eliot scholar, dressed in a pair of thick brown coveralls and heavy mud boots. A hunting cap with fur flaps encased his head. Like a swaggering plowboy (rather than the professor who famously required his students to spend an entire class period speaking in iambs), he jogged out of the barn.

Not knowing what else to do, they shook hands.

"So," Glenk said. "You want to take a look at the farm."

Fitger glanced longingly at the homely little rambler, the wind whistling through the cloth of his coat. "Of course. A quick look ... I suppose you grow things here in the summer?"

"No. It isn't that sort of farm." They turned and walked through the breezeway, the scent of manure thickening the air. "I have a pot of tomatoes and basil on the step but that's it. The only reason for the farm is the donkeys."

Donkeys?

"*Miniature* donkeys," Glenk said, as if the idea of a full-size animal would be absurd. He had been raising miniatures, and selling them, for a dozen years. He kept a very clean studbook. Normally the jennies would be out in the pasture but Glenk had just given them a ration of alfalfa and brought them in, because of the cold.

Glancing up at the rafters in case of a hidden camera, Fitger learned of Glenk's preference for the draft-horse body type ("the rump is wider," Glenk explained). Then, on the lookout for a chance to shift the conversation to matters of business (e.g., the Shakespeare requirement and/or Glenk's possible acquaintanceship with any Nobel-winning writers or scholars who might be interested in delivering a lecture for free), he followed his colleague into the barn. "Martin," he said, "I'm hoping you and I can—" Both his feet and his sentence came to a stop.

"They're something, aren't they?" Glenk asked, as Fitger gazed disbelievingly at the strangely mythical-looking creatures, two to three feet tall, lifting their snouts from a series of wooden troughs.

He almost expected the donkeys to speak. "How many of these things do you have?"

"Twenty-six of them," Glenk said, beaming as if he had sired the oddly foreshortened beasts himself. Some of the donkeys were enclosed in stalls, but others wandered freely through an indoor arena. One of them ambled over to Fitger, pushing a dove-colored nose into his pocket and leaving a foot-long smear of saliva behind.

Stroking their ears and their suede faces and proffering endearments, Glenk led Fitger on a tour of the barn. He discussed the problem of cow hocks and parrot mouth while Fitger fended off a trio of animals that trailed closely behind him, one of them nipping now and then at his thigh.

"You don't want to let them take advantage," Glenk chuckled, when Fitger discovered a rip in his pocket. "They'll try to get away with bad behavior. By nature, they're gentle, but given the chance to be naughty . . ."

Fitger high-stepped over a clump of turds and tried to put Glenk between himself and the donkeys. "Martin," he said, "I hope we can find some time this afternoon to discuss some issues in the department."

Glenk nodded but seemed not to have heard. They walked to the far end of the arena, where, through a cobwebbed window, Glenk pointed out the boundary of his estate: a decrepit grain silo at the edge of a field. There was still a good hour of daylight ahead, Glenk said. Would Fitger like to go for a ride?

Another nip at his thigh. "Ow! Yes." The rip in his pocket was getting bigger. He felt for the car keys in his coat, imagining a three-mile trip down a country road to a homey café.

But Glenk had entered a shed in the corner. One of the donkeys turned its head, staring at Fitger with an ex-convict's lopsided grin. "Martin, I'd be happy to drive if—" The other animals, perhaps alerted by the anxiety in his voice, had begun to approach. "Martin!"

Glenk backed awkwardly out of the shed—the tide of animals dispersing—and Fitger saw that he was pulling behind him what could only be described as a donkey buggy or mini-cabriolet.

"Astonishing, isn't it?" Glenk asked.

Fitger agreed that it was. Glenk, busying himself with halters and bridles, handed Fitger a whip, which he explained was "mostly for show." Fitger was glad to accept it, but it did occur to him that, given the nefarious gleam in some of the animals' eyes, he would have been safer with a two-by-four or a gun.

Soon both men were seated, pressed together, in the mini-carriage, with two mini-donkeys in harness and ready to pull. Glenk gestured to the whip in Fitger's hand. "Just a touch," he said. "Right there on the flank."

Fitger stroked one of the donkey's buttocks with the tip of the instrument: nothing. Glenk made a kissing sound with his mouth; ears rotating like TV antennae, the donkeys picked up their stocky, truncated legs and started to trot. They jounced in a dust-filled circle around the arena, Fitger feeling that his bones were being rattled free of their sockets. The cabriolet's seat was an icy board.

"I hear I'm not the only member of the Payne faculty who asked about visiting you this week," Fitger said.

"You're referring to Roland?" Glenk flicked the whip in the air between the two donkeys, and the carriage headed out of the arena and onto a small frozen path. "He didn't visit; we ended up talking on the phone."

A herd of animals had followed behind them and, gradually picking up speed, were on their tail. Shades of *Planet of the Apes*, Fitger thought. "What did you talk about?" he asked.

Glenk took a corner somewhat quickly, one side of the carriage almost lifting off the ground. Apparently Roland knew something about horses, and had sympathized regarding the problem of finding a farrier. "Mainly, though," Glenk said, "he wanted to talk to me about retirement."

"Why is your retirement any of Roland's business?" They took another sharp turn, and Fitger noticed that the mini-stampede of donkeys was gaining on them.

Glenk smiled. "They get excited when they see the carriage."

"Excited in what way?" Fitger was remembering the folk-tale about wolves chasing and devouring the members of a wedding party, picking off carriages one by one in the snow. Was that in *My Ántonia*?

"Apparently, Roland's committee, QUAP, has some discretion in regard to retirement incentives," Glenk said. If he agreed to retire within the next twelve months, he could end up with enough money for a heating and cooling system in the barn.

"We don't have heating and cooling in Willard," Fitger said, as they headed toward a stand of trees. "This is bribery, Martin. And you can't retire yet: we haven't gotten permission to replace the faculty who have already left."

That might be true, Glenk said, but the money would be welcome; and who would look out for Martin Glenk other than Glenk himself?

A donkey war cry arose from the trees on their left. Besides, Glenk said, he was tired of the chaos and ill will in the department, and he wasn't alone. Tyne was thinking about retirement. And Sandra Atherman had long complained about the English faculty's failure to mark important disciplinary occasions and to take an interest in one another's hobbies and areas of research.

Remembering Atherman's fondness for nineteenth-century garb, Fitger made a mental note: *Find out about the Brontës' birthdays.* A cluster of beasts was closing in on the starboard side.

Glenk cracked his whip in the air and the donkeys galloped, hell-for-leather, toward the barn.

"Martin? Should we slow down?"

No, they were fine.

Clutching the carriage with frostbitten hands, Fitger said he was glad to have had this chance to learn about Glenk's very stimulating hobby; and he hoped that Glenk wouldn't make any sudden decisions regarding retirement. Roland and QUAP weren't to be trusted. Their aim was to divide and destroy English. Look what they had done to the conference room! If the English faculty were able to unite around the SOV and—

Glenk cut him off. He preferred not to talk about work while he was relaxing down at the farm.

TWELVE

STUDENTS "SMARTING" FROM TRAUMA-
INDUCING MATERIAL IN APOCALYPSE CLASS

—by L. R. Young

The Campus Scribe (January 11, 2011): Two undergraduates enrolled in an English class taught by department chair and professor Jason T. Fitger have lodged complaints with the university's Office of Mental Health and Wellness about traumatizing material required by the syllabus.

The students, who have requested anonymity, claim that the reading list for the fall class—on the "Literature of Apocalypse"—was detrimental to their mental health and "psychologically hostile." One of the students has reportedly consulted a family lawyer.

Sophomore Yvetta Curtin, who was *not* enrolled in the class but had seen a copy of the syllabus, suggested that the selection of novels was "irresponsible" and could be dangerous for students with emotional issues or PTSD.

"This is part of the faculty's systematic disregard for

the well-being of students," Curtin said. "We shouldn't have to put up with this kind of insensitivity."

Professor Fitger, who designed and taught the controversial death-based class, was not available for comment.

At 3:26 a.m., in bed with a 40-watt bulb attached via elastic strap to his forehead, Fitger was reading this latest depiction of himself in the *Scribe.* Where had that photo—it made him look like a yeti—come from? And did the *Scribe*'s reporters (the name L. R. Young was faintly familiar) have a mandate to portray the chair of English as a hideous fool? He had a suspicion regarding the identity of the article's two anonymous plaintiffs—one of whom had failed his class by attending less than half its sessions; the other having mentioned the legal/adversarial careers of his parents at least four or five times—but who the fuck was Yvetta Curtin? Furthermore: How could a class on the subject of apocalypse be personally triggering, when none of his students had yet lived through the end of the world?

He turned slowly and gingerly onto his side, the mattress beneath him emitting a squeak. At any small sound or even a glimmer of light, Kentrell would bestir himself downstairs. Nearly three weeks after his release from the hospital, he was still living with Fitger. There had been a setback, including a twenty-four-hour rehospitalization; then, on the day when Fitger was getting ready to load his colleague's belongings into the trunk of his car, they got a call from Kentrell's neighbor: a pipe had burst, and Kentrell's bathroom and a nearby closet were flooded with ice. The neighbor asked if someone had turned off the heat. Kentrell didn't think so, but Fitger recalled an image of his own fingers, a few days after Christmas, spinning the dial.

In the *Scribe,* the article detailing Fitger's malicious treatment of freshmen was followed by a perfunctory little squib about President Hoffman's commitment to "efficient, cost-saving measures and the need to eliminate duplication across departments." This was coded language, of course, foreshadowing the day when Hoffman—prepped by Roland and QUAP, and ill-disposed toward Fitger's department— would stroll through campus, swinging a scythe to eliminate entire disciplines. Education was expensive and inefficient; teaching students to think and write clearly was the same. But Hoffman, a business school graduate with the single-cell mind of a banker, had never taught anyone anything. Her ultimate plan would be to reorganize the campus into two simple units: "Numbers" and "Words."

Fitger let the paper slide to the floor and snapped off his headlamp, staring into the dark. He wondered whether English would survive until the end of the year. Marie Eland had sent him an e-mail the previous morning, asking if he had heard about the end-of-semester event and the announcement soon to be made by his gladiatorial neighbor upstairs: a Very Large Gift to Econ from two mega-donors. She was referring, she said, to the kind of money that could alter the minds of presidents, deans, and provosts, allowing them to free themselves of all scruples.

He had thanked her for the heads-up and immediately drafted an e-mail to Janet: What could she tell him about

Roland and Econ? His fingers paused over the keyboard. He deleted the message, replying again, instead, to Marie Eland. Would she like to get together for that long-delayed drink?

Perhaps in February or March, she answered. She was preparing for a trip out of town.

Fitger refolded his pillow, which had developed a wafer-like and inelastic quality. The spring semester, now under way (he was teaching an undergraduate class on Narratives of Adventure as well as pinch-hitting a section of comp for Kentrell), promised to be no easier than the first. Tossing and sleepless, he wanted to go downstairs to retrieve his briefcase (which he believed he had left in the kitchen, near the bottle of bourbon by the sink) but Kentrell had the hearing of a hunting dog, and at the slightest hint that Fitger was awake he would emerge from the study and begin a meandering conversation.

Still, all was quiet downstairs . . . and now the concept of leaving his bed had sent an urgent body-gram to his bladder, which over the years had become a thimble-sized organ with an impetuous streak. He lay studiously inert for several moments; then, giving up, he swung his pajama-clad legs out of the covers and, without turning the light on, began to grope his way down the hall. Almost immediately he heard the parallel shuffling of Franklin Kentrell heading toward the toilet downstairs. The two bowls flushed in synchronicity.

"Jay?" Kentrell flipped the switch on the klieg lights that illuminated both the upstairs and downstairs hallways, capturing Fitger at the top of the steps. "I thought I heard something," he said. "Are you up?"

Of course he was up; why would he sleep when there were

new humiliations to be endured? Fitger shaded his eyes and descended the stairs, heading for the kitchen. Where was his briefcase? Hadn't he left it right there on the counter? He was probably losing what was left of his mind, due to Kentrell's prolonged convalescence, which was even more unpleasant now that he wasn't as sick. Still claiming he was too weak to teach, he seemed to treat his visit to Fitger's place as an in-town vacation. He watched TV or relaxed in the study; he left his toothbrush, bristles splayed, at the edge of the sink; he sampled the wares in the kitchen; and left the indentation of his oily, rectangular head on the pillows and chairs. He seemed to enjoy the status of invalid: though he walked fairly well without his walker, he occasionally unfolded it and used it, as if indulging in a sentimental mood.

Aha: there was the briefcase, half hidden beneath a dish towel on a kitchen chair. On top of it was a sticky note he had written to himself and forgotten: *Wilcox,* it said. Shit. Wilcox was Janet's development officer friend; he had meant to follow up on their earlier non-conversation, to ask if she might be harboring a rich and childless Payne alum on life support, or if she knew of any prize-winning authors who might want to help the Department of English improve its image by delivering a lecture or giving a reading for free.

Kentrell sidled into the kitchen, already yammering on about something. His conversational style was a slow-motion list of random autobiographical tidbits, his mind like a kitten with a ball of yarn. He popped the tab on a can of Ensure and put a pillowcase, some (borrowed) socks, and something that looked like a corset into the dryer. Fitger was determined not to ask questions. He was going to burn all his linens in a great flaming purge the day Kentrell got the OK on his flooded row house and finally moved home.

It was probably no use contacting Perrin Wilcox—during their only previous interaction, she had impressed him mainly because of her ability to speak in code—but he owed it to Janet to make an effort; she would surely ask him about it (she would have returned by now from her amorous respite in the Caribbean) at their annual divorce anniversary meal.

Kentrell was trimming his fingernails at the kitchen table, blue bathrobe sagging open between bony thighs. He was rambling on about a grandfather's ranch in Wyoming, where he had spent his childhood summers: *yadda yadda split rail fence yadda yadda pronghorn yadda yadda rattlesnake in a boot.*

In an effort to drown out this mini-marathon of non sequiturs, Fitger twisted the cap off the bourbon, muttering to himself. He had to stop Roland and Econ. He needed money, he needed faculty consensus, he needed President Hoffman off his back, he needed a world-renowned donor-novelist to drop out of the sky. Forget the novelist; he would even settle for a playwright or, god forbid, a poet.

Scattering fingernail shards across the table, Kentrell began to interleave his own rambling remarks into Fitger's. No, there weren't many poets of renown, at least that he knew of, in Wyoming—other than his own childhood friend, Orest Weisel. Weisel—Fitger, undoubtedly, had heard of him—had grown up only a few miles away, on a neighboring ranch.

"Weisel?" Fitger turned to face his colleague. "I don't know his work."

Kentrell sipped at his Ensure and then licked his teeth—a

jagged mountain range in shades of gray. He was surprised that Jay hadn't heard of him. Weisel was fairly well known. He was famous, really. He had won multiple prizes and had quite a following. Of course, he didn't need to make a living as a poet (Kentrell chuckled): his family had made a fortune in oil in North Dakota, so Orest could write or not, as he chose.

Fitger took a seat at the table across from Kentrell and filled a glass with two inches of bourbon. So: Orest Weisel, he said. Maybe the name did sound familiar. And his family had oil money? How many books had Weisel published?

Oh, at least eight.

Really? And were he and Franklin still in touch?

Kentrell tugged on his earlobe with his fingers. He hadn't seen Orest for a few years, but as boys they'd been close.

What kind of close?

Well, they were friends. This was Buffalo, Wyoming; there weren't hundreds of children around. Orest had moved away at fourteen, but they'd stayed in touch. Only a few years ago, it seemed, Orest had sent him a condolence card when Kentrell's uncle Wally died. Uncle Wally had taken them fly-fishing during the summers, and . . .

Fitger sluiced some bourbon into his colleague's Ensure. "I'm just thinking aloud, here," he said, "but let's say you contacted Weisel and invited him to campus."

Kentrell crossed one hairy leg over the other. "What for?"

"He could give a lecture. Or read from his work." English wouldn't be able to pay him, but since he and Franklin were friends . . . A poet of renown wouldn't want to see a literature department starve or suffer. And of course Kentrell could introduce him. Perhaps, during his visit, given his family's financial situation, Orest Weisel might make a contribution to the English fund.

Kentrell bobbed his slippered foot up and down. His mind moved slowly, like a cutworm inching through an ear of corn. He would have to think about it, he said. Did Jay have any bread? He wasn't usually hungry at this hour, but he suddenly thought he might be up for some buttered toast.

Fitger stood. He opened the bread box and found two matching heels from a loaf of dark rye. He put them both in the toaster. "Jam?" he asked.

Butter was fine. But perhaps a soft-boiled egg if there was one?

Fitger, envisioning Orest Weisel's check for $100,000 made out to English, set two eggs in a pot of water on the stove. He put a small plate and the butter and salt and pepper on the table.

"I suppose I could reach out to him," Kentrell said. He sipped at his drink while Fitger busied himself at the counter, humming softly and waiting for the *ding* of the timer that would signal that the eggs were done.

Janet's lawyer had assured her during the divorce that her soon-to-be ex-husband's stipulation of two yearly meetings—one on their wedding anniversary, August 6, and the other on the anniversary of the divorce itself, February 3—was not legally binding. But Janet had agreed to it anyway, perhaps having more respect for the dissolution of their marriage than for its vows.

She was nervous. They had toasted their other divorce anniversaries over lunch. But lunch didn't fit their schedules this year, so they had ended up—probably a mistake—with an early dinner right after work. She watched Fitger shrug himself out of his jacket and stuff his scarf (a dark blue cashmere; it looked expensive) into a sleeve. "This is a cushy little place," he said, looking around. "I haven't been here before. Is it new?"

"Somewhat." On top of his artfully folded napkin, Janet had set a copy of the most recent *Scribe,* opened to reveal letters to the editor airing complaints about English and its incompetent chair.

Fitger glanced at the letters, then tossed the paper onto a nearby table. "I didn't think to bring *you* a gift," he said. "But happy divorce anniversary."

"To you also." Janet examined a strip of sunburnt skin on her wrist. "Jay, I need to tell you something," she said.

Fitger heard the apprehension in her voice and froze. She was going to tell him that she had gotten married to that heffalump of a boyfriend; that's what the trip to the Caribbean had been for. She would soon be showing him her wedding photos: Hinckler carrying her into the ocean, Janet carving their initials (*J.M. & P.H. 4-ever*) into a coconut shell. It pained him, that she would divulge this unwelcome news on a significant date and at very close range—ostensibly out of kindness, but perhaps also in order to enjoy the sight of his dismay. Fortunately, planning ahead, he had already rehearsed several potential reactions. He could choose from among mild congratulatory interest (tepid smile, head inclined forward); doubtful concern (head tilted back, one eyebrow lifted); or rank bewilderment (both eyebrows lifted, and hands palm-up toward the ceiling—the international symbol for *what the fuck*).

In the end, needing time to strategize, he opted for delay-of-game. "Hold on," he said. "We just got here. How was your day?"

How was her day? That was a very un-Fitger-like question. It was a day like a thousand others, she said. It had begun with caffeine and ended in a desire to slam her head into the drawer of her desk.

"And how about your blood pressure?" Fitger asked. He hoped she was taking regular readings, keeping track.

A waiter arrived before she could answer. "Good evening. Have either of you dined with us before?"

"I don't see why that matters," Fitger said. "We know what a restaurant is; we know how it works."

Janet hadn't intended to order a drink—she wanted to keep her wits about her—but found herself requesting, on an immediate basis if at all possible, a large glass of red wine.

"Yes! Two of those," Fitger said.

The waiter nodded. "If you need anything," he said, "my name is Beck."

"I assume your name is Beck even if we *don't* need anything," Fitger said. He turned to Janet. "At least he didn't use that horrible phrase about taking care of us, as if he were our nurse."

Janet reached for the breadsticks and snapped one in half. Fitger jumped as if startled. "What?" she asked.

"Nothing." He had seen her left hand: *no wedding ring*. So they hadn't gotten married in the Caribbean; but of course it was still possible that the dean, inspired by sun and surf and sand (or his hatred of Fitger), had knelt down and proposed. Would Janet accept him? If Hinckler bought her a ring it would probably be large: diamonds like mushrooms erupting from a hollow log. Fitger's leg was bouncing a jig beneath the table. He watched Janet nibbling at her breadstick. She looked good. She always did; physically speaking, she inhabited a point on the spectrum midway between comely and austere. A silver rivulet of hair swept left to right above her forehead. They had both entered the cocoon of middle age, from which they would one day emerge in the form of the cobwebbed creatures they were able now to observe from a distance: the men with drooping bellies and oversized ears, the women with spun-sugar coiffures and furrowed flesh.

Why was Fitger staring at her? Janet wondered. He looked older all of a sudden. The parallel runways of baldness on his head had widened, leaving a peninsula of almost colorless hair in their wake.

Beck arrived with their wine.

Janet thanked him, then collected their menus. "I'll have the salmon, and this rude person across from me would like to order the special pasta, with a Caesar salad on the side."

"I haven't had a chance to look at the menu yet," Fitger said.

"That's because you were late. Don't worry; I got you something soft, for your teeth."

Beck walked away, and Fitger probed a molar with his tongue. This was the amiably banal sort of dialogue, he thought, in which he and Janet would have indulged if they had stayed married. Over dinner, they would have discussed hemorrhoids and cataracts and the replacing of knees. "Just tell me they didn't put quotation marks around 'special' pasta," he said. "You know I can't eat things that are badly punctuated or misspelled."

Having finished her breadstick, Janet seemed to be preparing herself for conversation again. Fitger quickly forestalled her. "How are things at the office?" he asked. "How does Angela like her internship?"

Janet planted her elbows on the tablecloth and massaged her temples.

"Headache?" he asked.

"No. Angela's in your class again this semester, isn't she?"

"Yes." Fitger agreed that she was.

"Have you noticed anything different about her?"

"Different?"

"About her appearance," Janet said.

Fitger sipped at his wine. *Did Angela Vackrey look different?* Undergraduates were always adorning themselves and revising their self-conceptions, adding tattoos or piercings or arriving in class wearing combat gear or a shirt made of rubber bands and string. But for obvious reasons, he had always been careful to cultivate an impassive demeanor in regard to students' bodies and clothing (which was sometimes a challenge: he had once sat for thirty minutes across from a senior who was wearing a T-shirt that said, I DON'T GIVE A FUCK ABOUT YOUR IDEAS). He strived never to glance at any student below the neck, and couldn't imagine Angela taking drastic measures with her appearance. Shy, of course, and lacking in sartorial skills, she nevertheless exuded a clarity and a consistency . . . He smiled. It still happened sometimes: he found a student who surprised him, and whom he admired. "You like her too," he said. "Don't you?"

Yes, Janet said. It was almost impossible not to like Angela. Her face was an ingenuous canvas; she was bright but naive; her fingernails had been nibbled down to their blood-flecked moons. On her first day in the office, Janet reviewed with her the information she gave all the interns—but in Angela's case, she'd had to make an effort to refrain from additional counsel: *Don't get married in your twenties; don't take a job at a university; use the word "underwear" and not "panties"; learn to speak in statements rather than questions; don't waste your time being impressed by people (usually men) who are already adequately impressed by themselves.*

Fitger had begun talking about an essay Angela had written for his apocalypse class. She hadn't turned anything in yet for his Narratives of Adventure (which began with Jules Verne and ended—in case Janet was curious—with Ursula Le Guin), but based on her—

Janet interrupted. "Jay, for god's sake, she's pregnant."

"What?" Fitger put down his wineglass. "Really? Angela? She told you?"

"I *asked* her. You just have to look at her. She's four months along."

"Four months." Already too late for a reversal of fortune, Fitger thought, if she'd hoped to have one. He counted backward: October. In class, they'd been struggling through *Riddley Walker* in October. He wasn't sure why that mattered, but he felt that it did.

"She hasn't told anyone," Janet said. "She said she stopped by your office last week but lost her nerve."

"She was going to tell *me*?" he asked. "Why?"

Janet had asked Angela the very same question and had concluded, after hearing the girl's whispered, convoluted answer, that, having misunderstood the role of the academic adviser, she hadn't been able to think of anyone else.

"Well," Fitger said. "You ended up talking to her. What will she do?"

Coworkers in Janet's office occasionally suggested that someone else—other than Janet—should take on the burden of supervising the interns; but Janet liked working with students. She liked interacting with people who were at an earlier stage of their lives, and in a more malleable condition. And (Fitger had been right) she found Angela particularly appealing. Coming upon her one day in the copy room, and noticing the pill-covered sweater over the girl's shoulders, one sock slipping down the shapeless plank of her leg, it had occurred to her that the new intern was precisely the age that a child conceived by herself and Jay would have been. They had never intended to have children, but occasionally they had been less than assiduous in their efforts to avoid them; and during one single long weekend Janet had kept to herself the tantalizing suspicion that she might be pregnant—a possibility that, several days later, had proved not to be. It was during that moment in the copy room that she knew, without being told (why had her eyes overflowed at the thought?), that Angela was pregnant herself.

"I'll tell you what she's going to do," Janet said. First, she was going to make an appointment at the clinic and ask for a referral to an obstetrician. Second, she was going to find herself a campus therapist. Third, she was going to buy some maternity clothes and figure out what to say to her parents, whoever they were. And fourth, she was going to check in on a regular basis with someone she trusted. This person, oddly enough, appeared to be Fitger, whose new job it would be to listen carefully and empathetically, making sure that Angela found the courage to do all the previously mentioned things that she needed to do.

Beck brought their food. He set Janet's plate gracefully in front of her; then, from a height of several inches, he dropped Fitger's—a Caesar salad and a carpet of cheese covering some sort of pasta—onto the tablecloth with a thump. Fitger stared disconsolately at the salad, which Janet had apparently forgotten was not his favorite. Caesar, he thought, often smelled of seaweed left in the sun.

"Is there a boyfriend involved?" he asked. "That is, for Angela?"

Janet was carving up a forest of broccoli. "I'm not sure I'd give him that title, but it was consensual, she says. She met him at a Bible study group. She says they had sex only once; I don't think she's seen him much since then."

"Once?" Fitger found that he disliked the idea of Angela having sex; she seemed too young even to know what it was. Without having given the matter much thought, he realized that he envisioned for her a bibliophilic future, as either a celibate librarian or (was she Catholic?) perhaps a scholarly nun.

"So. You'll talk to her?" Janet asked.

"About what?"

"Whatever she wants to discuss."

Fitger sighed and, reluctantly, agreed—but he wouldn't

talk about pregnancy unless Angela raised the subject. Discussing intimate personal or sexual issues with a student was an absolute minefield; one misstep and his name would be listed at the head of a column of erotopaths in the *Campus Scribe*.

They had reached a lull in the conversation. "I didn't ask you how your break was," Janet said.

Fitger put down his fork. He didn't want to compare his holiday, playing nursemaid to a feculent colleague, with Janet's halcyon vacation: seven days on a beach, in front of her a turquoise body of water and behind her a well-used set of sheets and a satisfied dean.

Beck reappeared beside their table. "Is everything delicious so far?" Janet had eaten two bites of her salmon, and Fitger's plate was a rubbery island of cheese.

"Unparalleled," Fitger said.

Beck walked away.

Feeling morose, Fitger dissected his salad, pushing the croutons aside. He always looked forward to their divorce anniversary (even though the first of these had ended with Janet dumping a bowl of minestrone soup in his lap), and now their hour together—much of it spent talking about a student—was almost done. If Janet had news related to her Kama Sutra–inspired vacation, she was probably saving it for the end of the meal, he thought, planning to drop it and leave, as she had with the soup. He chewed a few bitter leaves of lettuce. Time to get it over with. "How's Phil?"

"Why are you asking?" Janet stiffened.

"Should I not ask? I'm curious. You're going out with him; he's the dean."

"So you're asking because he's the dean, or because I'm going out with him?"

She was angry; that was interesting. Where was their conversation headed? Fitger had lost track.

"What about you?" Janet asked. "How's your French friend?"

"My . . . what? No, she and I aren't—"

"Never mind. It's none of my business," Janet said. "I don't want to know." She went off to the restroom, asking Beck for the tab on her way.

Fitger ate one more lethargic bite of his salad. He had pissed Janet off—easy enough to do, of course, but his tone, when he asked about Phil, was probably aggressive. He put down his fork. How, after all these years, had Janet forgotten about his disinclination for Caesar?

When she returned to the table, they split the check. "FYI, for whenever you talk to Angela," Janet said. "She and this boy are thinking about getting married."

"Married? Legally?" Fitger was adding up a (small) tip.

"I guess he's religious," Janet said. "You and I were in our twenties when we got married, and even that was too young."

But we wouldn't have married if we were older and wiser, Fitger thought; and he was glad to have made that mistake when he had the chance.

Outside, new snow had fallen across the sidewalk. Janet touched the fringe on Fitger's scarf. "I remember this. Did I give it to you?"

"Probably. It's definitely nicer than anything I would have bought for myself."

She rubbed the dark fabric between her fingers, and he

stood still and hoped to remain in the doorway for a very long time.

"Happy divorce anniversary," she said. They engaged in a postmarital embrace, a thick buffer of winter clothes between them.

"Janet, I wish I had—"

"I'm glad you liked the food," she said.

This was an unusual remark, as they had both left at least a third of their dinners on their plates and refused the offer of a doggie bag. Fitger turned toward the restaurant's window, where the menu was posted. There were the misbegotten quotation marks on *"special" pasta;* worse, under *Soups and Salads* his vision was arrested by the word *Ceasar,* grossly misspelled.

Janet was walking through the snow toward her car.

"You did that on purpose!" He took off his scarf and waved it at her. Hope had lit a tentative candle within him. Janet remembered that he didn't like Caesar salad. She knew him and knew how to torment him—and wasn't such specific, intimate knowledge a form of love?

THIRTEEN

Fran enjoyed the average wedding about as much as a migraine, and the thought of Angela getting married left her depressed. In the English office, she and Fitger and Ashkir had all received invitations, Angela coming into the office to hand-deliver them, her stomach like half a basketball under her shirt.

PLEASE COME TO WITNESS THE MARRIAGE OF ANGELA
BERNICE VACKREY
TO TREVOR LOUIS THURLEY
Payne's Campus Chapel
Wednesday, March 30
3:00 p.m.
Thank you.

The "thank you," Fran thought, was a clear indication that Angela was handling the wedding details herself. Fran had looked Trevor Thurley up on P-Cal. Uh-huh: a skinny young fuck with an Adam's apple like a burl in his throat.

Ashkir, pausing in the doorway of her office, saw her

rereading the invitation. Would she be going to the ceremony? he asked.

Fran nodded. She had thought about trying to talk Angela
out of the wedding but decided against it. Marriages weren't
forever these days; and maybe it was preferable, legally or
for insurance reasons, for Thurley to own up to what he had
done. Like everyone else in the world, Angela would learn,
even if painfully, from her mistakes. Still: a wrong turn like
that at such an early age and a person could end up on a
decades-long detour, the map of life with its helpfully high-
lighted routes sliding straight to the ground. "I told her I
would visit her this summer," she said, "after the baby shows
up. Maybe in August."

She put the invitation back in her in-box and stretched,
careful not to disturb Rogaine, who spent most of the day
beneath her desk, at her feet. The university's rules about
dogs on campus being needlessly strict, she'd been forced
to be furtive about bringing him with her to work. Rogaine
was too big to be hidden or carried in a tote, so she made
him a vest with a logo (she created the vest from an old Girl
Scout sash and a collection of badges, including NEEDLE-
CRAFT, HOSPITALITY, and VISUAL ARTS) so that he could
pass for what in some sense he was (everyone knew that animals were very soothing)—a therapy dog. A side benefit of
the vest: Fran had sewn a Velcro loop on each side so that
Rogaine could carry her travel mug of coffee and sometimes
her purse. He was learning to behave himself around human
beings, at least most of the time.

Fran's ultimate object, of course, was to ready the dog for
adoption. Because of his biting history, Rogaine was consid-

ered "hard to place"; he hadn't bitten anyone in the office, though he'd snapped at Fitger once or twice—but only because Fitger had pushed him away from his office window, which was the dog's favorite vantage point from which to observe the comings and goings of campus squirrels.

But she couldn't think about adoption at the moment, because they had a boatload of things to take care of: graduation bureaucracy and next year's teaching schedule and various undergraduate complaints/possible lawsuits—and another installment of mousetraps for Professor Hesseldine's office. They were also required to follow additional security measures in the building because of Cassovan's "break-in" (which Fran suspected was not the work of a mischief-maker or thief, but evidence of the custodian's attempt, by standing on the flat of Cassovan's desk, to repair a broken ceiling tile or replace a dead bulb). The end of spring semester was (thank god) now only seven weeks away.

The newest task on the English to-do list (unbelievable, Fran thought, that Fitger might pull it off) was a speaker's visit, which Fitger had dropped onto her desk like a penny into a beggar's cup the week before.

"This is a lecturer who will come to campus?" Ashkir asked.

"I'm not sure I would call him a lecturer," Fran said.

"A writer, then."

"Sort of."

Ashkir stood ready with a pen and paper. "When will he visit?"

"We don't have a firm date yet because the . . . visitor has to check his schedule. But we're looking at the second week in April."

"Ah. And the visitor's name?"

Rogaine stirred, and Fran scratched his flank where the fur was beginning at last to come in. She took a deep breath. "Orest Weisel."

Ashkir frowned. She wasn't referring to the Orest Weisel who—

"Yes," said Fran.

Not Orest Weisel, whose poetry was—

Yes.

"But—"

Fran poured some kibble into Rogaine's collapsible bowl and explained that Orest Weisel was a friend of Professor Kentrell's, and that Professor Fitger had green-lighted his visit without bothering to find out that his poems were directed at the K–5 crowd, or that his most recent collection (Weisel was regularly lampooned on late-night TV for his bouncy educational jingles about everything from the rings of Saturn to Sojourner Truth) was entitled *Blue-Bellied Baboon*. "He's been invited, and he accepted. We can't uninvite him." (A few hours earlier, Fran had found Fitger in his office, studying Weisel's oeuvre, which included a waterproof book about the ocean that could be read in the tub. She often wondered if he would make it to the end of the year.)

With Ashkir looking on over her shoulder, she clicked her way to Orest Weisel's website. On his homepage the poet, holding an oversized umbrella, was dressed as a cloud. "I just work here," she said. "I don't make the decisions. We'll need to get the word out to the local elementary schools."

Ashkir picked up his pen and his pad of paper again.

What sort of help did Fran need, he asked, with the upcoming event?

What did she need? Well, all campus events were a pain in the tail, requiring arrangements for venue, travel, hotel, per diem, microphone, bottled water, allergen checklist, advertising and media coverage, and notification of the campus police; and typically, they were planned at least six months ahead. Though Weisel was forgoing an honorarium (Fran was relieved to know that she would not be required to cut a bad check), there was almost no time to iron out all these details. She thought about the professionally designed posters all over campus, promoting the end-of-year announcement to be made by Econ, with Roland Gladwell's pompous likeness on every one.

"The first problem," she said, "is that we don't have a venue. And Weisel has an enthusiastic kindergarten fan base, so we need something big—ideally the auditorium, but we don't have the money to reserve it."

"And you don't have an exact date yet?" Ashkir asked.

Rogaine finished his kibble and crawled under the desk.

"No. Weisel is rearranging his schedule, and he asked us to keep the second week of April open. To be safe, we should reserve the auditorium every night for five days. We might as well book the Taj Mahal."

Ashkir tented his fingers. Student activity groups were able—without cost—to reserve campus venues, he said. Each group was allotted one reservation per year.

"But the auditorium?" Fran asked.

Ashkir said he would look into it; he was an entrepreneurial studies major, after all.

As required by university policy, Dennis Cassovan had filed a report about his office break-in, which he assumed was related to the vandalism of his poster, despite Fran's belief that the rearrangement of the objects on his desk had resulted from the campus custodian's attempt to replace a faulty overhead bulb. This was possible, of course, but the bulb still didn't work—it flickered—and in any case, Cassovan preferred his green-shaded banker's lamp to the fluorescent glare from above. Furthermore, why would the custodian have positioned Cassovan's letter opener blade up and protruding from the center drawer? Curricular issues aside, Cassovan doubted that anyone cared enough about him to harm him; still, twice during the past few weeks, he had suffered the impression that someone was following behind him. Once, walking alone after dark from the library to his office, he had headed, chagrined at the direction in which his feet were carrying him, toward the blue security beacon behind Willard Hall and rested his trembling hand on the button. Feeling like a child playing olly-olly-in-come-free, he had stood quietly, catching his breath. *The fit is momentary, upon a thought he will again be well.*

Perhaps he *was* unwell; he continued to have trouble sleeping. For years he had risen every day at 5:15 a.m., worked for two hours before breakfast, and arrived on campus to meet with students or deliver a lecture by 9:00. Now, even though he still got out of bed, from force of habit, at 5:15, it seemed to take him hours to get dressed and read the paper, and when the draft of his book was in front of him, he gazed at the pages without getting much done.

His conversation with Roland Gladwell (who had followed up with multiple e-mails) pricked and disquieted him. A required Shakespeare class divorced from English? It was a peculiar, incongruous thought. On the one hand, the idea of every undergraduate student at Payne taking a course on Shakespeare was extraordinary, almost enthralling; on the other hand, a universally enforced class might soon be considered, by the students, to be punitive and dull. Morever, who—other than Cassovan—would teach it? He had always enjoyed both the dedicated literature students as well as the skeptics who needed to be coaxed; but to teach several hundred students every semester . . . He would need teaching assistants for crowd control and for grading. It would be exhausting. He thought about Lincoln Young and about his students and their SOS buttons, and he felt very old.

He had been trying to reach Lincoln Young for the past few days in order to talk about the upcoming conference, but his RA, who was usually eager to fill up a time card, was uncharacteristically elusive. Discovering a flyer taped to his door that announced an SOS meeting in the student center with "Professor Young," Cassovan decided to attend, to seek Lincoln out.

The meeting was in process when he arrived, so he took a seat on a bench in the hall. Though the door nearby was open, he could hear only part of what was said. The discussion seemed to have nothing to do with Shakespeare, the students (with Lincoln Young interceding now and then, and emceeing) expressing frustration not with literary or curricular issues but with injustices, global and local, of all different stripes.

Meeting concluded, Cassovan waited for the group to disperse; then he flagged Lincoln down.

The younger man seemed surprised to see him. He had been busy. Professor Cassovan had sent him an e-mail? Yes, of course; he would respond tomorrow. He would have invited the professor to the meeting but he assumed . . . Had Professor Cassovan noticed how many of the students were wearing SOS buttons?

"Yes, the buttons," Cassovan said. It was impossible not to notice them; one saw them everywhere now, around campus. He had discovered a button half-crushed in a parking lot only that morning, and had picked it up to find an image of Shakespeare snarling and lifting his middle finger. Other buttons, festooning the students' outerwear and backpacks, made obscure references (one depicted President Hoffman astride an oversized feather pen) that Cassovan found unsavory as well as absurd. The buttons had begun—didn't Lincoln agree?—to betray an indeterminacy of purpose.

No, not at all, Lincoln said; that was just the undergrads' natural high spirits. The students were all about supporting Shakespeare. Had Professor Cassovan seen them taking photos of themselves in front of his office?

Yes, it was hard not to see them. This was one of the reasons he couldn't work in his office anymore, and why he was falling further behind. Personally, he failed to see how posing for photographs in front of a blemished poster—

"Let me show you." Lincoln pulled out a phone and diddled with its screen, then held the device in front of Cassovan, who beheld a video of a student pulling up his shirt to reveal an undecipherable slogan lipsticked in red on the plank of his chest.

Here was the future, Cassovan thought. Out with considered argument and nuance; in with publicity stunts, competitive righteousness, and the thrill of rage. He stood up and tested the grips on his shoes, which could sometimes be slippery indoors. "I've had a change of heart about our conference submission," he said.

Lincoln tucked his phone into his pocket. He was standing in front of a bulletin board covered with thousands of multicolored slips of paper that advertised clothing swaps, rideshares, essays-for-hire, recovery groups, athletic clubs, tutoring services, cultural awakenings, bike sales, nature walks, political forums, drum circles, religious and pagan ceremonies, and prevention programs for venereal disease. How did students find time for academic work, Cassovan wondered, while they were at college?

A change? That was okay, Lincoln said. He had a few last-minute thoughts of his own. He was considering, for example, the idea that he should rewrite his bio. Had Professor Cassovan read the one he had written? Was it too long? And what about the edits Lincoln had suggested to the final section of their paper? He had meant to send the clarifications Professor Cassovan had requested; but, in the meantime, what did he think?

They had walked down the hall to the exit. Hand on the handrail, Cassovan summoned the conference paper—"The Problem of Augury in *Titus Andronicus*"—into his mind. Lincoln's edits, belatedly submitted, were either negligible or fallacious, and Cassovan had lacked the time to set them to rights. It was his book, *Anamnesis in Three Roman Plays,* and not the conference paper that mattered. The paper was irrelevant, or at least incidental. The book—he could envision the first chapter now (only when he was away from it did it assume a cogent shape in his imagination)—had to be the object of his remaining energies. He might never see it in print (even as a much younger scholar, he had been afraid that he would die before seeing his book through to publication), but he knew that almost everything else in his life had become a distraction he could no longer afford.

"I'm withdrawing the paper," he said. "I thought I should tell you in person."

Lincoln had just swigged the last of a cup of coffee and tossed the empty container—wasn't Styrofoam banned on campus?—into the trash. "The paper?" He stopped abruptly in the doorway. "But it's already submitted. Our names are both on the program."

"It's better not to submit than to have your name on something subpar," Cassovan said. "It's not good enough."

"But I can work on it over the weekend," Lincoln said. "We still have almost three weeks. We can—"

"No," Cassovan said. The first chapter of *Anamnesis in Three Roman Plays* flared to life like a phantom at the back of his brain. Perhaps if he moved those troublesome paragraphs from what had once been the middle section to the preface . . . "You're still free to attend the conference," he said. "I'll cover your registration fee. But I'm going to cancel my flight and hotel. Perhaps we can try again another year."

Lincoln Young was dumbfounded. He understood that Professor Cassovan had reservations; but wasn't that what a conference was for? To ask for feedback from other scholars? Besides, it wasn't just about the paper anymore. Didn't the professor want to find out about curricular battles being fought at other universities? To learn whether other schools were doing away with their Shakespeare requirements, or considering the idea of teaching Shakespeare in departments other than English?

"Who spoke to you about Shakespeare being taught outside English?" Cassovan asked.

Lincoln lifted his lip in a half snarl. "No one," he said. Given budget cuts, it was just an idea that he assumed scholars were batting around.

Outside, the wind was gusting between buildings (*The air bites shrewdly,* Cassovan thought), bringing a sparkling new veil of snow. After watching Lincoln Young thrash his way across the quad in the direction of the facilities plant—one of the few areas where smoking was allowed on campus, and where a cluster of nicotine users could often be found huddled, like lepers, beneath a shelter—Cassovan walked alone in the other direction, testing the path ahead of him with a walking stick he had been assured by the woman who'd sold it to him was not a cane. He was eager to get home so that he could think more clearly about his book. Its discussion of memory and commemoration, he thought, was insufficient. Perhaps he could spend a few hours before going to bed— But of course the briefcase in his hand held fifty-five freshman and sophomore papers. Much of Cassovan's life had been spent grading papers, his career a never-ending attempt to inspire in undergraduates the idea that logically developing and clearly explaining an original argument—supported via relevant detail—was a desirable and significant skill.

He shuddered against the cold; it was early evening, but darkness had already thrown a cloak over the campus. He walked past the statue of Cyril Payne (attired in cowboy chaps and pleather vest) and ended up on the narrow sidewalk, flanked by lopsided pines, behind Willard Hall.

And here it was again: the sound, or strong impression, behind him, of footsteps. Cassovan knew that, in general, the campus was safe and, at his age, he was more vulnerable to a stroke or a fall in the tub than to the plot of an anti-Shakespearean. But the sense of a presence or a person following—*a dagger of the mind, a false creation?*—was vividly real.

The path narrowed ahead before opening into a tiny clearing that housed the blue emergency beacon. How often, Cassovan wondered, had some troubled student pressed the knob, fearful, asking for help? It was the unknown that most often frightened. Looking backward was sometimes painful; but only looking forward did one experience the dread and apprehension of the empty page. A flashlight's beam swept the path behind him and was quickly extinguished. Did he hear someone approaching? Or was that the hammering of blood in his veins? He slipped on a nugget of ice, then regained his footing and continued up the slope toward the beacon, a lovely blue lighthouse surrounded by snow.

Patience was not one of Roland Gladwell's primary virtues, so he had periodically to remind himself that Rome was not built in a day, and that even among economists, no undertaking could be perfect, glitches attaching themselves to the most well-considered plans. He had hoped to have Fitger and his department out of Willard (or at least shunted into the basement) by the end of the year, but delays dogged his efforts: the provost, according to Wu, his assistant, was still "considering" QUAP's recommendations, and President Hoffman was stagnation in human form. Dennis Cassovan was an additional source of annoyance: despite the carrots dangled in front of him and the sticks applied smartingly from behind, he had not yet agreed to Roland's plan.

But Roland had an ace in his pocket and therefore a reason to be optimistic. Following a grueling, yearlong series of meetings, which culminated in a visit to Manuela Pratt's oceanfront estate in West Palm Beach, he had secured a very sizeable gift—in fact, one of the largest in Payne's history—to be bestowed upon the Department of Economics at the end of the year. The combined largesse of Manuela Pratt and William Fixx (one widowed, the other divorced, they had met at an "Alumni of Distinction" gathering several years before) would be revealed to the campus and the public via a celebratory announcement early in May. The funds would secure the approbation of the president and the provost and would elevate Roland's department above all others, enabling the removal of the word ENGLISH from the facade of Willard Hall.

Roland strolled out of his office and into the reception area for a little chat about the Pratt-Fixx event with Marilyn

Hoopes. The posters had gone up and the media had been notified, well in advance. Had she checked the VIP list? Provost Rutledge (provided he could be located) and President Hoffman would be seated, of course, with the families of the donors. Catering should be lavish—but without alcohol because of the students. And he would need an extra pair of eyes to proofread his speech, though he wasn't yet certain that—

Marilyn Hoopes interrupted. "There's a problem with the event," she said.

"What kind of problem?"

She coughed politely, twice—a signal—and waited until the other women in the office stopped what they were doing and walked out the door. Manuela Pratt had called an hour ago, she said. She had offered apologies but said that she needed to change the date of the announcement: she had a grandchild who was competing in a water polo tournament, and she had promised him she would attend.

"Water polo?" Roland asked.

Yes. And Manuela had already compared her availability with that of Big Bill Fixx, and there was only one week when they would both be in town.

"We agreed on this date in September," Roland said.

Yes, Marilyn Hoopes was aware. But apparently the grandchild had gotten confused about his schedule, and Manuela had promised to fly to California to see him compete.

The announcement of a multimillion-dollar endowment displaced by a seventeen-year-old who didn't know how to read a fucking calendar: Roland waited for his indignation to subside. "All right," he said. "During which week does her grandson's schedule allow her to be here?"

"The second week of April." All the arrangements and the invitations would have to be changed. Even more important, Marilyn Hoopes pointed out, the paperwork associated with the gift wouldn't yet be complete.

"We'll put a rush on it," Roland said. "We don't have a choice." It would be ridiculously inconvenient, but they would change the date; they would find a way to make it work.

"I've been trying to make it work," said Marilyn Hoopes. She scrolled through a document on her computer. "I can't get a venue. The auditorium is booked."

Roland loomed like a thunderhead over her shoulder. "It's booked every day?"

"Every afternoon and evening that week. The only venue I can get is the gym."

He took the mouse from her hand and scrolled through the website. "Who reserved the auditorium? Who are these people? Are they student groups?"

It appeared that they were. The groups were Payne's Somali-American Cultural Society, the Future Millionaires' Forum, the Organization for Pregnant and Parenting Students, Banjos and Zithers Anonymous, and the university's chapter of Zombies vs. Radioactive Squid.

"These people don't need an auditorium," Roland said. "All they need is half a classroom. And they can meet any week of the year. Can't we shift them around?"

Marilyn Hoopes said she'd been trying to do so, but it was difficult to track down the members of the groups who had actually made the reservations. It was interesting, though: the groups had all handled their bookings within a few hours, on the very same day.

"What the hell does that mean?" Roland asked.

Marilyn Hoopes didn't know; but she was going to find out.

Fitger gave the Caesar salad episode several weeks' worth of an insomniac's careful attention. Janet had chosen the restaurant and made the reservation. And she had asked, again, about Marie Eland. Perhaps she wasn't planning to marry the bloviator, Hinckler. Was it possible, or faintly conceivable, that he and Janet . . . Should he call her? Invent a reason to swing by her office? At some time in the fall, she had called him *charming*. He sent her an e-mail. Neither of them had ordered dessert after their anniversary dinner, he wrote: Could he treat her to a *crème brulay or choclate tart*?

Several days went by before she answered. Was she ignoring him, or pondering? At work, trying not to think about the fact that he had invited a children's entertainer to campus, Fitger paced back and forth and checked his e-mail every ten minutes. Finally the response came: *I don't mind eating things that are mispelled.* Marvelous woman: she deliberately omitted the second *"s."*

He quickly replied: *Later this week? I'm free tomorrow.*

Again the delay before she answered. *No. Thanks.*

He subjected the "thanks" to a few days of scrutiny—the tone was encouraging—before trying again. It was important that he not sound overeager, that he strike a note somewhere between jocular and sincere. *I appreciated the heads-up about Angela,* he wrote. *I know you're busy at this time of year, but we could do dessert for lunch someday instead of saving it for after dinner. Apple Brown Betty? Funnel cake? What are you doing this weekend?*

My father's coming to town for a visit.

Fitger's relationship with his former father-in-law, "Bulldog" Matthias, had consisted mainly of a concerted effort to stay out of his way. So the weekend was probably out, but Janet hadn't given him a categorical refusal. Before he could formulate a reply, she e-mailed again. *Have you talked to Angela?*

Fitger slumped in front of the keyboard. It was baffling, he thought, that anyone would consider him to be the appropriate person to sit down with a pregnant eighteen-year-old and debate the idea of giving a baby up for adoption versus bringing it with her to school. But because Janet had charged him with this task, he had in fact made an effort, speaking to Angela twice, in his office. During their first conversation, he had spoken about the trajectory of her life in the context of the course syllabus: it was a narrative and, though not entirely in charge, she was its author. Even this indirect approach made the poor girl blush. During the second, they had ended up talking mainly about *Treasure Island,* a novel that thoroughly flummoxed most of his students despite the fact that it had been enjoyed, a century or so earlier, by ten-year-old boys.

I've tried, he wrote. *She *is* getting married.*

I know. I've got the date on my calendar.

Fitger glanced at the copy of Orest Weisel's *Blue-Bellied Baboon*—available in board book format as well as

257

hardcover—that Fran had left on his desk. In preparation for his childhood friend's visit, Kentrell had taken to stopping by on a near-daily basis to confer about the event's many details: Weisel always flew first-class, he said, and the hotel on University Avenue was preferable; they served tea and muffins in the lobby every afternoon.

Fitger obscured the book under a stack of files and reread, again, his e-mail correspondence with Janet. *Let me know if you need an escape hatch or a distraction while your father's in town,* he wrote. *I can be that needy, annoying friend you have to meet for a drink.*

No response. But two days later he got an e-mail the subject line of which read, *Drink Saturday night?*

Definitely, he answered. *How is your father?*

Dead.

What? He looked more carefully at the e-mail. It was from Marie Eland.

8:00 at your house, she wrote. *I will see you then.*

For reasons that, in Fitger's mind, remained somewhat obscure, Fran had impressed upon him the need for him to take care of Rogaine over the weekend. First she had mentioned something about a friend from out of town who didn't like dogs; then the story had shifted, involving a handyman repairing her kitchen floor.

Were there no kennels available? Fitger had asked.

A kennel was completely out of the question, Fran said. The dog needed to learn trust, and he was familiar with Fitger; sending him to a kennel would set him back weeks in his rehabilitation.

"You'd better behave yourself, you rock-headed varmint," Fitger said to the dog, when Marie Eland rang the doorbell on Saturday night. Rogaine had spent the afternoon deconstructing a new pair of shoes.

Marie Eland kissed Fitger on one cheek and then the other. "So you have a bodyguard," she said, looking at Rogaine and handing over a bottle of expensive-looking wine. "Things are so dangerous now in your department."

"Yes," Fitger said. "Anyone who comes within ten feet of me is in danger of mange."

They went into the kitchen, leaving the dog to grind its butt across the rug, presumably releasing some sort of larvae onto the floor.

While Marie Eland opened the wine and lit a cigarette simultaneously, Fitger offered condolences (a decade late, it turned out) on her father's demise. He wasn't sure what they should discuss, so they talked about death for a little while. Fitger's father had died fairly young, and his mother's (unfulfilled) last wish had been that she be embalmed and displayed in the window of Nordstrom, her favorite store.

Marie Eland clinked her glass against his. They sat down on the couch. "It's very clever—and brave, also—what you are doing." She tapped the ash from her cigarette into a potted plant. "A campus visitor, and a public event in the auditorium."

Fitger murmured something about the English Department's commitment to the non-university community and to K–12 education. "I don't know about 'brave,'" he said. "Orest Weisel is . . ." He wasn't able to finish his sentence.

"It is definitely brave." Marie Eland sipped her wine and considered him. "Brave but foolish. You are thinking, *My department is strong. I can play this dangerous game by myself.* But you are mistaken. You will need allies."

"Allies," Fitger said.

"Yes." She drew her bare feet up onto the couch. "You have locked your friend the gladiator from the auditorium. He is so angry."

"Roland is locked out of the auditorium?"

The couch was old and soft; its cushions caused her to migrate gradually toward him. One of her breasts grazed the back of his hand. "Consolidated Languages would like to partner with you," she said.

"Partner?" he asked. "I'm not sure that—"

She tilted her head at a skeptical angle, backing away. "There is something wrong with your animal," she said.

Rogaine was pacing back and forth across the rug in a semi-crouch. This was a telltale signal: Fitger could either take him outside or he would shit on the floor. "Do you mind going out for a quick walk?"

Marie Eland tossed her cigarette into the sink, refilled her wineglass to bring it with her, and they put on their coats.

Outdoors, Rogaine pulled at the leash, dropping into a squat every few yards but apparently not finding the ideal location to make a deposit. They walked through a playground.

"If you are going to fuck with Roland and QUAP," Marie

Eland said, "let us do it together. It will be best to share information, to tell what we know."

"I'm not sure I know anything," Fitger said.

"I am sure you hear things. You have conversations."

Rogaine selected a patch of ground and then locked eyes with Fitger while he did his business. Fitger scooped up the steaming burden with a plastic bag.

"I will give you an example." Marie Eland gestured with her wineglass. "Here is a piece of information I have recently learned: the dean is not going to be dean anymore. He will return to his beloved Department of Music—which will *not* be subject to a QUAP review."

"I thought every department was subject to review."

"No. Some receive—what do you call it?—immunity, because of favors traded back and forth. The dean has given something to Roland."

Rogaine led them to a malodorous area at the edge of the park, near a set of trash cans. Fitger tossed the bag of dog shit into one of the cans. *Given something to Roland?*

"So you see why we need to work together." Marie Eland took his arm as they stepped off a curb. "Anything you can learn, I promise to share only with Gusev and one or two others. You have such a source . . ."

"A source," Fitger repeated. He was conscious of a smear of shit on his sleeve. Was she referring to Janet? Because he couldn't . . . Or, rather, he had already tried to wrest information from her but could no longer put their ex-marital relationship to that kind of use. Where Janet was concerned, he wanted to have a clean conscience. He knew she was in intimate, daily contact with the dean—not that he understood what she could possibly see in Phil Hinckler—but the truth was, his feelings for his ex-wife were complex. In fact, he sometimes—

"No." Marie Eland tugged at his arm. They had left the park and the playground behind and begun to cross the street at a four-way stop. "There is the beauty. They are not together anymore. You didn't know? She has broken off their relations."

Fitger took the wineglass from her hand and drained it. "Janet broke up with him? With the dean?"

"Several weeks ago," Marie Eland said. "Watch: be careful."

A car pulled up at the four-way stop, and a familiar face turned aggressively toward them. It took Fitger a moment to recognize his former father-in-law, "Bulldog" Matthias, who formed a gun with his thumb and fingers and pointed it at Fitger, through the window. He was riding shotgun, with his daughter, Janet, who was looking at Fitger also, at the wheel.

FOURTEEN

The wedding wasn't going to be the kind with the white dress and the veil and the row of bridesmaids and grooms-men arranged by height in pastel colors. It wouldn't include matching nosegays or music from the pipes of an organ, or champagne served in skinny glasses, with people making toasts and tossing rice. But that was fine: Angela knew it wasn't the trimmings that mattered; it was the seriousness, the promises made in front of witnesses, the troth. Was that actually a word? "Troth"? Wiping her face on a clump of toi-let paper, Angela thought it probably *was* a word, but she would have to remember to look it up later. That was some-thing her mother had taught her from an early age: *Need to learn it? Look it up!*

But she couldn't think about her mother, not with the ceremony only fifteen minutes away; it would make her cry, and she had already spent most of the morning in tears. Her mother had prayed hard about her decision and finally told Angela that she wouldn't come to the wedding. Of course she loved Angela and always would. But there were moments when a parent had to stand up for and demon-strate her principles; and it was too painful, she said (at this point both Angela and her mother were crying), to see the values she had tried to instill in her daughter—as well as the dreams she'd had on Angela's behalf—cast so quickly and so carelessly aside. She had thought she knew Angela. She'd thought she could trust her. The fact that Angela had lied to her, all through the fall and especially at Christmas, not saying a word! And now she wouldn't even talk to her mother about her decision, or lack of decision, regarding the baby, which (who knew?) might be Angela's mother's only chance for a grandchild . . . Well, she needed some time by herself, to think things over. And she would be praying for Angela, as she did every day, but from a distance—the distance apparently being something that Angela had been wanting, herself. Besides, Angela's grandmother was running a fever. It was probably not serious, but the trip was too long for her just now; the hours in the car on top of the news of Angela's pregnancy (and they knew nothing about the boy, Trevor, she was marrying, or about his family)—it would be too much.

"Hey. Are you still in there? You don't want to make me get a crowbar, do you? Come on: let's see how you look." The voice on the other side of the women's restroom stall belonged to Angela's resident adviser, Brandi, who had offered to leave her Spanish class ten minutes early and help Angela get ready at the campus chapel. Brandi was the only student (other than Trevor, the groom) whom Angela had invited to the wedding—not because they were friends, but because Brandi, during a weekly check-in with all the girls on her hall (a ritual that typically involved advice about hangover remedies), had knocked on Angela's door and, with a thumbs-up for emphasis, recited her usual question: Was

Angela going to make this week a good one? Was she going to kick this upcoming week in the ass?

"I think so," Angela had told her. "I'm getting married on Wednesday." Brandi had tossed back her head, her mouth opening wide, as if on a hinge. *"Hilarious."* Then she noticed Angela's expression. "Are you shitting me, Glowworm?" She took a few wary steps into Angela's room, noting the bookshelf with its row of books in alphabetical order, the bed with its hospital corners perfectly made. Angela—who had been wearing an oversized pullover sweater for the past six weeks—had stood up and smoothed her hands over her stomach. "Oh. Okay. Wow," Brandi said. "So: I guess this is for real?"

They talked. Aghast at the idea that Angela had no bridesmaids or attendants, Brandi had volunteered for the job.

Now, in the women's lounge at the back of the chapel, Spanish flashcards in the pocket of her jeans, Brandi hummed *"Here comes the bride"* as Angela, eyes almost crimson from the effort not to shed tears, emerged from the toilet stall. "All right, then," Brandi said, looking Angela over. "So far, so good." Brandi had gone above and beyond her resident adviser duties by taking Angela wedding-dress shopping: they had started at a discount bridal store but ended up at Goodwill. They had ultimately settled—for seven dollars—on a lemon-colored knee-length shift with yellow-and-white cloth daisies at the neck and hem. In the store it had seemed to Angela a sweet and simple dress, appropriate for a modest afternoon wedding. But now, catching sight of herself in the mirror over the sinks, she knew the dress was more comic than graceful: it emphasized the bump of her stomach and might have been borrowed from an overweight ten-year-old girl.

"Okay, my turn." Brandi peeled off her jeans and pulled her T-shirt over her head, her breasts nearly tumbling over the scalloped rim of a black lace bra. She dug through her backpack. "I wore this for my cousin's wedding last October." She held up a red cocktail dress with a slit up the thigh and made a *va-va-va-voom* gesture with her shoulders. "Dang. We should have brought flowers." She pulled the dress on over her head (the black bra still visible, Angela noticed, but maybe that was a style), then discovered a plastic bouquet in a vase by the sink. She rinsed a few years' worth of dust off the flowers, shook the water into the sink, then ripped the bouquet in half at the stem. "The bigger one's yours," she said. "That's one more thing taken care of. Now: let's see who's here." She cracked the restroom door and peered into the chapel. "All right. We've got a few people in the second row. And, yup, there's your groom, Shy-Guy Thurley. That's a heck of an overbite. He sat across from me in Bio-Chem in the fall." She turned to face Angela again. "Are you sure you're okay about this? And is Thurley okay"—Brandi gestured toward Angela's stomach—"you know, with the bump?"

Well, there wasn't much he could do about it, Angela said. He was surprised, of course, when she told him. She had gone to his room to deliver the news, and had found him walking down the hall with a toothbrush (it was the middle of the day, but Trevor liked to brush his teeth after lunch). In order to be alone they had gone into the dorm's kitchen, which smelled like sour milk and burned food, and Trevor had stared at the floor, the toothbrush clutched in his fist, while she explained—it sounded so odd—that they were going to be parents. She was four months along. He hadn't doubted her or questioned her at all.

"So . . . he just stood there?" Brandi shook a few drops of water from the plastic flowers. "What did he say?"

"I don't remember. I was so nervous," Angela said. Trevor—even before she broke the news—had seemed nervous, too. When she said the word "pregnant," he twitched; when she finished talking, he told her he had to call his mother. Angela had followed him to his room (would his mother want to talk to her also?), but he asked her to wait in the hall. Their conversation—through the door, she could hear Trevor's voice rising and falling but she couldn't hear what he said—went on so long she eventually gave up and went back to her dorm. Several days later, Trevor e-mailed. His mother had spoken to their pastor, and in light of the sin he and Angela had committed it would be best if they married. Trevor had asked about Angela's class schedule and compared it with his, and it turned out that a Wednesday between two-thirty and four—Trevor offered to reserve the chapel—would probably work best.

"Pretty freakin' romantic," Brandi said. She outlined her mouth in a bright shade of red and held the lipstick out to Angela, who declined. "What is it?" Brandi asked. "What's wrong?"

Angela had pressed her hand to her stomach. There it was, that otherworldly sliding motion, a knee or elbow carving a subtle arc from within. She stood still in order to pay closer attention and felt it again—some half-formed creature navigating an ocean inside her, making her feel as if she had swallowed a globe. "I'm fine," she said. She blew her nose and clutched her half of the plastic bouquet.

Still studying Angela, Brandi cracked her knuckles and then moved up her skeletal chain of command, cracking her wrists and her shoulders and ending by wrenching her neck to the left, her bones giving way with an audible pop. "You know, I'm way over my head in all this," she said. "During the resident adviser training they didn't talk to us about students getting married."

"I appreciate your being here," Angela said—though she wondered if it might have been easier to have gotten ready alone.

Brandi opened the restroom door again, giving Angela a glimpse of the minister—someone from Trevor's family's church—making his white-robed way down the aisle.

"Are we supposed to go in now?" Angela asked.

"Not yet." Brandi stood in front of the door. She was taller than Angela and was wearing heels; Angela stood face-to-face with two sizeable breasts. "Before we walk out of this room, I want you to give me three reasons. Three *good* reasons, other than that"—Brandi nodded at Angela's stomach—"to explain why you're ready to marry this guy."

"Well," Angela said. She remembered lying on her back in the tangle of sheets, with Trevor's garlicky breath in her ear. She had thought that having sex would be graceful, like dancing, the way it looked in the movies, but she'd found the configuration awkward: she wasn't sure what she was supposed to do with her arms, and Trevor's knee had kept pinching the skin of her thigh. Their stomachs had slapped together once, making a farting noise, and when they were finished (it had only taken about thirty seconds), there was the condom, still partly rolled up, beached on the sheet like a fish at low tide. "He's smart," she said. "If he weren't smart he wouldn't be in college."

Brandi said something about Payne not quite being Yale, but told Angela to go on.

"And he's . . . a nice person. He didn't doubt me when I told him."

"The fact that he didn't call you a liar about being pregnant is a real plus," Brandi said. "But I wouldn't call that a reason. I'm going to say you're at one and a half."

Out in the chapel, a CD player switched on. Angela had asked Trevor to play "Joyful, Joyful, We Adore Thee"—one of her mother's favorites—but heard something dark and Wagnerian instead.

"He's—we have things in common," she said. "I mean, our backgrounds. I met him at campus Bible study." She hadn't returned to the Bible study group after the night of the party (what if the other group members knew what had happened?), but it counted for something, she thought, that she and Trevor had grown up with similar beliefs. Beliefs were a way of making decisions—or having decisions ready-made for you. Furthermore, Trevor, like Angela, had grown up at the edge of a farming town. Thinking about Vellmar, bordered by crops, Angela couldn't help but consider her pregnancy in agricultural terms. Trevor had planted a seed in her, and soon it would show itself and come to fruition. The only trouble with this analogy was the comparison of Angela's body to dirt.

Brandi sighed. "Okay. We'll call that two and a half reasons. What else can you come up with?"

Angela was having trouble thinking. The CD shifted from Wagnerian gloom to some sort of eerie Celtic music. Was that her cue? But Brandi and her breasts were still blocking the door. Brandi wanted to know about Angela's plans for her wedding night and her honeymoon. Angela's dorm was girls-only. Were they going to spend a romantic night sleeping on a couch in the student center? Or in a tent in the mud on the quad?

Well, in truth, Angela hadn't thought about that. She had only gotten as far as the fact that it was important to be married, because having a baby outside of marriage was a sin. She hadn't imagined sleeping in the same bed or even the same room (in twin beds?) with Trevor, and she would rather go to her chemistry lab than have sex again. The woman at the health clinic had told her that being pregnant might make her feel absentminded, and Angela had definitely found that to be the case. The only things she could keep her mind on were her classes; she sometimes even forgot, when she woke up in the morning, that she was pregnant, remembering only when she bent over to put on her shoes.

"Well, people are waiting out there," Brandi said. "Should I tell them you're coming? Or do you want to take a rain check and get married to somebody else in about ten years?"

Angela couldn't think. She had already told her mother that she was getting married. And she had told and invited

270

Professor Fitger and Ms. Matthias and Fran, and she had invited a few other professors, and the idea that they were sitting out there waiting, that she had told them to come . . . "Do we walk up together?" She felt her pulse thumping forcibly in her neck.

"Not unless you want me to give you away. Which I'm not going to do. I'll walk in first, and you walk behind me." Brandi opened the door. "But listen: if you decide to make a run for it, let me know; I can cause a distraction."

Angela saw Trevor at the front of the chapel, wearing a shirt and tie but no suit. Shouldn't the groom wear a suit? But she remembered her seven-dollar dress and unpolished shoes.

"This is it, then. Liftoff," Brandi said.

Angela followed behind her into the church.

Staring into the gloomy heart of Payne's campus chapel, Janet tried to remember—not that it mattered—whether the right or left side of a church was for friends of the bride. She had been in the chapel only a few times before: once for a terrible production of a student-directed play (the theater had been closed, as it often was, for repairs), and once or twice for a funeral. The building was more suited, she thought, to funerals: the wood was dark, and because of overhanging trees and an adjacent building, the windows admitted only a begrudging light on one side.

She had been hoping to arrive after Fitger was seated, in order to avoid him, but of course he was late. God, she was an idiot, playing that game with the Caesar salad. What had it led to? To her ex-husband e-mailing her at all hours, and to the evening when she and her father were driving home from that horrible superhero film he had insisted on seeing, and there was Jay, strolling cozily along in the dark with his little French friend while walking Fran's dog. Janet had endured, during the remainder of her father's visit, a Möbius strip of parental observations: *he never understood why Jan-Jan had married that loser; she was obviously better off without him; her ex was a self-satisfied clod and a jackass; and who was that sexpot he was walking with?* Fitger had left her a message the next afternoon, explaining that he had no idea she had broken up with Phil, and that he and the chair of Consolidated Languages had been discussing a—

Janet had hit *delete* without listening to the rest.

There weren't many people in the church. On the right, a handful of undergrads stared robotically at their cell phones. On the left, Fran sat with Ashkir, her entrepreneurial office assistant; just behind them were Dennis Cassovan and Helena Stang, Stang wearing what appeared to be a full set of typewriter keys (still attached to their metal levers) like an alphabetical fringe around her neck.

Assuming that Fitger would arrive midwedding and take a seat at the back, Janet sat near the altar, in front of Fran, who scooted forward to inform her of the obvious: that Fitger hadn't yet come.

"Nice to see you too," Janet said.

A minister glided past in his robe and plunked a missal down on the lectern.

"Ms. Matthias used to be married to Professor Fitger," Fran said to Ashkir.

Janet ignored the sharp intake of breath denoting Ashkir's surprise. There were no flowers in the chapel. Should she have brought some? No: better to have brought the gift of a check made out to Angela, folded neatly in half in a card in her purse.

Lugubrious music issued from two tinny speakers to the left of the altar.

Ashkir said he was sure that Professor Fitger would be there soon: it was a three-minute walk from Willard Hall.

"Three and a half," Fran said. She tapped Janet's shoulder. "Did you hear about our department event?" she asked. No? She nudged Ashkir; could he give Ms. Matthias one of their flyers?

Janet accepted a bookmark-sized piece of paper announcing the Department of English's end-of-year speaker. She turned around in her pew. "Orest Weisel?"

"He is Professor Kentrell's friend," Ashkir said.

"But—"

The music shifted to something Gaelic; Janet stuffed the flyer into a hymnbook.

"He'd better get here," Fran said. "I was hoping he'd be able to talk Angela out of this."

Ashkir said he was sure Professor Fitger would arrive very soon.

In his Willard Hall office, having told Fran that he would catch up with her at the wedding, Fitger was sorting through seventeen different versions of the Statement of Vision. Having fallen behind due to the upcoming visit of the nation's premier preschool poet, he had only a few more weeks in which to forge a faculty consensus. Rutledge, when he resurfaced, would probably approve QUAP's recommendations, and Econ's announcement of its soon-to-be-acquired millions would give Roland a power no other faculty member at Payne had ever known. The SOV would provide a meager, temporary protection. Fitger was therefore trying to assemble agreeable passages from the seventeen previous drafts of the document, each of which, when submitted to the faculty, had been roundly condemned.

The Department of English at Payne University, he wrote, *engages undergraduate and graduate students and faculty in the study and analysis and creation of literature* [he remembered that Stang objected to the word "analysis"] . . . *in the study and creation of literature that* . . . He paused. Someone—West?—had insisted on "literatures" and not "literature." He added an *"s." Emphasizing critical inquiry, aesthetics, and textual knowledge and appreciation* [Glenk disliked the word "appreciation," but might let it pass], *instruction in English spans centuries and disciplines* [Christ, he sounded like Carl Sagan], *from the Anglo-Saxon period to* . . . Cassovan would never allow him to use the term "Anglo-Saxon" if Shakespeare wasn't represented as well.

Through the ceiling, he heard the rolling thunder of Roland Gladwell's executive chair. QUAP had decimated Theater and chewed Gusev to pieces over in Classics, the committee's job becoming simpler after Roland had purchased Hinckler's nonintervention via an associate professorship in the French horn; the dean would return to the

Department of Music, his pockets weighed down with thirty pieces of silver, in June.

Fitger looked at his watch: fifteen minutes remained before Angela's wedding. Janet should have warned him about the dean; why didn't she tell him that Hinckler and his French horn would accept a payoff? Fitger picked up his pen and went back to the Statement of Vision, keeping in mind the preferences and particular needs of each of his colleagues. Of the twelve tenured or tenure-track faculty members in English, eleven, he thought, were, at least at the current moment, potentially receptive to compromise.

One was Hesseldine, rescued from Rodentia;

Two was Lovejoy, relieved of her masturbator;

Three was Brown-Wilson, never again to serve on a committee (Fitger had signed a contract to this effect) with either Tyne or Kentrell;

Four was West, never again to serve on a committee with Kentrell or Stang;

Five was Stang, given precedence for "childcare";

Six was Fitger;

Seven was Glenk, whose miniature donkeys had tentatively approved a reversal of position;

Eight was Atherman, whose birthday, as well as those of Charlotte, Anne, and Emily Brontë, was now denoted via a party hat on the calendar;

Nine was Beauchamp, given clearance to brew and dispense kombucha (to faculty only) down the hall in her office;

Ten was Tyne (Fitger cringed when he thought
of the Jiffy Maids who had confronted Albert's
shuddersome enclosure, what with the animal
cadavers and the bottles of urine collected over so
many years);
Eleven was Kentrell, who had been fed, housed, and
cosseted for the better part of a month.

Which left only Dennis Cassovan, whose portion of the
Shakespeare scorecard remained pristine.

Rogaine—Fran had left him behind in the office—was
snuffling at something in Fitger's briefcase. "Get out of
there, you hairless rascal. What are you eating?" The dog
had chewed a hole in a bag of confetti Fitger had purchased,
along with a gift certificate to the campus bookstore, for
Angela's wedding, after having been told that, for some sort
of environmental reason, it was no longer appropriate to
toss handfuls of rice. Rogaine had swallowed some of the
brightly shredded contents. Now he held his chin close to
the floor as if about to be sick.

"What's the matter with you? What do you need? Water?"
Fitger filled a coffee mug at the fountain in the hall and set it
on the floor in front of the dog. A thought occurred: Would
Dennis Cassovan be at the wedding? Angela had been in his
class as well, so he probably would be. Perhaps, before the
ceremony started, Fitger could talk to him for a few minutes.
Janet, of course, would be at the wedding, too.

Rogaine wheezed, a sprinkle of confetti chuffing out of
his mouth. "Look at you," Fitger said, aware that it was no

longer unusual for him to talk to the dog. "You need to drink something." He pointed with his toe to the mug of water, which Rogaine promptly knocked over with his paw.

Fitger consulted his watch again. "Shit." Weddings didn't generally start on time, did they? Fran had told him to leave the dog behind to guard the office, but fearing a confetti-induced asphyxiation, he clipped a leash to Rogaine's collar, and together they went to the chapel to see Angela wed.

Helena Stang, suffering from laryngitis, had felt unwell enough to make legitimate excuses and to skip her student's wedding, but she had rallied and made that extra effort, deciding to attend for intellectual as well as feminist reasons. Weddings were stunningly patriarchal, beginning with a parade of pastel virgins preceding the victim/sacrifice on her way to the shrine. Stang unwrapped and put a lozenge into her mouth while studying the young man with the face of a tapir, obviously the groom, who was currently escorting a middle-aged female version of himself to the front of the church.

Bagpipe music began to squeal from a CD player; Dennis Cassovan, in the pew beside her, stood. Well, this was interesting: rather than a full bouquet of maiden attendants, here came a single brassy young creature in a bright red dress, who stalked hips-first up the aisle like a majorette. Close behind her, walking alone (at least she wasn't being traded like a bargaining chip from one male arm to another), was the bride, looking fertile and anxious in a flowered smock. Angela, enrolled in Professor Stang's Feminism and Literature class, had spent two weeks studying institutionalized gender bias, after which she had knocked on her professor's door and handed her an invitation to her espousal. Stang had initially wondered whether this gesture might be a work of subversive theater; unfortunately, it was not. Angela was a bright young woman, but irony was a difficult concept for her to grasp.

Dennis Cassovan, at Helena Stang's side, had quietly signaled to the cluster of undergraduates (who looked as if they were about to be graded on an exam for which no one had studied) in the opposite pews, indicating that they should stand as the bride began to walk down the aisle. He smiled at Angela. He himself had married at twenty-eight; his wife, Louise, had been only nineteen. Back in those days, even seventeen or eighteen conferred adulthood; now, unbridled adolescence seemed to begin before puberty and to peak during the college years, extending through graduate school and beyond. When Angela came to his office with that handwritten wedding invitation he had immediately noticed the thickness at her waist and the careful, self-conscious way she sat down. He remembered Louise, pregnant with their son (how terrified he had been about the idea of being a father!), moving in the same way.

He thought about the portion of his book that focused on *Coriolanus. I am weary; yea, my memory is tired.* Impossible to alter the past, and yet the desire to amend it in one's mind was constant. Perhaps if he shifted the first chapter's discussion of cognizance to . . . Angela, her eyebrows pinched above the bridge of her nose, glanced quickly and, it seemed, anxiously in his direction. It wasn't the role of faculty to intrude on students' personal lives and decisions (the university hired counselors for that), but Cassovan shifted uncomfortably—*hasty marriage seldom proveth well*—as she took her place at the front of the church. Where was her family? Who was advising the poor girl? He would have liked to tap Fran on the shoulder and ask. The groom—who brought *Much Ado About Nothing*'s Dogberry to mind—stood near the baptismal font, as rigid and unmoving as a stave.

Dearly beloved, we are gathered . . .

Fran had been hoping that Angela might come to her senses and make a run for the exit, but now that the ceremony had started, that possibility seemed more remote. She probably felt trapped—a situation Fran knew a few things about—and was latching onto the idea of marriage like a drowning victim reaching for even a semi-inflated raft.

Fitger hadn't shown up. If he didn't get to the chapel soon, Fran would personally kill him, thus lending a sense of satisfaction to the end of her week. Angela looked very cute in that dress. She was such a sweet kid. Fran saw her flash an interrogatory half smile at the boy she was marrying, who responded with terror or surprise, as if someone had slammed his finger in a car door. Fran would happily kill him, too, at any indication that he was unkind to Angela. It was too easy to get married, she thought, whereas a number of painful years were usually involved in coming to the realization that one's spouse was a dud.

Let us pray.

At the back of the chapel (he hadn't missed much; the wedding had just started), Fitger took a moment for his eyes to adjust to the gloom; then, wanting to evade responsibility for the confetti-filled dog, he made a beeline for Fran. Man and dog clattered into the pew beside her.

"What's that on his face?" Fran hissed. "What did you feed him?" Rogaine appeared to be wearing makeup; his lips and whiskers were flecked with blue.

Fitger tried to explain, but a woman whose spine was curved like a shepherd's crook had tiptoed toward them to say that dogs and other pets were not allowed in the church.

"This is a guide dog," Fitger said, pointing to Rogaine's Girl Scout sash.

"A therapy dog," Ashkir added.

Amen. You may sit.

"Rogaine, sit," said Fran.

Everyone sat. The woman with the crooked back walked away.

The all-wise Creator in the Garden of Eden—

Fitger gave Fran the leash and control of the dog, then harrumphed once, wanting Angela to know he had come. Janet was sitting directly in front of him. His gaze immediately settled on the back of her head, which had always struck him as pleasantly shaped: there was something of the old-fashioned lightbulb about it, with a cup at the nape like a small oval pool. He remembered their wedding, performed by a justice of the peace in a ceremony that lasted about forty-three seconds. A sudden rainstorm had kept them from leaving the courthouse when it was finished, so they'd had quick, furtive sex (probably recorded by surveillance cameras) in a basement corridor, under the stairs. It was a memory that returned to him during weddings; he wanted to ask her if she thought about it also, but he needed to talk to Dennis Cassovan, seated diagonally behind him, first.

Then the rib which the Lord God had taken from man He made into a woman . . .

Fitger leaned, uncomfortably, over the back of his pew. "Dennis," he whispered. "Do you have a moment?"

Cassovan was still thinking about *Coriolanus;* his mind was wandering.

"Dennis, I'm writing another version of the Statement of Vision," Fitger whispered. "And I'm hoping you might be willing to—" Stang (what was she wearing around her neck? Fitger wondered; it looked like a typewriter that had been flattened by a train) was flapping her hand to get his attention.

"Just a minute, Helena," Fitger said.

She had scribbled the word *OBJECT* in the margins of the previous Sunday's program ("Art Thou Weary, Art Thou Languid," Fitger noticed, was the week's chosen hymn) and was thrusting it toward him.

"Uh-oh, watch it," Fran said. Rogaine coughed up a pile of blue mulch.

At the front of the chapel, the minister spoke at some length about God's separate, divinely sanctioned plans for wives and for husbands.

"Dennis, wait," Fitger said. Cassovan removed himself to the far end of the pew, while Stang continued to press the previous week's program on Fitger, pointing at the word *OBJECT* with her thumb. A noun or a verb? Fitger wondered.

Fran said it was no way to treat a dog; Fitger needed to keep a better eye on Rogaine if he was going to adopt.

"Who said I was going to adopt?" he asked. The minister paused and looked up.

"Sorry." Fitger helped Fran cover the vomit with a collection of tissues. He sat facing forward in the pew. There was Janet's well-shaped head again, just in front of him. "I didn't know you broke up with Phil," he said.

Janet scratched at an earlobe.

"He sold out to Roland. But I guess you knew that." Fitger leaned closer.

Continuing to read from his zealot's playbook, the minister reminded Angela that, in wedlock, she would be "submitting to the headship" of her future spouse.

"Is he talking about blow jobs?" Fran asked. "I never heard of that being written into the wedding vows."

Stang's typewriter necklace was rattling; she kicked the underside of the pew.

"I took your advice all year," Fitger murmured, still speaking to the back of Janet's head. He wasn't sure whether he was pleading or scolding. He told Janet he had done everything she suggested—not always because he thought her suggestions were good but because they were hers. He had gone door-to-door through the building, he had networked with other department chairs, he had conferred with Wilcox, and now he was going to humiliate himself by staging a campus event that would be of interest mainly to those who hadn't yet learned to count to ten.

"And Marie Eland and I aren't dating," he said. "You can ask her."

Janet's head revolved, slowly, on the stem of her neck. She proceeded to tell him, speaking in a whisper reminiscent, in Fitger's mind, of a samurai sword, that she didn't care if he was dating or not dating, and she had tried to tell him at their divorce anniversary dinner that Phil had sold out to Roland and QUAP but he had refused to hear. And as for her suggestions, she had offered them against her better judgment while bending university codes of conduct. In addition to providing him with a year's worth of sound administrative advice, she had put up with his neediness and had hired his student; and she was not responsible for his selfish ineptitude or for his department being eviscerated by QUAP. Maybe he should have spent more time advising his students instead of flirting. And she hoped to god he didn't flatter himself by imagining that he or English had anything to do with her decision to break up with Phil.

At the altar, perhaps fully persuaded that she was at fault for the Fall of Mankind, Angela handed her plastic flowers to Brandi.

Would Trevor, as first among equals, promise to have and to hold, to guide and to tutor—

"We need to talk. I want to talk to you," Fitger said. Would Janet meet him after the service?

"Fuck you, Jay," she said. She would not.

—and for her portion, would Angela promise forever to honor and to render obedience to Trevor L. Thurley?

Angela had heard Professor Fitger enter the church (she was glad that he and her other professors were there), and during the wedding she had been reassured by the sound of his voice occasionally rising and falling behind her, as if he were a participant in the service or the prayers. Based on some of his comments in class, she didn't think he was religious; but there were things he strongly believed in and, during his Narratives of Adventure class, he talked about character and success and failure and virtue in a way she admired. They had finished discussing *True Grit* and he had spoken about Mattie Ross and the arc of her life as if she were real. That was what Angela loved about books: that she could live within them and through them.

The minister had asked her a question and seemed to be waiting.

When Angela had met with Professor Fitger in his office, he had told her that she might think of her life as a book, with herself as its author. She had told him that she couldn't imagine writing a book, and he had said that lesser people than she had done it, and she wrote very well. She looked past Trevor, who had been clutching his tie for the past ten minutes, and toward the pews on the left side of the church. There was Professor Stang, with her typewriter necklace; Professor Cassovan in his black suit with the handkerchief peeping out of his breast pocket; there were Ms. Matthias and Ashkir and Fran. The thing Angela had worried about had begun to happen: they were all waiting for her to say or do something, but she couldn't speak. And when the minister repeated his question and Angela saw that the daisies on her dress had begun to shake as if to remove themselves from the fabric, Professor Fitger stepped into the aisle and asked if she would like to sit down or take a moment—because it would be fine if she needed to do so; she was in charge, but he would walk with her, if she liked, back down the aisle and out of the chapel. He came toward her and extended his arm.

The minister, starched in his cassock, looked at Fitger, who was wearing an ill-fitting jacket and had dog vomit splattered over one of his shoes. "You presume to advise this young woman?" he asked.

Fitger said, "I do."

FIFTEEN

Major Gift to the Department of Economics Announced

—by L. R. Young

The Campus Scribe (April 11, 2011): Roland Gladwell, Professor and Chair of Economics, will announce a major gift to his department this week, during an event which is open to the public and the Payne community. Gladwell, reached in his office, was tight-lipped about the amount of the gift and the use to which it will be put, but claimed it will be a "game changer" for his department, located on the second floor of Willard Hall.

"It is deeply gratifying," Gladwell said, "when donors from industry and the community recognize the excellence of our teaching and scholarship."

President Nyla Hoffman echoed Professor Gladwell's sentiments and encouraged Payne's students, staff, and faculty to attend the announcement, which will be followed by a special recognition of Professor Gladwell's work on behalf of the university.

"The Department of Economics is clearly superlative," Hoffman said. "I know that everyone at Payne will share in the pleasure of its success."

Tossing the *Scribe* into the recycling bin in the hall, Fran wondered whether "sharing in the pleasure of Econ's success" might include access to their women's bathroom, which sported a sign asking faculty and students in English to use their own facility on the lower floor. Econ's plan (Roland hadn't bothered to obscure it) was to evict English from Willard and—like a fat man in an airplane seat—to spread into the space rightfully belonging to someone else. And where was English supposed to go when it was pushed out of Willard? To the racquetball courts? Fran imagined her office turned into a dressing room for Marilyn Hoopes. On a flyer on the mailroom door, she was confronted by Roland Gladwell's smug expression; his face was plastered on glossy posters everywhere around campus. But every advertisement for Econ's announcement of the Pratt-Fixx gift bore a corrective banner: NEW DATE AND LOCATION! *Thank you, Ashkir,* Fran thought. The event would unfold—in fact, was unfolding right now— against a backdrop of socks and deodorant, in the gym.

It was Friday afternoon and the building was quiet, the students preparing for their evening inebriations and the Econ faculty and staff having strolled off in a self-congratulatory cluster to learn of the riches that would soon rain down upon them from above. Fitger had left the office with Rogaine, muttering something about not wanting to hear, from his window, the roars of bloodlust coming from the gym.

She reentered the English Department suite. A few minutes later Angela came in, her final essay for Fitger's class in her hand.

"Look at that," Fran said. "So you finished, huh? And ahead of schedule."

Angela gave her the essay—"Ambiguous Role Models in Adventure Literature, by Angela B. Vackrey." She told Fran that she needed to get everything done early. "I'm going home today," she said. "I have to be on partial bed rest, my doctor says." They stood in the anteroom together; Angela looked at the closed door of Fitger's office. "He isn't in?"

"I'm not sure where he's wandered off to," Fran said, dropping the essay into the slot on his door. "He's been hard to find since the Orest Weisel performance on Tuesday. I don't think it fit very well with his self-image."

"It was fun to see all those little kids in the auditorium, though," Angela said. "They were so excited. And Professor Fitger was a good sport in that skit at the end."

"Yeah, I never expected to see him dressed as a peppermint tree. But every day here at Payne I learn something new. Speaking of which: Do you want to see the new animal I've got in my office? Someone abandoned her, the poor thing."

Together they peered through the narrow window in Fran's office door.

"Wow. What is it?"

"Monitor lizard," Fran said. "She's not full-grown; otherwise it would be hard to bring her to work. But she's adjusting; I set up a heat lamp there in the corner." The animal—almost three feet long, with a dust-colored mountain range that extended down the length of its spine—turned away from a food dish full of what appeared to be sizeable insects and, with a sociopathic expression, lunged for the door.

"Not family-friendly yet," Fran said. The lizard clawed itself upright and glared at them with a mineral eye through the window. "But think about how far Rogaine has come. I'm willing to bet he'll have an owner by the end of next week." She put her hand against the glass. "Well, enough about me. How are you feeling these days? Are you getting enough sleep? You're taking vitamins?"

"Yeah." Angela scratched at her stomach. "Mostly I feel hot. And big. My feet are huge."

They both looked at her feet, in a pair of white sneakers. Next to Fran's feet, in their rubber sandals, they looked tidy and elegant, almost demure.

"You look wonderful; I mean it," Fran said. "I want you to let me know if you need anything—baby clothes, books, whatever."

Angela thanked her. "I still haven't—I know it probably seems late, but—" She looked at Fran. "I'm still not sure if I'm going to keep it. To keep him. That sounds strange, doesn't it? I found out it's a boy. Obviously I need to decide soon. I can't wait until—well, I don't know exactly how long I can wait."

Fran asked if she needed a lawyer—Ms. Matthias would definitely find one for her—or if she wanted help extracting money or maybe some pints of blood or a testicle from Trevor L. Thurley.

"No. Actually, Trevor has decided to transfer," Angela said. "He's going to Saint Silas next year."

Fran limited herself to a subtle murmur of response, quelling what otherwise would have been a thorough condemnation of the sanctimonious son of a bitch who had knocked Angela up, then tried to bully her into a misogynistic excuse for a wedding.

"His mother is still angry," Angela said. "She told Trevor she won't pay tuition for a secular university where the teachers are atheists and no one has values." Besides, Trevor would be happier at Saint Silas, she said. He had asked Angela (without telling his mother) to transfer also—though he had cautioned her that it was a very strictly faith-based school.

"Amazing that he felt confident enough of his own moral standing to be able to advise you," Fran said. She resisted the urge to suggest that every mile Angela could insert between herself and the father of her future child would be a boon. It was a three-hour drive between Payne and the incorruptibles at Saint Silas; Fran indulged in a brief agnostic prayer that Trevor would be denied access to any and all modes of transportation—cars, vans, buses, bicycles, camels, scooters—and that any contact between his family and Angela's would consist only of generous, regular installments of cash.

"I wouldn't want to go to Saint Silas anyway," Angela said. "And I wouldn't have a scholarship there."

"So you'll be coming back to Payne in the fall?"

"I'm not sure yet. But I haven't withdrawn. Will you still be here, Fran?"

"Me? I've ordered a manacle so I can be fastened by the leg to my desk. Hey, that reminds me. Professor Fitger and I got you something." She went into Fitger's adjoining office and came back with a small paper bag. "I didn't wrap these yet, because I didn't know you'd be coming by."

Angela opened the bag and held up two T-shirts, one a medium adult and the other a newborn. Both were emblazoned with the word PAYNE. She held the newborn shirt in front of her. "I love them. Thank you. Would you tell Professor Fitger goodbye for me?"

Fran said she would. "Is someone coming to get you?"

Angela looked at her watch. "My mother and grandmother. They'll be here in an hour."

Fran gave her an apple. "A snack for the road," she said. "Do you want me to hide in the trunk of their car? Or in a suitcase? I could probably fit."

No. Things were calmer now, Angela said, between herself and her mother; she was almost looking forward to being at home. "Tell Professor Fitger I'll write him a thankyou note," she said. "I mean, for the T-shirts. And for advising me. And for standing up at the wedding and walking outside with me and saying it didn't matter if everyone was in there waiting, Trevor and his mother and the minister and Professor Cassovan and you and Professor Stang and everyone else. He said, 'Let them wait'—and we sat and talked for almost an hour! And I told him I didn't know what I was doing, I've been so confused all year, and then we talked about Robert Louis Stevenson, because I didn't come to college to get married, I came to get an education, and to—"

"It's all right," Fran said. "It's okay; don't cry."

Angela wiped her eyes on the T-shirts and put them away. She thanked Fran again. "When you see Professor Fitger," she said, "please tell him how lucky I feel, that I drew his name as my adviser at the start of the year."

Outside the gymnasium, which Marilyn Hoopes had done her utmost to refresh and disguise, Roland Gladwell was getting ready to make the most significant speech of his academic career. At one end of the gym, students eagerly shouted back and forth (a free buffet would follow the announcement of the Pratt-Fixx gift) and thumped their feet in the wooden bleachers; faculty and VIPs were seating themselves in chairs, facing the hastily erected platform at the other end. A blue-and-white Payne banner hung from the ceiling over the podium. Manuela Pratt and William Fixx and their families had taken their places and were chatting with President Hoffman in the front row.

Roland conferred briefly with Marilyn Hoopes and his other assistants. This was the moment when the Department of Economics would forever distinguish itself from the quagmire that was Payne. Roland would soon be chairing a unit that would attract and hire illustrious scholars. For the price of a few curricular tweaks that would steer both faculty and students toward a greater appreciation of the market economy, the department would become a magnet for excellence: even better, the donation from Manuela Pratt and William Fixx (he would be sure to pronounce their names slowly) would enable him to begin the process of ejecting Fitger and his riffraff colleagues from Willard Hall.

Was everything ready? Roland's speech was in his breast pocket, and President Hoffman had taken her seat, accompanied by a potpourri of deans. Of course the auditorium (currently in use by seven members of Banjos and Zithers Anonymous) would have been a much more appropriate venue; but given Manuela Pratt's water polo appointments, the gym would suffice. Roland felt uneasy about the paperwork: because of the last-minute change to the date and the slothlike pace at which everything occurred over in Legal, the final documents hadn't been signed. But Marilyn Hoopes assured him that the ink would be more than dry by the following week.

Marilyn opened the door closest to the dais and touched his shoulder by way of a go-ahead. The podium was stocked with three bottles of water and the mic was live, so he should simply follow the red carpet on his way to the stage, remembering to—

"Wait. What is that?" Roland asked.

Jouncing up and down on its furry haunches beside the podium—in fact, now summoning Roland with the mindless joie de vivre of a game-show host—was Payne's mascot, Pup-Dog, cheered by the crowd.

"Pup-Dog comes with the venue," Marilyn said.

"What do you mean, he comes with the venue?" Roland asked. "Does he live in the gym? This is his home?"

"There's nothing I can do about it," Marilyn said. "All public events in the gym involve the mascot."

On the dais, Pup-Dog dropped into a squat and did some push-ups, then leapt to his feet again, beckoning to Roland. In the bleachers, the students yipped and rollicked and made digging gestures in the air with their hands.

"I can't make a speech with that thing prancing around,"

Roland said, as Pup-Dog swung his hips from side to side and mimed the delivery of remarks at the mic. "How do we get him to leave the stage?"

"I have no authority over the mascot," Marilyn said.

Sweat dampened the collar of Roland's shirt. What kind of sense did it make, at an institution as hierarchical as Payne, for an undergraduate in a rodent costume to be overseen by no one, a free agent entirely lacking in supervision? Roland followed the red carpet onto the stage. Did he have his speech? Yes, it was in his pocket. He simply needed to— On impulse, he veered from the podium and approached the mascot, who—perhaps startled—spun his polyester head in a circle, then darted away.

"Hold still," Roland growled.

Pup-Dog spun his head in the other direction and kept the podium between them. The students laughed.

Roland signaled for Marilyn Hoopes to bring a chair, which she did—setting it up a few feet from where Roland was to give his speech. Pup-Dog started toward the chair but before he could sit in it, Roland pushed it farther from the podium, toward the edge of the dais. Pup-Dog briefly looked dejected, then sat down, as if sulking, with his back to Roland. On the gym floor below, a reporter was taking pictures with a flash.

Roland went back to the microphone and unfolded his speech. Was someone supposed to have introduced him? No; he should probably introduce himself. In the first row, President Hoffman said something to Manuela Fixx; that is, to Manuela Pratt. Roland barreled through his opening paragraph. *As Chairman of the Department of Economics here at Payne, I take great pride and pleasure in* . . . The filthy mascot had straddled the folding chair and scooched a bit closer to the podium. *Very few universities are fortunate enough to* . . . Damn. Roland had accidentally omitted a sentence. With the mascot leering in his direction, he cleared his throat and began again.

In an empty classroom in Willard, Jason Fitger sat in a lop-sided wooden chair, defeated, with Rogaine (exiled from Fran's office by an overgrown lizard) asleep at his feet. Fran claimed the dog had taken a shine to him; had Fitger read the articles she had sent him about the benefits of the human–animal bond. Fitger didn't mind if Rogaine accompanied him around campus—sometimes the dog even followed him into the men's room, helping himself to liquid refreshment—but he wasn't prepared to become the animal's *forever home.*

It was four-fifteen. By now, Roland would have made his announcement and would be writing eviction notices and getting ready for the tar-and-feather ceremony for English. "Prepare yourself; it's not going to be pretty," Fitger said, running the sole of his shoe over Rogaine's mottled fur; the dog enjoyed anything that involved human feet. "The first thing they'll do is push us out of the first floor into the basement," Fitger said. "And when they run out of storage space for their new money, they'll probably convert the basement into a vault."

He looked out the window. The weather was dismal. The statue of Cyril Payne, appropriately dressed in lime-green swimming trunks and a snorkel, had presided over three days of rain that had left the sidewalks crosshatched with worms. Fitger had distributed yet another version of the SOV with a ballot attached but was not optimistic. Cassovan had apparently been bribed with promises of his own free-wheeling Shakespearean kingdom, and Roland continued to offer retirement incentives to both Tyne and Glenk (Glenk was suffering an expensive year with the miniature donkeys, what with laminitis infecting the herd).

One way or the other—this thought cheered him somewhat—the semester would be over soon, and the Payne campus would resemble a sparsely attended park. With the students gone, he would be able to work part-time at home, taking an inventory of his remaining teeth and asking himself whether it would be preferable to chop off both of his hands with an axe or continue to serve as department chair. Again he looked out the window, expecting at any moment to hear riotous pecuniary huzzahs or to see Roland's likeness etched into the heavens by skywriting planes above the gym.

Rogaine wagged his stump of a tail and emitted a flatulent groan of contentment.

"You are disgusting." Fitger picked up the leash. "Do you think it's time to go back to the office?"

Rogaine did. Together they walked down the hall past the W LC ME O ENGLI H sign and, opening the door, found Janet, in a blue raincoat, talking to Fran. Fitger stared. Water dripped from his ex-wife's raincoat onto the floor.

"There you are," Fran said. "We were just talking about the

Orest Weisel event. I told Janet it was definitely a hit with the preschool crowd. We even made money on the visit."

"Really?" Janet looked at Rogaine.

Yes, it was true: because of Ashkir, they didn't have to pay for the auditorium, and Weisel, after waiving his usual fee, had, post-sing-along, even made a donation. "I think I have it here in my wallet." Fitger took a check from his billfold: fifty dollars, made out to the Department of English.

Fran dropped it into her in-box. "I need to leave a little early. Octavia is going in for a checkup." She bobbed her head in the direction of the monitor lizard, then said something to Janet about the dog's evening meal. "Has Rogaine had a chance yet, today, to do his business?"

"If by 'business,'" Fitger said, "you mean chewing the decomposing carcasses of squirrels or humping my briefcase, yes, he's enjoyed the opportunity for both." He looked at Janet. "Are you . . . taking him home?"

"For the weekend." Janet held her hand out to the dog, and Rogaine licked some rain from her skin.

"Traitor," Fitger said, while she scratched the dog's skull. "He never puts his ears back nicely that way for me."

"Maybe that's because Janet doesn't talk to him about euthanasia," Fran said. She handed him a manila envelope. "Here. You've probably been trying to forget about these."

Fitger felt a tide of weariness wash across him, a liquid torpor taking the place of the blood in his veins. Did he feel queasy, too, about Rogaine?

"What's in the envelope?" Janet asked.

"Ballots," said Fran. She explained that the English faculty had been given a week to read Fitger's most recent sixteen-word version of the Statement of Vision and, by checking *Yes, No,* or *Abstain,* to cast their votes by Friday at two. Here were the results. Fitger tucked the envelope under his arm.

Janet looked at him directly for the first time. "Aren't you going to open it?" she asked.

"He can't," said Fran. Department policy clearly stated that ballots had to be opened and counted in the presence of two members of the English faculty and one member of staff. And it was now 4:25 on a Friday and Fran was late for a veterinary appointment, and they weren't likely to find any faculty still in the building. They would have to wait until the following week. She went into her office and came back a moment later clutching what looked like a small cloth suitcase—a carry-all, Fitger saw, for the monitor lizard. A hole in the back allowed for a furfuraceous tail.

"I'm a member of staff," Janet said. "Does the staff have to be Department of English?"

Fran raised her eyebrows. "No, I guess not," she said. "But you still have to find a second faculty member. And if you do dig up someone"—she looked severely at Fitger—"you have to count the ballots *twice.* The chair writes the final tally down and then signs it." She started toward the door, the lizard's tail lashing behind her like a rope. "If you have any questions—"

"I'll be fine," Janet said. She knelt on the floor to untangle the leash from Rogaine's paws.

Fitger stood by and watched; he hadn't seen Janet since Angela's wedding—or non-wedding. He had wanted to call her or stop by the law school, but understood that she preferred he stay away. But here she was, kneeling on the ragged carpet in the English Department office, reviving in him the hope that she didn't revile him; that in fact the Caesar salad episode (he understood, now, that she had probably been trying to tell him about Hinckler) was evidence of an evolution in her feelings for him; and while perhaps she wasn't fond of him, per se, she was able to think, as he did, about their marriage and their years together with affection, and would therefore allow him to tell her (even though he was half a dozen years too late with this declaration) that he had missed her every single day since the divorce and, in his own flawed and rudimentary way, he loved her still.

"Angela came to talk to me a few days ago," she said. "I wanted to thank you for recommending her as an intern."

"You're welcome." Fitger couldn't parse her expression. "Janet, I—"

She cut him off. "I came here from the Econ event," she said, looking up. "I assumed you wouldn't be in the audience."

"No. Rogaine and I considered attending," he said, pulling a burr from the dog's ear. "But other matters kept us here in the office. How was it? Were there seven or eight zeroes on the check?"

Janet stood up. The rain had stopped. She looked out the window. "You know they moved the event to the gym?"

Yes, Fitger knew.

She paused. "It didn't go well. Roland . . . misspoke."

"What do you mean, he 'misspoke'?"

Well, he had some sort of altercation with Pup-Dog, and his obvious dislike for the mascot made the students unhappy. Then—maybe he was rattled—he mispronounced the donors' names. "And not just once," she said. "After the second time he did it, Pup-Dog covered his eyes with his paws and crawled off the stage. The local papers were there, and I think half the students in the audience caught it on film."

"I don't understand. He mispronounced 'Pratt' and 'Fixx'?"

"Into the microphone. It was loud. There was no mistaking what he said."

"Pratt-Fixx?" Fitger asked. "The Pratt-Fixx Endowment?"

Janet pinched the air with her thumbs and fingers and moved her right hand over the left as if rearranging words and letters in the air.

"Pratt-Fixx . . . Fatt—"

"And apparently the agreement wasn't signed yet," Janet said, "and word on the street is that the money is going to be redirected to a 'worthier cause.' "

Fitger shook his head as if to clear it. *The Fat Pricks Endowment. The Department of Economics in Fat Pricks Hall.* "President Hoffman was there? And Rutledge?"

"I didn't see Rutledge," Janet said. "But Hoffman was sitting next to the donors; when they walked out, all in a row, she brought up the rear."

Fitger envisioned a thread of hope dangling in the air before him. With Roland disgraced and Econ bereft of its windfall, English would remain, at least for the immediate future, in Willard. He felt almost fond of the building. He and Janet sat in silence for a while.

"Thanks for bringing the news," he said.

Janet said he was welcome, but she had something else to discuss with him as well. A proposition.

"Oh?" He tried to quell the surge of optimism that quickened his heart.

"Now that Phil and I aren't together anymore," she said, "I spend a lot of time alone. For a while, I thought about getting a cat. It turns out I'm allergic."

"Ah. Interesting," Fitger said.

Rogaine licked some crumbs from the carpet.

"So I was talking to Fran, and I told her I didn't want a dog, because I'm not home often enough. You have to walk a dog and take care of it."

"Right," Fitger said.

"But then Fran told me that some people who don't want sole responsibility for a dog co-adopt. They co-own it. The dog would have two separate owners and two separate houses; it would go back and forth."

As if aware that he and his kind were being discussed, Rogaine yawned, showing the cave of his mouth.

"I thought we might try it, if you were interested," Janet said. "It's just an idea. We'd have to work out the logistics, but if you were willing, we could share him. Take some time, and let me know what you think."

Fitger understood the openheartedness of her offer: she was telling him that she didn't love or intend ever again to love him; but it was possible that from the stupidest move of his life he might be freed and forgiven. He looked at Rogaine. If they co-owned the dog, might Fitger walk him to Janet's house on the weekends and, like a divorced co-parent, be invited in for an ex-marital consult regarding the problems of canine behavior, over a beer?

Probably not. But the possibility would sustain him and he would try to be satisfied with it; for now, it would do.

Janet picked up the loop of Rogaine's leash (the dog

behaved much better for her than it did for Fitger) and suggested that they look for a colleague who could help with the counting of ballots. Out in the hall, she headed toward Fitger's old office, from which, as always, one could hear the *clickety-clack* of computer keys.

"That won't work. There's a Norwegian in there," Fitger said. "It has to be a member of the English department."

"Why are you harboring Norwegians?"

"I don't know. He doesn't have a department." Fitger had become convinced that Arnljot had recorded a tape of someone typing and was playing it, in an endless loop, while he napped on the floor.

"Kick him out," Janet said, as Rogaine sniffed at a trash can. "Wield some power; after all, you're the chair."

"I suppose that's true."

A custodian waved to them from the end of the hallway.

"The Fat Pricks Fellowship," Fitger murmured.

"It does have a ring to it," Janet agreed.

"Payne University's Fat Pricks Prize in Economics."

The custodian, a cart full of fluorescent lightbulbs behind him, was hurrying in their direction. "Professor? Please. Would you please come with me?"

The study of literature, Dennis Cassovan had always thought, was a preparation for death. By definition, the literary scholar was continuously engaged in a scrutiny of the arc that gave shape to existence, via Aristotle's beginning, middle, and inevitable end. *Our little life is rounded with a sleep.* How had he managed to persuade himself that his own demise, like that of a literary hero, would arrive in dramatic form—rather than softly, while he worked by the light of his father's lamp in his office, alone?

Cassovan's hand—he had trained himself to write with the left, after the childhood polio weakened his right side—had been in the act of annotating the essay questions (his undergraduate class would be tested, among other things, on vengeance in *Titus Andronicus* and *Hamlet*) for the next week's exam. Observing the sudden, involuntary jolting of his pen, he had suffered a spasm of disappointment; he would not be grading the exam himself, or explaining his absence, unexcused, to his students. He envisioned them on Monday morning waiting in their seats, irritated, restless, and eventually picking up their books and heading back to their dorms. He made a final effort to rise from his chair but his body remained oddly immobile. Even his breath had come to a quiet close—and how strange it was to realize that the ghostly footsteps he believed to have dogged his progress around campus for the past few months had been tracing instead a simple path toward his heart.

He understood, or was given to understand, that this final transition would not be difficult. His affairs had long been in order, and he had tried to make peace with sadness and put conflicts to rest. Of course there would always be tasks not completed. Most personally painful was the fact that his book—*Anamnesis in Three Roman Plays*—would remain unfinished, his study of retrospection and memory never granted a final form. (Lincoln Young would attempt, unsuccessfully, to appropriate the first chapter, but would misread and misinterpret Cassovan's notes, which were color-coded and neatly organized and rubber-banded in his left-hand drawer.)

Strange: the overhead lights (had he turned them on?) had begun to flicker, and his wooden chair had suddenly reminded him of a cradle. There on his desk (whose missing right front foot had been replaced, forty years earlier, with a brick) were the incomplete essay exam, the banker's lamp with its green glass shade, his mother smiling while she pinned up her hair, a black rotary phone, his wife admonishing their son about the washing of hands, an apple cut into perfect quarters, a velvet curtain splashing onto the stage at the end of the play, and a five-dollar clock purchased at a hardware store by his son, Ben—a Father's Day gift—about six months before he died at the age of fourteen. Such small but lovely souvenirs; such—

The fur on Rogaine's spine rose up, from just behind his ears to his tail. He had smelled dead things before—tire-tracked squirrels, rabbits, possums, birds, mice—but this odor was heavier, and different. Cautious, he extended his nose and flexed his nostrils. Fruit-blood-eggs-urine-dirt-sweat-bread-ink-wool-soap-rain . . . and the body-with-clothing smell of a very old man. He had never smelled a dead human. He tugged at his leash and lay down with his nose by the door.

Fitger touched Cassovan's wrist; it was cold. Cassovan was wearing what he would likely be buried in: his traditional black suit, white shirt, and black tie. His rawboned fingers were still gripping a pen; and on his face, Fitger couldn't help noticing, there was a look of mild but not unpleasant surprise.

"We should call 911," Janet said.

Pinned to the blade of Cassovan's letter opener, which rested precisely next to the stapler, was a ballot. It was not filled out.

"Jay?" Janet asked.

Fitger picked up the letter opener and plucked the ballot from its tip. Then he tore open the manila envelope Fran had given him and spilled the rest of the ballots onto Cassovan's desk. He remembered Fran's admonition: ballots had to be counted in the presence of two English Department faculty members and one representative of the university staff. Department policy made no mention of both faculty members still being alive. *Do you approve of the Statement of Vision for the Department of English as stated below?* Check *Yes, No,* or *Abstain.*

Rogaine crawled forward, dragging his belly along the floor, and sniffed Cassovan's shoe. Setting Cassovan's blank ballot aside, Fitger counted the others. Eleven to zero. A unanimous *Yes.* He counted them a second time to be sure.

Janet picked up the phone. Rogaine whined. On Cassovan's bookshelf, Fitger saw an SOS button. Save Our Shakespeare. He slipped it into Cassovan's pocket. *Keep this man safe,* he thought, contemplating his colleague. *I had rather have such men my friends than enemies.*

Janet called his attention to something out the window.

At the edge of the parking lot behind Willard Hall, Angela Vackrey was sitting on a suitcase, eating an apple. She was immersed in a book.

The first order of business in the coming year, Fitger thought, would be the reestablishment of the breastfeeding lounge.

Acknowledgments

A thousand thanks to my wonderful editor, Gerald Howard, who didn't care for the original version of this novel and persuaded me to start over. Let's be honest: I wasn't happy about it at the time, but he was right in the end. Also at Doubleday, thanks to Emily Mahon (I apologize for being a pain in the ass about the cover), and to Nora Reichard and Lawrence Krauser and Nora Grubb and Sarah Engelmann and—especially—Michael Goldsmith.

Thank you, again and again, to Lisa Bankoff, who has the strength and tenacity of a hundred merely mortal literary agents.

At the University of Minnesota, sincere thanks to my colleagues in the Creative Writing Program and the Department of English (who truly are *not* represented in the pages of this novel): Kim Todd, who handed me the title during a lull in a faculty meeting one afternoon; Katherine Scheil, who offered valuable insight into all things Shakespeare and even allowed me to grill her undergrads in my search for material; Charles Baxter and Patricia Hampl, who championed this book in its early stages (I hope I didn't let you down by not getting that Guggenheim); John Watkins, whose perspective on academic and department politics is always refreshing; and Andrew Elfenbein, department chair par excellence. Thank god you're serving as chair, so that I don't have to.

Thank you to everyone at Ucross, for that beautiful studio. I threw out most of what I wrote while I was there (see paragraph no. 1, above), but I loved every second of my time in Wyoming.

Thanks to Alison McGhee, for near-continuous moral support; and to Kate DiCamillo, for thinking both versions of the opening chapters were good.

Thanks to Jon Baxter Williams, for his knowledge of tarantulas; and to Karie Swenson, for passing that horrible knowledge (with illustrations) along.

Thanks to the members of my book club, who encouraged me to use their names for various unsavory minor characters.

Thanks to Emma and Bella, who didn't exactly help with this book that I can remember, but that's okay because they inspire me in a hundred other ways, and I love them for simply being themselves.

And finally, thanks to Moo, Hazel, and Vince, who provided hours of bewhiskered companionship while I typed up this book. Any errors in the work are theirs alone.

About the Author

Julie Schumacher grew up in Wilmington, Delaware, and graduated from Oberlin College and Cornell University, where she earned her MFA. Her first novel, *The Body Is Water*, was published by Soho Press in 1995 and was an ALA Notable Book of the Year and a finalist for the PEN/Hemingway Award. Her 2014 novel, *Dear Committee Members*, won the James Thurber Prize for American Humor; she is the first woman to have been so honored. She lives in St. Paul and is a faculty member in the Creative Writing Program and the Department of English at the University of Minnesota.